THE TINDERBOX

Jo Bannister titles available from
Severn House Large Print

The Fifth Cataract
The Primrose Switchback

THE TINDERBOX

Jo Bannister

SEVERN HOUSE LARGE PRINT
London & New York

Essex County Council Libraries

This first large print edition published in Great Britain 2007 by
SEVERN HOUSE LARGE PRINT BOOKS LTD of
9-15 High Street, Sutton, Surrey, SM1 1DF.
First world regular print edition published 2006 by
Severn House Publishers, London and New York.
This first large print edition published in the USA 2007 by
SEVERN HOUSE PUBLISHERS INC., of
595 Madison Avenue, New York, NY 10022.

British Library Cataloguing in Publication Data

Bannister, Jo
  The tinderbox. - Large print ed.
  1. Missing persons - Fiction 2. Homeless persons - Fiction
  3. Detective and mystery stories 4. Large type books
  I. Title
  823.9'14[F]

  ISBN-13: 978-0-7278-7619-5

Printed and bound in Great Britain by
MPG Books Ltd, Bodmin, Cornwall.

The city is like a mountain, like an iceberg. You only ever see the top.

The top of the mountain, the crown of the berg, high up in the crystal air where the sun shines and the rainbows dance, is the country of the chosen. It is possible to be richer, more powerful, more demonstrably alive in the upper reaches of the city than anywhere else on earth.

But nine parts of an iceberg are under water and the mountain has deep roots. Beneath the city of the great is another place – a limbo, a half-lit *between* – where the small unseen live with squalor, darkness and crushing weight under the heedless tramp of a million feet scurrying about important business.

But if they cannot share in the city's success, still they may for a time evade the worst consequences of failure. Down here at gutter level people with nothing left but a sense of self, the stubborn refusal to accept their own worthlessness, can make a home of a kind. They have no aspiration. There's no prospect that they'll ever climb the mountain, breathe untainted air or feel the sun. They live the only way they can, for as long as they can, and sing strange songs in the darkness.

PART ONE

THE MAN

One

Feet scurrying lightly on the landing, the clatter of plates in the kitchen.

'It's on the table.'

The plaintive wail down the stairs: 'I'm not *ready*!'

Jan's voice, flat and faintly humorous, reassuring in its refusal to panic. 'Well, it's ready for you.'

The long dark hair pouring into the stairwell as Cassie leaned over the rail. 'I haven't got *time*!'

'You've all the time in the world.' Earthquakes wouldn't disturb that massive calm. 'Beethoven wrote the "Eroica" in less time than you've got to get into town and play it. Now come down here and eat your breakfast.'

'Oh, *Mum*!' The light feet stamped downstairs. The tall slender figure – this year she had grown nowhere but up – trailed into the kitchen and, sinuous as a cat, slipped between table and chair. Long agile fingers toyed with the teaspoon. 'I couldn't eat a thing.'

Jan ignored her, leaning over the deal table to pour the tea. 'Another thing about Beethoven,' she said as if she'd known him personally. 'He never wrote a symphony without first having a proper breakfast.'

Cassie looked at her through the long hair she refused to tie back, stubborn and shy like a deer peeping through cover. 'I'm not doing Beethoven. I'm doing Mozart.'

'Mozart!' echoed Jan triumphantly. 'A two-eggs-a-day man if ever there was one.' She raised her voice. 'Tom, I'm not running a café here; come and get it or I'll give it to the cat.' This was an empty threat. They didn't have a cat.

Still not eating, and with the heavy patience that emphasizes how much more people know at fifteen than they do at forty, Cassie said, *'Mozart* practically *starved* to death!'

'But only after his mother stopped cooking his breakfast.' The tilt of Jan's head, the tone of her voice, indicated that the discussion was over. 'Now eat.'

Laurence Schofield observed them in silence, smiling secretly into his toast. He craved no part of their conversation, was content only to watch and enjoy them. His wife and his daughter. Love for them filled his heart. Their radiance dazzled him. He loved Tom too, of course he did, and understood him and shared views and interests

10

with him in a way that made them closer than either could ever be to the artistic, intuitive female half of the family. Still there was something very special about his first child growing towards womanhood. When he found time to drink her in like this, when he sat back and considered her as more than the principal client of his one-man taxi service and the sitting tenant of his bathroom, she took his breath away. He couldn't think how, even with Jan's help, he'd managed to produce anything so lovely.

Jan's was a different kind of beauty: strong, competent, indefatigable. When Schofield had collected her for their first date, twenty years ago now, she was wearing Wellington boots with her panne velvet party frock because her father's bullocks had broken out. Pragmatic, unflappable.

By contrast, the Schofields were worthy but boring. They wore suits. In every family photograph, suits were all you saw. Undertakers in dark suits and doctors in brown suits and lawyers in pinstripes, and eccentric Uncle Keith who ran a coffee plantation in Kenya and came to family weddings in a safari suit – but always suits, from the very dawn of suitdom. Respectable, dependable, hard-working, unimaginative: that was the Schofields. Laurence – and it *was* Laurence, never Larry let alone Lance – was an architect. Jan bought him casual clothes for site visits and meetings with trendier clients, but his soul craved suits.

Yet somehow the blending of their genes had produced a magic child who moved like a fairy dancer in a bubble of music. It was entirely beyond Schofield's comprehension. It took the arrival, four years later, of Tom, with his stocky farmer's build and his passion for games involving balls and mud, to restore his father's belief in the principle of heredity.

As happened so often after losing an argument with her mother, Cassie appealed directly to her father. Her voice still held a trace of the childish whine that had undermined his resolve more times than he cared to remember. 'Daddy ... I don't think I can do this.'

Jan's fine dark eyes flashed at him in a mixture of warning and laughter. She knew all his weaknesses.

Schofield slid his hand across the table to capture his daughter's wire-thin wrist. 'It's a music exam,' he reminded her gently, 'not trial by ordeal.'

She tried to smile. But the agony in her eyes flayed him. 'I know. But I'm so nervous!'

'You're always nervous. And you always do well. Look at it this way: by lunchtime it'll be over, and you'll be on top of the world.'

She wasn't convinced. The fact that they'd

been through this so often, and the outcome was always the same, failed to mollify her. 'I could *die* before lunchtime! Up there on the stage, with everyone look at me – listening, waiting for me to make a mistake...' She was gasping for breath, her chest tight with terror. 'If I freeze up there – or drop the music – or lose my place...'

Schofield nodded solemn understanding. 'That's the least of it. You could blow spit all over the judges. You could take too deep a breath to start with and pop the buttons off your blouse. You could put the reed in back to front so it sounds like Mozart played on the kazoo. You could—'

'Oh, Daddy!' But he'd coaxed a smile to her narrow, fine-featured face. She had his bone structure and Jan's colouring: the best of both of them. Tom had his mother's sturdy build topped with a thatch of his father's straw-coloured hair, a design more functional than elegant, but their first child had drawn all the best cards to emerge as they saw her now – a dark girl with eyes like jewels, the slim, swift body of a woodland elf, and long, strong, deft fingers to draw soaring melodies from a dead thing of metal and wood.

That surprised them most of all. No one in Schofield's family was musical, and while Jan had a good singing voice she'd never had the ambition to please anyone but herself.

13

They wondered sometimes if Cassie was a changeling, if somewhere in the Midlands a concert pianist was raising a plump straw-thatched teenager with Van Gogh's ear for music.

'Listen,' said Schofield solemnly. 'This is supposed to be fun. Any time you're not enjoying it you can stop. You don't have to do this exam. You need never pick up a clarinet again, or only for your own enjoyment. It's your choice. But I think if you don't go you'll wish you had.'

Not looking at him, slowly she buttered toast. 'If it doesn't matter...' Her eyes were hidden behind the silk screen of her hair.

'Yes?'

She looked up with a quick, scared grin. 'If it doesn't matter, I might as well go and make a fool of myself.'

Jan saw them to the car and waved them off. She didn't care whether Cassie passed her clarinet exam. She cared how failure would make her daughter feel. So she made a point of keeping occupied for the next couple of hours. Schofield had a site meeting in Birmingham so she made Tom keep her company in the garden. Moving sideways up the border on their hands and knees, rooting among the sweet rocket with forks and trowels, they talked about school and football and summer holidays, and Cassie's improbable gift for music.

'You never think you'd like to take up an instrument, Tom?'

'No!' He said it with the fine disdain of the eleven-year-old soccer fanatic who knows that music is something for girls.

'Or something a bit more macho?'

'Football.'

She peered down her nose at him. 'You already do football. You do football at school, you do football at the club, and after that you meet a few mates to play football. Wouldn't you like to try something else?'

At least he gave it some thought. 'Like what?'

'Anything. Karate. Horse riding. Rock climbing. How about skiing? You enjoyed that day you went from school to the dry ski slope.'

The boy gave a sturdy shrug. 'It was all right.' Suddenly he grinned. 'The best bit was when Mr Perkins broke his thumb. You could hear the crack halfway across the slope. Then he went white and threw up.'

Jan laughed affectionately. 'You *are* a ghoul.'

'What's a ghoul?'

'Someone who likes the bits they cut out of TV programmes so they can show them to kids.'

He liked that. He beamed. 'I could go to ghoul classes. I could go to night-ghoul classes!'

15

His mother shook her head in despair. 'Tom dear, you could *give* ghoul classes.'

Jan expected Cassie to call after the exam, to say how it had gone, and took it as a bad sign when she didn't. When she missed lunch, Jan supposed she'd stayed in Birmingham for some retail therapy. At three, and again at quarter past and half past, she tried Cassie's mobile. But it was switched off. Plainly, she wasn't ready to talk yet.

Schofield was late home too. The site meeting had turned into a pub lunch and it was four o'clock before he got away. Still there was no word from Cassie. They agreed to wait till after tea before starting to worry. If she'd met friends the afternoon could have gone by without her noticing. It was inconsiderate of her not to call but still well short of sinister.

At six o'clock Jan called Cassie's music teacher to ask what time she'd left the exam. At six twenty he rang back to say that no one at the hall had seen her. That was when Schofield called the police.

There was no wailing of sirens or cordoning of roads. The police listened politely to his concerns, rang round the hospitals without finding an accident victim answering Cassie Schofield's description, then expressed tactful surprise that her father should be anxious about a fifteen-year-old missing in her home town for a few hours on a Saturday. They promised to contact him if they learned anything but were quietly confident that Cassie would be back by bedtime.

They sat up until four in the morning but she didn't return.

The next day a policewoman came. She took more details about Cassie and her life, and looked over the house. 'She had nothing with her? Clothes, money?'

'Her clarinet and her purse,' said Jan. 'She might have had thirty pounds, probably not more.'

'A change of clothes?'

'No. It was a music exam, not a concert tour! She should have been back for lunch.'

'Was she anxious about the exam?'

Schofield nodded. 'Yes. But no more than usual. Why, what are you thinking?'

'When kids run away, usually it's because something's upset them. Something and nothing half the time – the last straw breaking the camel's back. Maybe they've been unhappy for months and said nothing, then they run away because someone else gets the plastic toy in the cereal packet. If Cassie's been unhappy, the music exam could have been the last straw.'

'Unhappy?' Even thinking about it, Schofield had seen no sign. 'She's nothing to be unhappy about.'

'Were you pushing her to do well with her music?'

Jan shook her head firmly. Her face was grey with worry and lack of sleep, but she was holding her focus. Right now answering this young constable's questions accurately was the best she could do for her daughter. 'No. She does it because she wants to, because she's good at it. We told her she didn't have to do the exam if she didn't want to.'

'Then she was upset.'

'She was nervous. As nervous as she always is, and no more.'

The constable nodded, turned to Schofield again. 'You drove her into town. Where did you drop her? What time?'

'Opposite the hall, about forty minutes before the exam. She had ample time to check in, tune up – whatever it is you do at music exams.'

'Perhaps she had too much time,' suggested the officer. 'Time to start worrying – to lose her nerve.'

'Then why didn't she come home?'

The constable smiled, a kindly, reassuring, professional smile. 'I don't know, Mr Schofield. We'll ask her when we find her.'

The direction of the interview changed. Had Cassie a boyfriend? Did she seem to know a lot of boys? Did she put a lot of effort into her appearance? Did she seem to have more money than her parents gave her?

Jan said quietly, 'You're asking if my daughter's a prostitute.'

Schofield hadn't realized that was where the questions were leading. He stared between the two women, ashy with disbelief.

The constable was glad to have a difficult subject out in the open. 'Yes. Could she be?'

'No,' said Jan with certainty. 'I always know where she is. There's no time in her schedule for anything like that. If she isn't at school or working on her music, she's mostly with girl-friends. Yes, there are boys too, but no one she's serious about. I know there are girls who're fifteen going on twenty-two, but Cassie isn't one of them. She uses make-up on special occasions. She sleeps in a Winnie the Pooh tee shirt that she keeps in a fluffy rabbit on the end of her bed.'

The constable nodded again, and seemed satisfied.

For three days they listened for their phones and the doorbell. Every hour, through the night as well, they called Cassie's mobile. But it never rang.

Tom quietly made his own meals and got himself off to school. Only when Jan saw him washing his football kit in the sink because he didn't know how to use the washing machine, and saw the pinched face under his thatch of straw-coloured hair, did she realize that Cassie's parents weren't the only ones affected by her disappearance, and that her brother was as shocked, confused and fright-ened as they were.

She pulled the wet clothes out of his un-resisting hands and dumped them in the washer. Then she pulled Tom into her arms and they clung together, crying, for what seemed an age.

By then there seemed no prospect of Cassie just walking back through the front door. It had passed beyond that. A detective inspector visited the Schofields' home and talked frankly about the possibilities.

'Something happened within a few minutes of you dropping her. There are really only two alternatives. Either she decided not to do the exam and left of her own volition, or she was taken away.'

Of course they'd considered it. From the first night that was the spectre haunting them, the unbearable thing, the thing they dared not confront. Schofield caught his breath. Jan's lips pinched tight.

The detective kept talking, leaving them no time to dwell on it. 'Now, I can't tell you that doesn't happen, because it does. But it's a rare event. Particularly with a girl Cassie's age. If a man's drawn to teenagers, there are enough available that he doesn't have to risk his liberty by abducting one. And the time, and the place, and even the fact that she was carrying a clarinet case she could have hit him with, all make it less likely we're dealing with an abduction. Not impossible, and we'll go on treating it as a possibility until we can rule it out, but pretty unlikely.'

Schofield let the breath go in a ragged sigh. The detective had done this before, knew what he was talking about, and Schofield was anxious to accept his professional assessment. But where did that get them? The image of Cassie's frail body left defiled and broken in a ditch had tortured them, but what was left if it was erased? Ransom?

The inspector read his thoughts and smiled gravely. 'No offence, Mr Schofield, but kidnap for money usually only affects people who're conspicuously rich. Not comfortably off, not doing nicely – buying Caribbean islands. The Hearsts and the Gettys. Also, you haven't had a demand. That's significant. As often as not the demand comes before the kid's been missed. The kidnappers don't want the family to have called the police before they get their instructions. They don't want us advising on how to handle it.

'The other thing you should know,' he went on, 'is that murder is an uncommon crime to start with, and most murders occur within the victim's family or social circle. The random murder of someone by a stranger is much rarer, and because there's no connection with the victim there's usually no great need to hide the body. There are exceptions to every rule, but the statistical probability is that if Cassie had come to any harm we'd know about it by now.'

Jan began, very softly, to cry.

'Then what are you saying?' Schofield's voice was as thin as a reed. The last few days had reduced him to a husk. 'You don't think she's dead and you don't think she was abducted. What do you believe? That she got out of my car, said she'd see me later and, tucking her clarinet case under her arm, walked through a brick wall into another universe?'

'No. But perhaps she thought she'd like to see more of this one.'

'She's fifteen years old, Inspector!' snapped Schofield. 'She's hardly spent a night away from us – a holiday arranged by the school, the odd weekend at a friend's house, that's it. She couldn't manage on her own for twenty-four hours. You think she's set off to see the world with thirty pounds and a clarinet?'

The detective sighed. He was a solid individual of around forty-five, a man with children of his own. As a father he knew he wouldn't believe it either. As a policeman he knew it happened all the time. Often it was children from broken or violent homes, children with nothing to lose. Sometimes it was children with a keen sense of adventure, seeking fame and fortune amid the bright lights, ending up in reality earning small change in a tangle of dirty sheets.

But just occasionally it was ordinary children from nice homes, well brought-up, well educated, with no problems to speak of and a bright future ahead of them, who for no reason that ever came to light one day stepped off the edge of the world. The detective couldn't imagine how he would feel if it was one of his children. But in Laurence Schofield's face he could see the worm at work: incredulity warring with grief, the sense of betrayal with the sense of guilt.

He said, 'That's the likeliest explanation, yes. That she had some kind of personal crisis – maybe to do with the exam, maybe not – and she just felt the need to get away. If that's what happened she could come to her senses at any moment, and phone and ask you to pick her up. Or maybe she'll get involved in a bit of mischief and we'll find her that way. Her clarinet may turn up in a pawn shop and give us a lead.

'I know it's no use telling you not to worry. But she'll manage better than you think. She's old enough to get a job in a shop or on a market stall so she won't have to turn tricks just to eat. That's the problem for the younger ones – the only work they can get is the last kind they should be doing.'

'What can we do?' asked Schofield weakly. 'Advertise in the papers? Hire a private detective?'

The inspector shook his head. 'I wouldn't advise it. You'll attract every creep and chancer within a hundred-mile radius. We'll keep looking. All you should do is make sure you both have your phones turned on all the time. If Cassie gets the urge to call I'd like her to get through at the first attempt. I don't want her having second thoughts – worrying what you'll say, deciding it'll be easier to stay away than to come home ... One thing. If you get any strange phone calls where nobody speaks, don't assume they're nuisance calls. They could be her. Keep the line open. Try talking to her even if she doesn't talk back. Be calm – whatever you do, don't get angry. She'll know what she's put you through without being told. If she daren't face you for fear of recrimination she may never come home.'

That night in bed, lying sleepless and hollow through the cold dark hours, Schofield felt a tremor beside him and knew that Jan was awake too, awake and crying. He turned to her, folding his long arms around her. Her body was soft and warm as ever but she didn't come to him, seemed almost to recoil from the comfort of his touch.

He whispered into her dark hair. 'Don't give up. Whatever's upset her, it'll pass and she'll come home. We just have to wait. The nightmare will pass. We will get her back.'

Her hair moved against his cheek as she shook her head. Her voice was a low moan. 'She isn't coming back. We'll never see her again.'

Part of him wanted to hold her like a hurt child and part of him wanted to shake her. 'That's nonsense. She's fifteen; she can't vanish into thin air. For a few days, a couple of weeks, maybe. But then she's going to need us and she'll be back. She didn't plan to run away. Something happened – a brainstorm, loss of memory, something like that. She isn't responsible for that – it's an illness, it just happened. And it'll pass. We just have to hang in there and wait.'

Quite a long time later Jan murmured, 'I wish you'd gone into the examination hall with her.'

It was dark. That didn't stop him staring at her. The words were like a knife under his ribs. 'I never went into the examination hall with her! Not since she was twelve years old.'

'I wish you'd gone in with her this time.'

He had to fight the tears for a voice that was recognisably his own. 'Don't do this, Jan. What happened isn't my fault any more than it's Cassie's or yours. Don't let's hurt one another looking for somewhere to lay the blame.'

She just said it again, into the pillow, her back to him. 'I wish you'd gone inside.'

Finally they slept. But when they rose in the morning they were changed people. The thing had come between them, levering them apart.

Two

Craig Perkins, his thumb long since mended, taped the programme on homelessness for a lesson on social psychology.

He used it in sixth-form classes on the political, economic and social dynamics of the capital city. He wanted his senior pupils, many of whom would go from here to university and several of whom would find their way from there to the capital, to know about London. He didn't want to discourage them from seeking their fortunes in what was still one of the great cities of the world. He did want them to be aware that, while the city is quick to recognize and exploit ability, it can be hard on the less well-equipped. That for every penthouse there's a basement. That once you turn your back on home, not only does nobody owe you anything but nobody cares whether you have anything or not.

Those who'd known him longest knew that Perkins had not always taken such an interest in the subject. It dated back to the week Cassie Schofield was absent from school, and police officers had interviewed her schoolmates and teachers, and hushed rumours had flown around until her father made an appointment with the principal and told her what he knew: that Cassie had failed to return from a music exam and the police suspected she'd run away to London.

Cassie Schofield hadn't been one of Perkins' star pupils. She was polite but uninterested, contributing little unless pressed. He had students he'd have missed more. But the manner of her going had affected the whole school to greater or lesser degrees. Ever since, Craig Perkins had found ways of incorporating the subject in his lessons. He wanted his pupils to spread their wings. But he didn't ever again want to hear that one of them had disappeared into the London street-scene armed with thirty pounds and a clarinet.

London is the perfect distance from Birmingham to be a serious temptation to children bored at school or stressed at home. It's near enough to get on a train and be there before common sense has had time to intervene, but far enough away to seem exotic. A place where different rules might apply, where a teenager with nothing to offer but a pretty face and a quick wit might somehow find herself being showered with opportunities.

After Cassie Schofield went, Perkins heard

children as young as eleven talking – only half seriously but with excitement in their eyes – of seeking fame and fortune in London. He wanted them to see what it was like living on cold streets in a cardboard box. After he'd shown the video to his social psychology students he asked colleagues to show it throughout the school. Over the course of about a month he reckoned every child had seen it at least once.

He didn't get much feedback. There was a certain amount of sniggering in back rows, and the passing of little notes suggesting that Mr Perkins had a crush on reporter Briony Fellowes. Perkins sighed and bore the jokes stoically. The issue of homeless children was important enough to endure a little teasing for. Whether they recognized it or not, that fifty-minute video was vitally important to every child who saw it, and even if he didn't know half their names he cared about all of them.

Tom Schofield was one of those who saw the programme twice. The first time was in social psychology, when he took copious notes and concentrated on the commentary's facts and figures. The second time was in a sports period rained off by a March downpour. He watched through half-hooded eyes as the reporter interviewed a boy of fourteen who'd stabbed another boy for stealing his cardboard boxes.

Tom had already heard the boy's whining self-justification. On a cold night a few layers of cardboard between the sleeper and the street could be a matter of life and death, worth fighting and even killing for. But he hadn't seen the pictures. The boy's shrunken face, and the way his hands never strayed from the warmth of his armpits. The pathetic little brazier lit in a hubcap, and the ragged crowd that gathered to its meagre heat. He hadn't seen the young girls passing glue and a plastic bag between them. And all the time a desultory parade of dirty children and young people in strange clothes and old men in black coats belted with rope wandered past in the background, wondering what the camera crew were doing and whether there was anything in it for them.

When the bell rang the class shouldered its unused sports kit, shrugged off any intro-spection the programme had engendered and headed for the school gate. Only Tom Schofield hung back while Mr Finch re-wound the video.

After a moment the former Welsh rugby reserve felt eyes on him and looked up. 'You waiting for me, Schofield?'

'I wondered if...' He was seventeen now, starting to look like a rugby international himself. 'I'd like my parents to see that. Can I borrow it?'

Davy Finch sniffed. 'That's Mr Perkins'

pride and joy, that is; there'll be hell to pay if it gets lost.' Then he remembered the Schofields' particular interest in the subject and nodded. 'Give it back to him tomorrow morning. Only for God's sake don't tape over it. I don't think Mr Perkins is interested in female mud-wrestling.'

'Not as much as you are, anyway,' Tom murmured to himself as he left the gym with his trophy.

He wasn't sure how to broach the subject at home. If he could have watched again on his own he would have done. But since the arrival of DVD, the only VCR left in the house was in the kitchen, and he couldn't banish his mother without explaining why. So that evening after Schofield got home he sat them both down at the kitchen table.

'I've something to show you,' he said quietly. 'A TV programme. I got it from school. I'm honest to God not sure if I'm seeing what I think I'm seeing or not.'

So they watched together. Schofield couldn't imagine what Briony Fellowes had to say on the subject of London street kids that he hadn't heard before. But Tom didn't ask for much: if he wanted them to watch his tape they'd watch.

It felt odd. Difficult and painful, yes, but most of all it felt odd. This was something they never did. They never discussed Cassie's disappearance now. They never mentioned her name. It was as if everything they had to say on the subject had been said in the first few months when they still believed she'd come back – if not now then soon, if not soon then sometime. There were a series of family milestones – the first birthday they celebrated without her, the first Christmas, the first time they went on holiday and had to book for three instead of four – that kept the memories fresh. They made a point of talking about her then, even if it hurt, of continuing to include her in family life. 'Do you remember when Cassie said...?', 'Cassie always liked...', 'If Cassie was here...'

But when a year had passed without word of her – not a phone call or a postcard, or a sombre policeman with a few scraps of clothing and a broken clarinet – it seemed to take more and more effort to keep a place for her at the family table. Schofield was appalled when he realized he was avoiding saying her name. He knew of bereaved parents who'd created shrines to their lost children, and while that wasn't healthy either, it had to be healthier than trying to pretend they'd never existed.

The worst thing was the barrier it raised between him and Jan. Not because she wanted to talk about Cassie and he didn't: so far as he could tell Jan had been ready to put the toys and the clothes in the trunk in the attic before he was. But you can't make a tidy parcel of feelings and memories in the same way, and put it where you won't keep tripping over it. Undiscussed and unresolved, their feelings became something else they couldn't mention for fear of a dam bursting. An elephant at a dinner party, studiously ignored by people who had no idea what to do about it.

So they got on with their lives – with raising their son, with the everyday minutiae that add up into weeks and years – but they did it almost without talking. They lost more than a daughter that Saturday. They lost one another.

Now after six years Tom was breaking open the attic and hauling out the trunk, making them look at its contents, forcing them to think again about Cassie and what she'd done to them. Laurence Schofield knew he must have a good reason. But he couldn't see how it could be good enough.

Halfway through the video Tom reached for the remote control and sat cradling it lightly, his strong square face intent on the screen. When Briony Fellowes began to interview the boy about the cardboard boxes he leaned forward, his eyes combing the background. When he saw what he was waiting for he hit the pause button. 'There. Behind the man in black.'

Schofield saw it too. He sucked in an involuntary gasp and his fingernails dug into his thighs. In his veins the blood turned to ice. His words were like ashes in his mouth. 'Dear God...'

Jan rose to her feet. She'd become bulkier in the last six years, and the sparkle that once animated her had faded. Perhaps she'd just grown tired, but it was as if the burden of loss had ground its way into her bones and her body had grown heavier in consequence. Schofield couldn't remember the last time he heard her laugh.

Quietly, insistently, she said, 'Turn it off.'

Tom's head jerked round to stare at her. 'But, Mum, it's...'

Her fine dark eyes were angry. 'Is it? I don't know. I can't tell. It's been too long. Turn it off.'

In another moment Tom would have had to either obey or defy her. Schofield stood up and took the remote from him. Without looking at his wife he moved closer to the screen. 'I'm not sure. She's ... older. Different. Do you think it's her, Tom?'

As tall as his father and half as broad again, the teenager was uncomfortable at having to pick sides. But he'd known this would be uncomfortable when he decided to bring the tape home. He shrugged helplessly. 'I don't know. I thought it was. When I saw it at school it nearly knocked me off my chair. Now I don't know. I think it could be.'

Schofield was far too close to the screen to

focus the image. 'She's twenty-one.' It had been Cassie's birthday a couple of months earlier. They'd done nothing to mark it. 'She looks older. But living like that, you'd grow up fast.' He turned to his wife. 'Jan, look at it. I need you to tell me what you see. Is it Cassie? What do you think?'

'I think you should turn it off,' Jan said again. Her voice was calm but also determined, its very flatness a kind of passion. 'Please, Laurence. Turn it off. Now.'

He didn't understand. Anger painted a flush on his thin cheeks. 'It's Cassie, Jan. It's your daughter.'

She breathed steadily, forcing the air down deep enough to suppress the scream building inside her. Without taking her eyes off Schofield she said, 'I'm sorry, Tom, but I want to shout at your father and I'd rather do it in private.'

He wasn't a child, wasn't used to being dismissed, felt they had no right to privacy when they were going to talk about his sister. But six years of keeping his feelings to himself had left him without the words to argue his case. He rose awkwardly and headed for the door.

But before he was quite out of the room she'd started – not shouting but arguing vehemently. 'Laurence, think what it is you're doing! Don't start something none of us can finish.'

They confronted one another like gladiators across the frozen screen of the television. 'All I'm doing,' snapped Schofield, 'is asking you to look at your daughter. Is that so unreasonable?'

'Not unreasonable,' agreed Jan fiercely, 'but God, how unwise! Yes, that may be Cassie under that flyover, and if we look at the pictures long enough we may be able to see that it is – or at least persuade ourselves that it is. Then what? Six years ago this family was torn apart by knowing she was out there somewhere – God knew where and who with – taking hard streets, hard weather and whatever else the city threw at her as the price of getting away from us. Do you really want to put us through that again?'

Schofield simply didn't understand. 'Jan, we've found her! Six years ago we lost her. We didn't know where she was, what had happened, whether she was alive or dead. That's what tore us up. Now there's a chance to get some answers. If that is Cassie – and like Tom, I think it is but I'm not sure – we know she's alive and in London. The chances are she's living somewhere near that flyover. She looks ... OK. Better than most of them. So maybe she isn't homeless. Maybe she was just passing by and went to see what the fuss was all about. Jan, she could be married – she could have children. Don't you want to know?'

For six years they'd communicated less and less. What had begun as a means of managing their grief had seeped into every aspect of their lives and then set, like concrete. They never shared their innermost thoughts now. They'd believed it was better for everyone not to give in to their emotions. Later it became the template for their marriage; they each dealt with the bad times privately. It worked well enough. It was better than sharing their misery whenever the black dogs gathered. But after six years Jan struggled to express how she felt.

'When she was here,' she said carefully, 'when she was our child, I'd have given everything I owned – I'd have given pieces of my body – to know that Cassie was safe and happy. And if she'd left in the normal way, with love, all the years from then to the end of my life wouldn't have broken the threads between us. Of course I'd want to know where she was, what she was doing, if I was a grandmother.

'But it wasn't like that. Even after all this time, only the merest accident has given us this tiny insight into her life. If it *is* her life. God help us, we're so estranged now we can't even be sure we recognize her! She never expected us to see that, Laurence. She didn't want us to see it. If she'd wanted us to know where she was she'd have called or written sometime in the last six years. She put us out of her life.

'So what are we supposed to do now? Pretend we're all one happy family again? In six years, all we have of her is a grainy image on a video-tape – and that's all we'll ever have. What are we supposed to do with it? Show it at family gatherings? If it's her, if she's alive and well and just a hundred miles down the M1, we have to face the fact that she let us wonder for six years rather than tell us she's all right. We didn't give up on her, Laurence. She gave up on us.'

Schofield stared at her, shocked and appalled. 'When did you become so bitter?'

Jan barked an incredulous laugh. 'Of *course* I'm bitter! She ripped the heart out of me and left it bleeding in the sink. Now you want me to be happy because we've seen a few seconds of her in a TV programme? I'm sorry, it means nothing to me. Only one more twist of the knife she left in me – a bit more blood, a bit more pain. I'd be happiest, really, never to see her or speak of her again.'

Schofield could understand his wife's anger. What he couldn't understand was her not caring. After the same years, the same hurts, the same silence, he still cared deeply what had become of his child. He'd have gone anywhere in the world at a moment's notice for the chance to see her. He could hate what she'd done and still love her. Words stumbled out of his mouth. 'She's our *daughter...'*

'That's right,' snapped Jan. 'Someone who shares our genes. A relative. Not family. Being family involves certain obligations, and she's made it clear how much she cares about us. Not a friend – you'd shut your door on a friend who treated you the way she's treated us. And after six years, not even an acquaintance. We don't know anything about her now. She's a stranger.'

Schofield was stunned by her intransigence. His voice trembled. 'If this tape tells us nothing else, it tells us she's alive. Doesn't that mean *anything* to you?'

'Honest to God?' asked Jan. 'Not much. Do you know what I've wanted more than anything for most of the last six years? I wanted that policeman to be wrong. I wanted him to find a body. Don't you see? If she was taken, if she was killed, that's a tragedy but it's the fault of someone we don't know, that we'll never know. We had her until she was fifteen, and all her life we loved her and she loved us. But if she ran away, we haven't even got that. What was she thinking all those years that she could do that to us? She couldn't have loved us the way we loved her. She wasn't a daughter, she was a lodger. I'm not glad she's alive, Laurence. I'd rather have lost my daughter to a homicidal maniac than have spent fifteen years raising a stranger.'

'Where did that come from?' whispered Schofield. 'Why are you so full of hate?'

'Because I tried love,' cried Jan, her strong face tugged into ugly creases by the power of her passion. 'See where it got me!'

Three

From his office the next morning Laurence Schofield phoned the TV company. He found himself referred through a succession of secretaries and assistant producers, each more suspicious of his motives than the last.

Schofield wasn't prepared to be fobbed off. 'There's something in that footage that's very important to me. I think one of the kids you filmed is my daughter. She's been missing for six years. I need to find out where the film was shot, how you found the people to interview, how long ago all this was done. And I need to see any footage that wasn't in the finished programme. I'll be at your offices at nine o'clock tomorrow morning, and I'll wait until someone involved in the project – the producer, the cameraman, the presenter – can find time to see me.'

Then Schofield made his apologies to his partner. 'I'm sorry to take off like this, but I don't feel I have any choice.'

'Today?' Surprise lifted Ken Broadbent's voice and his eyebrows. 'You're going today?'

'Tonight. I want to start looking first thing tomorrow.'

'You've a meeting with the planners scheduled for tomorrow afternoon. The Rosebowl people are big clients; they'll expect to see you there.'

'Cover for me,' said Schofield, somewhere between a plea and an order.

'I don't know anything about the project! It's been your baby from the start. I've seen the model, that's about all.'

'Then reschedule the meeting,' said Schofield, tight-lipped, 'because I'm going to be in London tomorrow afternoon.'

'Go tomorrow night.'

Schofield tried to explain his sense of urgency. 'It's months since that film was shot. I'm scared the trail will have gone cold, that even another week's delay might make it impossible to find her. This is a chance I never expected to get, Ken. If I don't take it ... I have to take it, it's as simple as that. I can't let anything stand in the way.'

Ken Broadbent and Laurence Schofield had been friends longer than they'd been partners. Broadbent was Cassie's godfather. He carried her on his back when she wanted a pony and encouraged her musical ambitions long before her fingers were deft enough to justify them. He remembered the terrible weekend she went missing. It had taken patience, tolerance and a degree of toughness to drag Schofield through the despair of that time, all of which gave Broadbent an interest in the Schofield family over and above Laurence's value to him as a colleague. It wasn't the prospect of annoying an important client that bothered him most.

He had two concerns about Schofield rushing off to London in pursuit of the girl in the film. He was worried about the disappointment if she couldn't be found or if it wasn't Cassie. Clearly, however much he was trying to be realistic, in his heart Schofield believed that fate was offering him a chance to bring his daughter home. All his hopes were invested in it. If it proved a mirage, Broadbent was afraid he'd slip back into that desolation of the soul he'd barely survived six years ago.

He was also worried how his partner would feel if he did find the girl, and it was Cassie, and she didn't want to come home. He knew how much this mattered to Schofield. It mattered too much. The price of failure would be too high.

Schofield saw the misgivings behind his eyes and gave a tight, brittle smile. 'I'm not going to vanish up the Tottenham Court Road, Ken. I'll be gone for a few days. Look, today's Thursday. I'll try to be back on

Monday. If there's a trail to follow I can find her in that time; if there isn't there'll be no point staying. I need you to deal with the Rosebowl people tomorrow, and update the Simpsons on the progress of their barn conversion on Saturday morning. Two meetings. Three, maybe four hours. That's all I'm asking. You can manage without me for one weekend.'

Broadbent couldn't argue with that. Nor could he express his doubts in a way that would make sense to Schofield, afire with hope as he now was. He conceded with a shrug. 'OK. Do what you need to. Take whatever time you need. Just don't...' He ground to a halt.

'Don't what?' Schofield cocked a fair eyebrow.

'Don't do anything foolish, Laurence. Don't expect too much. Don't set yourself up for disappointment. Don't make yourself unhappy.'

Schofield was surprised and touched. They'd been friends for twenty years, partners for ten. But it had never been the kind of relationship that led grown men to throw their arms around one another. He turned the brittle smile down a few kilowatts. He knew he wasn't behaving entirely rationally. He also knew that the circumstances dictated his response. He had to try. Even if he'd known that his efforts would be unsuccessful, he'd still have had to try.

'I know it's a long shot,' he said quietly. 'I'm not expecting to go to this flyover and find Cassie still leaning against it. What I'm really doing is making a last effort, so when it comes to nothing I can draw a line under it and move on. I'm not going to get drawn into a wild-goose chase, if that's what's worrying you. London's a city of seven million people, and I have one lead. If it comes to nothing I'll come home. There'll be nothing else to do.'

He booked into a small hotel in Victoria. He'd never lived in London so his knowledge of the city was limited to the tourist sights. He and Jan had brought the children here a couple of times, and this was where they'd stayed. It was quiet and respectable, the service amiable rather than effusive, and importantly they knew him. If he turned up here with a young girl they'd listen while he explained. If he stayed anywhere else the porter would have dialled 999 before Schofield could produce the MISSING poster that he always carried.

It was terribly dog-eared now. In the first year it was in and out of his wallet so often the folds began to dissolve. For the last five years he'd kept it mostly as a memento. But before leaving the office he ran off fifty more on the copier, just in case.

He took Jan's car, leaving her his BMW.

The middle-aged Renault would be easier to park and less likely to attract thieves. Also, if he picked up a trail he might find himself winding down his window to ask questions of young women on street corners. A middle-aged Renault with a *Save the Whale* sticker and a tartan rug on the back seat was his best defence against an accusation of kerb-crawling.

He didn't allow enough time to find the offices of the TV company. By the time he'd found somewhere to park he was sweating with the fear that the people he'd come to see would have grabbed the excuse to be somewhere else.

He was mistaken. He was met in the foyer by the programme's presenter, Briony Fellowes. He started to greet her as if they'd already met, then realized what he was doing and blushed. She didn't know him from Adam and actually, he didn't know her either.

She flicked him a reassuring little smile. 'Why don't we go up to the reporters' room? You can tell me how I can help.'

Schofield was expecting a glazed expanse full of hammering typewriters, populated by men in trilbies with press cards tucked into the hatband, women in sharp suits and high heels, and hurrying copy boys. He thought Briony Fellowes had shown him to the broom cupboard by mistake.

It was the size of a living room, lined with cheap metal shelves bearing a small reference library and a collection of box files labelled *Morgue*. Half a dozen desks, garnered from a variety of sources and not even the same height, held not typewriters but computer terminals whose cables booby-trapped the floor. There were no copy boys. The men didn't wear hats and the women didn't wear heels. The preferred option for both seemed to be tee shirts for comfort, with a decent jacket to smarten themselves up if the need arose.

The reporter said, 'You were expecting something classier.' There was laughter in her green eyes.

Schofield tried to demur, but he wasn't very convincing. And Briony wasn't offended. 'We're only a small operation. We can't afford a couple of storeys at Canary Wharf. When we make a profit we upgrade the cameras, not the furniture.'

She evicted a colleague from the desk next to hers and tilted her screen so Schofield could see it. Then she showed him the footage he'd asked about. That took him by surprise. He'd expected to have to start afresh, telling her what he needed and why. He'd have been even more surprised to learn she'd been in the editing suite until one o'clock that morning finding all the material they'd shot for the *Streetwise* programme and putting it together in a way that would make sense to an outsider.

They watched the footage in silence until the small crowd under the flyover appeared. A couple of dozen waifs and strays, both sexes, two thirds of them very young and the remaining third apparently very old, idling round a meagre fire while a well-meaning reporter made a documentary about their plight which none of them would ever see. Long before *Streetwise* was screened, most of those featured in it would have forgotten it was ever filmed. That was nothing: some of them couldn't remember how they came to be there, or where *there* was, or where they had come from, or even their proper names.

When the girl appeared, Schofield's whole body jerked. 'There,' he whispered. He reached out an unsteady finger to touch her...

A tall, slender girl with pale skin and long dark hair, with great dark eyes that either moved very quickly or stayed very still. She wore amorphous clothes of black trimmed with red and kingfisher blue. Schofield couldn't be sure if they were ethnic chic or rags. A quiet surrounded her, which might have been a kind of serenity or ultimate despair. Once she leaned forward to speak to a man in front of her and something like a smile touched her lips, painted with something darker than lipstick. Then the shot ended.

Briony ran the film back and played it again, and stopped it when the girl appeared. She isolated the face and blew it up, then sharpened it. 'What do you think?'

Still Schofield couldn't be sure. 'I need to find that girl. Is it my daughter? I don't know. I don't think I'm *going* to know until I see her in person. How do I find her?'

But Briony shook her head, red-gold hair dancing in corkscrews on her shoulders. She might have been a year either side of thirty. 'These people don't have permanent residences with their names beside the doorbell. Most of them will have moved at least once since we shot that in November; some of them will have moved a dozen times. What we can do is go back to the flyover and try to find someone who knows her.'

Schofield's heart gave a little leap. November. He'd come within four months of her, and as recently as that she'd been alive and apparently well. 'Her name is Cassie.'

Briony gave a sympathetic little shrug. 'That may not be much help. They don't use names – at least, not the ones they were born with. It's a kind of self-defence. They're afraid of being identified.'

'You did a lot of work on that programme, didn't you?' said Schofield. 'I didn't realize. I thought you were just the presenter...' He didn't mean that to sound as rude as it did.

47

The woman managed a professional smile. 'I told you, we're a small operation. That was my story from the beginning. I researched it, wrote it, presented it. I was working on it for three months.'

'Then you probably know things about my daughter that I don't,' said Schofield. 'How she's been living the last six years. Where. Who these people are – *all* these people – and why nobody does anything about them.'

Briony nodded slowly. They were reasonable questions. Some she could answer, some she would answer, some she could really only guess at. 'First off, there are a lot of homeless people in London. There are a lot of homeless people everywhere, more than you'd suppose, but London is like a Mecca for them. They come here from all over the country. God help them, they really do think the streets are paved with gold. They're young, for the most part – some of them younger than Cassie was. On average between fifteen and twenty-five. Both sexes. And while many of them are from unstable backgrounds – some of them horrendously unstable – others are from perfectly ordinary families who have no more idea how this happened than you have.'

Schofield almost didn't dare to ask. 'What happens to them after they turn twenty-five?'

Briony wasn't going to lie when the truth

might be all she had to give him. 'Some of them don't make twenty-five. The cold gets them, or the glue gets them, or they go off with men no professional hooker would touch with a bargepole and are never seen again. But others make a life for themselves. Maybe not the kind of life you'd want for your daughter, but better than the streets. They get a job and a room, and find a partner and have kids. And yes,' she said, seeing what he was about to ask, 'some of them go home. Even after years. It doesn't happen often, but it does happen.'

'How do you *know* this?' he wondered aloud. 'I've been asking these questions for six years. No one could answer them.'

She gave a cool professional shrug. 'I talked to them. At length. Some I visited a dozen times, gaining their confidence, getting them to open up. Most of them have been let down in the past – or at least, think they have,' she amended, remembering who she was talking to. 'They don't like talking to strangers. Some of them wouldn't talk to me at all. Some would talk, but only about their lives now – not who they were before. But some wanted to talk about it, as if talking helped them remember. I think those are the ones who might one day go home.'

The reporter became aware that Schofield was watching her with a particular kind of curiosity, his narrow head tilted to one side.

49

She was used to being watched but not like that. She lost track of what she was saying. 'What?'

'I'm sorry,' said Schofield, contrite. 'I was just thinking ... you care about these kids, don't you? They're not just a story to you.'

'What's that supposed to mean?' she demanded. 'That most of what I work on is just a meal ticket? Yes, I care about them. That's why I made the programme. Maybe you'll find your daughter because of it, and that's great, but it's still only one girl. What they need is for their situation to be tackled. For councils to provide them with shelters that don't close a week after Christmas. For social services to break the vicious circle that stops them drawing income support because they haven't got a proper address and stops them getting somewhere to live because they haven't got an income. These kids are destitute in a way that no one in our country is supposed to be, and no one's doing anything about it. I'm sorry to be blunt, but I was less concerned with acting as a missing-persons bureau than trying to get someone to take responsibility. So yes, I care. And being a journalist means I can do something to help. I'm not going to apologise for that.'

Schofield felt a jolt of fear. He'd managed to anger the one person who could help him find his daughter. He stumbled. 'I'm sorry, I ... I hardly know what I'm saying. You must know how grateful I am – for your time, for your help...'

Briony Fellowes' lips were pressed thin. 'Don't worry, Mr Schofield, I'm not going to storm off in a huff. I'll help you all I can. Even if you think a reporter's pretty much like a rat catcher. Jolly useful people when you need them but you wouldn't mix socially.'

Schofield said carefully, 'I'm an architect. Some of my best friends are rat catchers.'

She couldn't stay angry, tossed her lion's mane with an exasperated chuckle. 'Yeah, right. Tell me, what do you suppose these kids need more than anything else?'

'They need to be home with their families,' Schofield said with conviction.

The reporter shook her head. 'Actually, no – or only some of them. A lot of them need their families like they need a hole in the head. What they need is money spending on them. Not the kind of money you and I and a hundred like us could come up with – big money. Government money. They need to be treated like the refugee problem they are. If they all looked and sounded the same, and came in on relief flights from the Third World, and sat around Heathrow waiting for Immigration to agree a response with the UN, everyone would understand the scale of the disaster they represent. Until all the government departments, welfare agencies, charities and their supporters understand what's going on here, nothing that's done for them will make any lasting difference.'

Her green gaze was intent on his face. 'And that, Mr Schofield, is where I come in. In one programme, if it's good enough, I can tell everyone who matters about the plight of the homeless on the streets of London. I can ensure that those whose job it is to find solutions can't use ignorance as an excuse to do nothing. I can touch consciences up and down the country so there'll always be someone who wants to know what's being done for these kids, how much money's being spent, why it isn't more. I can inform, mould and mobilise opinion in four million living rooms. That's worth more to street kids than a tea-and-sympathy stand that only opens when the middle-class volunteers have nothing better to do.'

Schofield nodded, abashed. 'I'm sorry. I never thought of it that way.'

'No one does,' said Briony tersely. 'They think all we're interested in is ratings. Of *course* I'm interested in ratings – ratings mean people are watching my programme and hopefully being moved to help. The more people I reach, the more help I can generate. I've spent time with these kids – I've seen how they live, what they're up against. Every day is a battle for survival. We should be doing more for them. Not just for

Cassie – for all of them.'

Schofield turned his gaze once more on the frozen screen on Briony's desk. The tall girl, slender as a reed in her long dark dress. He stared so hard it was as if he was trying to crawl into the picture with her. Slow tears gathered in his eyes and made his voice hoarse. 'I think it is. I think it's her.'

The reporter nodded. 'Then let's go find her.'

Four

She took him to a London he had never seen. Or rather, that he had seen only fleetingly, on his way to somewhere else, thinking it had nothing to do with him or his comfortable middle-class existence, and had dismissed so completely he was now unaware of having seen it at all.

He hadn't expected the reporter to head for the glitter of the West End, or for the thronging streets and quiet alleys of the City where the national financial institutions of a thousand years had always jostled for a footprint and now fought for space in the sky. Even Schofield would have noticed if a thousand nomads had set up camp among the spectacular buildings that featured in the architectural journals.

He had supposed, when he dared think about it, that people like Cassie – people with no homes they cared to go to – ended up in places like the Bermondsey waterfront, slinking through red-brick canyons where rotting warehouses leaned together like dying giants over damp alleyways that the sunlight never reached. In all that crumbling majesty he supposed there must be shelter of a kind: places where the wind and rain didn't penetrate, where a few friends could pool meagre resources in a makeshift semblance of a home, where there would be rubbish enough to fuel a fire that would keep the worst of the winter at bay.

Schofield could imagine living like that. He could not imagine enjoying it. He couldn't imagine preferring it to any alternative other than repeated physical abuse. He didn't know, couldn't guess, how long he could survive like that. But he could just about imagine how it would be.

In fact, he was imagining a London that was already gone. The crumbling warehouses have become showcase apartments, the alleyways jammed with cars designed for autobahns, and a clever use of glass and mirror-finished steel shines sunlight into every corner. London is too prosperous a city to cede space anywhere near its heart to those who don't make the grade.

Briony Fellowes, navigating while Schofield drove, didn't take him to the sort of area that Dickens would have recognized – some expanse of vacant mouldering warehouses, somehow in the wrong place or lacking the right views to be snapped up for redevelopment. She didn't take him to one of those oddly abandoned areas south of the river, which were once deep-water docks for the trading capital of the world. Instead she headed for the motorway.

Juggling the traffic, Schofield flicked her a surprised glance. 'I thought you made the programme in London.'

'We did. This London.'

He looked about him. The roofs they had been travelling among were dropping from sight. All he could see were other roads, elevated on great concrete piles that strode across the broken bones of a landscape too impoverished to be called suburban. 'I don't understand.'

'You will. Take the next exit.'

As they dropped back to the level of the living, Briony guided them through streets that were half houses, half shops, buttressed at intervals by the substantial edifice of a Victorian pub. It was not a salubrious district. Half of it had been sacrificed to the road system, and more of the fractured terraces had fallen down in sympathy. The

55

upper windows of the surviving houses had the aloof, secretive look of eyes behind which nameless deeds are contemplated.

The reporter had him stop for a minute while she went into a shop. She came back with a plastic bag which she threw on to the back seat. Then they went on through the ruined neighbourhood. Finally the concrete legs of the striding motorway loomed ahead, and between them, bizarrely, the wire-net enclosure of a tennis court. The gate was locked and the key must have been long lost because someone had clipped an alternative entrance with wire-cutters. No one played tennis there, but someone had dragged inside a three-piece suite.

'Stop here,' said Briony. There was a quiet tension in her voice, as if they shouldn't have been here; as if she'd brought him poaching.

There were a couple of small businesses in the shadow of the roadway: a monumental mason and scrap-metal yard where gutted cars were piled in improbable towers. The endless rumble from above was a reminder of the real world – young professionals speeding along in glossy cars only a few metres up in the air, quite unaware that waiting like dogs at the table were two little independent traders who would get their business in the end.

In the fifty-metre stretch between the tennis court and the scrap yard were half a dozen cars which had been too tired to complete their last journey and weren't worth pushing inside. Schofield went to park behind them, then thought better of it. He didn't want to come back and find his wife's wheels gone. He turned and drove back to the tennis court, and parked facing the way they'd come in case they needed to make a fast get-away. Through the open window came the acrid scent of exhaust smoke, burning tyres, wet ash and neglect.

'Now what?'

'Now we talk to some people.' Briony looked at him, her green eyes candid. 'Mr Schofield, it's important that we shouldn't seem too ... eager. If we crowd these people they'll just clam up. We'll learn more if we play it cool. And if you let me do the talking.'

It made sense. But there was a problem. 'Briony, there's no one here.'

Her smile had an uneasy quality which Schofield – had he not known better, had he not known that Briony Fellowes was a hard-bitten reporter accustomed to going anywhere the job took her – might have taken for fear. 'Someone's here all right. They'll show themselves when they recognize me.'

She got out of the car. Schofield got out too, but stayed in the angle of the open door, ready to get in and lock it at a moment's notice.

He didn't know what there was to be afraid

of. He was a stranger here, wary as befits a stranger in a strange land but lacking the local knowledge that would have told him if he was trespassing on some unofficial preserve. He was uneasy mainly because Briony was, and he didn't know her well enough to judge if she was afraid of a ripe curse, a ripe tomato or Armageddon.

She raised her voice. 'Tonto? Can I talk to you for a minute? You know me – Briony Fellowes, from the TV.'

Nothing happened. After a couple of minutes, when still nothing had happened, Schofield was about to get back in the car. But then a hinge creaked nearby and a door swung open, and a boy got out of one of the abandoned cars, unfolding thin limbs like a stick insect.

He might have been any age between fourteen and twenty. His body was undernourished, undeveloped, the skin pinched and white as if he hadn't been warm since last summer. By contrast his face was old beyond expectation, wary, sly and weary, the narrow eyes beaten. It was the face of an old man but without any kind of wisdom except how to survive in a hostile world. The face of an old monkey who knows his way round his bit of the forest as well as any creature alive, and still knows that one day he'll lose his grip and fall.

He wore denims, the jeans and jacket

clearly made for two different people, one taller than him, the other fatter. Under the jacket was a thick sweater he may actually have killed for; on his feet were trainers with holes in them, on his hands he wore fingerless gloves. He asked suspiciously, 'What you got?' and Schofield thought he detected the tatters of a Glasgow accent.

Briony reached into the car for the plastic bag, held it out. 'Chocolate, smokes, a six-pack.' But when he reached out a tentative hand she held back. 'Is Winston about?'

'I'll tell him you're here.' The boy took another step towards her, stretching out his skeletal fingers. His muddy eyes were cunning. 'I'll take him the stuff, will I?'

But Briony Fellowes was nobody's fool. 'That's all right, Tonto, I'll carry it. You lead the way.'

The boy was crestfallen but hardly surprised. His life was a procession of disappointments. 'Aye, OK.' Returning his hands to the warmth of his pockets he shambled past the cars and across the wasteland under the motorway.

The visitors followed. Schofield whispered, 'Tonto?'

'I told you,' said Briony, 'they don't use their own names. This one teamed up with a bigger boy when he first came to London. So they called him Tonto.'

'What happened to the Lone Ranger?'

The reporter shrugged. 'No one seems to know. He may have moved on. He may have gone home. Or...' She glanced quickly at him, then fixed her eyes resolutely on Tonto's back.

Schofield said quietly, 'Or he may be dead?' After a moment she nodded. 'Briony, you don't have to protect me. I'm aware of the possibilities. I've considered them all, one at a time and all together. I'm here because I think my daughter's still alive, but I could be wrong. My wife thinks I'm wrong. No, my wife *hopes* I'm wrong. She hopes Cassie's dead.'

Briony broke her stride momentarily, then picked it up again without looking at him. 'I can understand that.'

'Can you? I can't.'

'If you take Cassie home, she won't slot neatly back into the space she occupied before the music exam. She's been growing away from you for six years. By now you'll barely speak the same language. You'll have to break down walls to even start getting to know one another again.'

'I'm ready for that,' insisted Schofield.

'I hope so. Because the only thing I can promise you is that it won't be easy. Cassie didn't prick her finger on a spindle; she hasn't slept away the last six years. She's been living in a place like this, with people like these. People like these have been her friends and lovers. It's a different world to the one you've been living in. She may feel – when the novelty of clean sheets wears thin – that it'll be too hard learning to be your daughter again. Maybe that's the risk your wife doesn't want to take.'

She caught his look, startled and aggrieved. 'You have to be realistic, Laurence. Yes, some of these kids will eventually go home, resolve the problems with their families and never come back. But others will go home for a week, or a month – I met one boy who didn't last twenty-four hours – and then they'll be back here, passing a joint round the fire, with people who're just like them, and nothing short of dynamite will shift them again. What they have here suits them. They have friends, freedom, and the certain knowledge they'll never disappoint anyone ever again. When you're all at rock bottom you can't. That's reassuring to kids who struggle under the weight of family expectations.'

Schofield couldn't help feeling that was a criticism. 'Cassie wasn't under any kind of pressure at home. We loved her; we thought she loved us. What happened came from nowhere.'

'I'm sure it did,' said Briony, conciliatory. 'I'm really not talking about your family. But I talked to a lot of these kids when I was making that programme; I'm telling you what they told me. Fear of disappointing someone was a recurring theme. You have to remember, a lot of them are very young. Teenagers aren't famous for thinking rationally. What they felt as pressure may only have been people trying to do their best for them.'

Schofield looked around him, helpless and angry. 'And this is the answer? This is what's better than people who love you wanting the best for you?'

'For some of them,' nodded Briony. 'Otherwise they'd go home. In a strange way they feel safe here. They're all in the same boat, there's not much of a caste system here, and once they've been accepted there are certain benefits. They are a genuine community. They look out for one another. They make friendships that survive real hardship. How many friends do you have, Laurence, who even when they're hungry would give you half their last meal? Any? I doubt if I have. But Cassie will have. The people she lives with may not have much, but they make a point of sharing what they have. They may go hungry, but they're never hungry alone.'

'You sound as if you admire them. As if you see some merit in their way of life.'

'Not that,' said the reporter slowly. Schofield thought she was trying to answer him honestly. 'If I lost a child to this, I'd be as distressed as you were, and as eager to get her back. But there are things about them to admire. They're stronger than you or I – or they – would ever have thought. And they stand up for one another with a fierceness you can only explain if it comes from a kind of love.'

He would have made her justify that, except that by now the boy Tonto had brought them to a nexus under the motorway, where one flyover leapfrogging another had created a kind of concrete spinney with the road's smoke-stained under-surface for a canopy. The road existed in two parallel universes. From the tarmac up its function was to rush thousands of people every hour from where they were to where they wanted to be – except for rush hour, when the best they could expect was to dawdle. But from down here, the clear purpose of the concrete canopy was to keep the wind and rain off the communal bonfire.

It struck Schofield as curious that the free spirits of the homeless community should work similar hours to those in the regular world. But if you live primarily by begging, with a little petty larceny thrown in, you can't do it when no one's about. This family's breadwinners had to rise as early as he did in order to catch the commuters coming into the city, and stay out later to catch the clubbers going home. It made for a long day so they tended to work shifts. He was struck by the irony of these rebels emulating so closely the way of life they had rejected.

Because it was now midday the afternoon shift were on their way to work while the morning watch had yet to drift back, so the camp under the motorway was largely deserted. There were a couple of young boys – younger than Tonto – playing marbles. There was a girl who appeared to be ill, wrapped in a sleeping bag and huddled beside the fire, who looked up sullenly at the visitors' approach. And there was a fat man in tight jeans and a vast shapeless sweater, sitting beside the fire in a folding chair, toasting sausages on a long metal spike. Older than the others, he was clearly some kind of leader. He might have been twenty-five.

Briony gave him a casual nod. 'Hi, Winston. How's things? We brought you a few supplies.'

He didn't get up, but he did favour her with a friendly smile. 'It's Miss Fellowes, isn't it? Wanna sausage?'

Schofield wondered how she'd excuse herself without causing offence. She didn't even try. She took two sausages off the spike and passed him one. He stared at it as if he could see the listeria marching up and down it.

He felt her eyes on him, realized with a guilty start he was causing offence. He bit into the sausage with as much enthusiasm as he could muster.

The fat man went on watching him. 'So,' he said calmly. 'Who he?'

Briony told him who Schofield was and what he was doing there.

As she spoke Winston's face became ever more guarded. 'I haven't got your daughter, man.'

Briony fielded that before Schofield had the chance to answer. 'We don't think anyone's got her. We think she's living with one of the tribes round here – or at least, she was about four months ago. Even if we find her, I don't expect she'll want to go home. But Laurence and his wife need to know that she's OK. One meeting, hugs and kisses, then he'll go back to Birmingham. He has the right to one meeting. Actually, so does she.'

Winston's broad face remained impassive. But his eyes were thinking about it. 'What does she look like?'

Schofield produced two photographs: the dog-eared one that he'd used on his posters, and the new one Briony had culled from her film. 'Like this.'

The other man looked but made no attempt to take them. 'Why'd she leave home?'

'I don't know,' said Schofield honestly.

'Why do you want her back?'

Alien as this situation was to him, Laurence Schofield knew that Winston was a figure of authority and what he thought mattered. Schofield's answer mattered. He framed it carefully. 'I *do* want her back. But mostly I want to know that this is what she's chosen for herself, that she isn't afraid to come home. That she doesn't need anything that I can give her. She's twenty-one now – she's a woman. She's too old to drag back home if the life she's made here is genuinely what she wants.'

Apparently it was the right answer. Winston nodded. 'Yeah, I've seen her.'

Schofield's heart skipped a beat and then raced.

'The day we made the film?' asked Briony. 'Or more recently?'

The fat man shrugged. 'I've seen her around. Passing through. She doesn't live here.'

'Do you know where she does live?'

He shook his head. There was no way of knowing if it was the truth.

Briony wasn't ready to give up. 'Can you tell us anything that'll help us find her?'

He gave it more thought before answering. When he decided to, he spoke to Schofield. 'Not everyone wants to be found. Not every home is worth going back to. People got phones: anyone who wants to call their mummy and daddy can do. So no, I won't tell you anything to help you find your daughter. What I will do is ask my kids to look out for her. We'll get a message to her, see if she wants to see you. If she does, she can tell us where she'll meet you. Come back here in a week, maybe I'll have something for you then.'

'A *week*?' Schofield's voice soared. 'I'm due back at work...' Belatedly he realized this wasn't an argument that would carry much weight with the homeless.

Winston raised an eyebrow. 'Maybe she isn't worth coming back for. It's got to be – what – a hundred miles to Birmingham, must take all of three hours. And petrol's expensive.'

Schofield flushed. 'I didn't mean ... I've waited six years, of course I can come back next week. But I want to know *now*. I want to see her today. If it's a question of money...'

Winston wasn't offended by the offer, but he wasn't impressed either. 'Sure, we'll want paying. We haven't found a way yet of living without money. I'll tell you what it's going to cost you when I have some news for you – though a down payment always makes people think you're serious. But it won't speed things up. I don't know where this girl is. She could be out of town. I don't know how long it'll take to find her. Could be days, could be weeks. We don't have the kind of addresses that make it easy to leave a message. Finding someone takes luck, and it takes time. I'm sorry if it's being more trouble than you expected.'

Schofield had the sense not to rise to that. Winston might not have much to offer but he was the only one offering anything. If he wouldn't be bribed and – having nothing that could be taken from him – couldn't be threatened, Schofield would have to curb his impatience and go at the fat man's pace. He wasn't going to be rushed. He seemed to think he had a duty to protect the homeless youngsters around him even from their own families, and if to Schofield he cut a poor father figure, perhaps any was better than none.

Reluctantly he nodded. He took some notes from his wallet and passed them to Winston without counting them. 'Expenses. If you're successful, I'll pay more for information. I'll come back on Monday.'

'Won't have anything for you by Monday.'

'Then I'll keep coming back until you do.'

As they were leaving a thought struck him and he turned back. 'The girl in the picture. Do you know what she's calling herself?'

Winston thought for a moment. 'Yes.'

'Can you tell me?'

'No.'

Five

A toasted sausage only goes so far. Schofield took Briony Fellowes for lunch before she returned to her office. As they ate he asked, 'Who else can I talk to?'

She didn't understand. 'About what?'

'About Cassie, of course!' He flicked the fair hair off his forehead in an impatient gesture he should have grown out of twenty years ago. 'If our fat friend is going to be a week making enquiries, who can I talk to in the meantime?'

Briony looked puzzled and a little troubled. 'Laurence, I don't think you should talk to anyone else. Winston's your best bet. If he hears you're seeing other people he may be offended. I think you should do what he said – go home and come back next week.'

'Home?' He sounded as if he'd never considered it. 'I'm not getting this close to Cassie and walking away. I came to London without much hope of finding her. I felt I had to try, but I never expected to find people who actually knew her. Now I have, everything's changed. My business can go to hell; my wife can...' He stopped just short of saying it, but Briony heard it just the same. Schofield took a deep breath. 'Maybe Winston will find her. I hope he does. But if he doesn't I don't want to have wasted a week. There must be other groups – tribes? – I can talk to.'

'Yes,' she said slowly. 'Lots of them. But I don't know any of them the way I know Winston's. I don't know which you'd be safe visiting and which would cut your throat. This isn't like anything you know, Laurence. There's no law here. Each tribal chief makes his own rules. Winston's a model of probity compared with most of them. That's why I worked with him. I don't know anyone else I'd have felt comfortable taking you to see, even in broad daylight.'

He dismissed her concerns. The morning's events had left him dangerously over-confident. Although he'd approached the interview with trepidation, the fat boy had failed to make his flesh creep. If he hadn't left the camp under the motorway with all he'd hoped for, he had certainly got more than he expected. No one had tried to rob or even threaten him. He thought – or at least a stupid, arrogant bit of him thought – it was because they didn't want to tangle with him. As if being a man of substance in his community, a member of his local Chamber of Commerce, meant something to these people. As if they cared that he'd played golf with an Assistant Chief Constable. He thought Briony was exaggerating the risk, and that as long as he exercised a little caution he could walk into any street camp the way they'd walked into Winston's.

'I only want to show them some pictures, ask some questions – I'll pay for the answers. Why should that cause a problem?'

The reporter stared at him, only now beginning to appreciate the depths of his ignorance. 'Laurence, in the Tinderbox, people die for asking questions. They die for the coins in their pockets. They die for straying into the wrong area, or being seen by the wrong people. They *die*. You wander off alone round here, you're never going to be seen again. They'd kill you for *having* pictures of one of them. They'd queue up to kill you for the money you're carrying. If you walk into a camp where you're not known, and flash your wad and demand a meeting with a girl who may or may not be your daughter, you're a dead man.'

He still thought she was exaggerating, gave a superior little smile. Briony had to stop herself hitting him. 'Try to understand! These tribes aren't a kind of summer camp for kids who hate nature trails. They're gangs of outlaws. Some of them are worse than others. Some of them live this way because of circumstances beyond their control, but on a day-to-day level they try to maintain a certain level of decency. Maybe they're not what you'd call honest, upright citizens – they live by begging, dealing, stealing and turning tricks – but they're not out to hurt anyone. They're just trying to get by.'

'Tell that to the kid who was knifed over a cardboard box,' said Schofield snidely.

'On a cold night, a cardboard box is the difference between living and dying,' Briony said quietly. 'You'd fight too for the things you needed to survive. If you had a knife you'd use it. That wouldn't make you vicious, only desperate.

'But some of the tribes are made up of people who don't know what the word *decency* means. They aren't like you and me, or even Winston and Tonto. They don't need an excuse to put a knife into someone. They're here because no law-abiding community would tolerate them, and because however low they sink there are always people here they can prey on. People who have just enough to be worth stealing. People who can't defend themselves; or who try to defend themselves with a knife and find themselves gutted with a machete.

'I spent months researching that programme,' she said forcefully. 'I talked to a lot of people besides the street-kids – police, social services, clergy, charities. I heard a lot of bad things, and one or two names. I wouldn't know where to find people like Rommel and the Pagan – I sure as hell never went looking for them – but one thing I did learn: you don't walk into anyone's camp unless you know you're welcome. This is their world, and they behave pretty much as they choose.'

'I think it might come as a surprise to the Metropolitan Commissioner,' Schofield said loftily, 'that there are parts of this city where the rule of law doesn't run.'

Only the certainty that if she abandoned him Laurence Schofield would be dead by the end of the day kept the reporter from walking out. He was an intelligent man; she couldn't believe she was having such trouble making him understand. He was like a little boy who couldn't see why he shouldn't play on the railway tracks. Her voice quivered with the effort to get through to him. 'Laurence, if you come back here alone someone's going to rip your throat out for your clothes and your wallet, and no one will even hear you scream. You'll end today bleeding your life away in a gutter. If your body turns up – which it might not – the police'll put on a show of investigating, but they won't find the killers and they won't expect to.

'Winston's not your *best* chance of getting what you came here for; he's your *only* chance. He'll ask questions you'd be killed for asking, and he won't follow you up a dark alley after you've paid for the answers. Go home, Laurence. Come back in a week. If I hear anything before then I'll call you. But don't risk your life hunting in this jungle. You don't know enough about the game.'

Still sulking, Schofield dropped her at her office and returned to his hotel. He sat on the edge of the bed for an hour, thinking about what she had said and what he had seen, weighing her advice against the ache in his heart to be doing something – anything – that might bring Cassie home. At the end of the hour he took out of his bag the things he'd begun packing into it.

But something of Briony's advice stayed with him. Instead of commencing a scenic tour of all the derelict sites within a mile of Winston's camp he tracked down the nearest police station.

He explained his mission, showed his poster, and the duty sergeant expressed his sympathies and then tried to get rid of him. Only when Schofield was still there after half an hour did he put in a call to Sergeant Parker.

'Who's Sergeant Parker?' asked Schofield.

'A brave and occasionally foolish man,' said the duty sergeant stolidly, 'who's taken on the role of community police officer to the Tinderbox. It doesn't mean the same here as it means in your nice leafy suburb of Cheltenham—'

'Birmingham,' Schofield corrected him levelly.

'Birmingham,' acknowledged the sergeant. 'But he's still the only police officer I know who'd attempt to walk a beat round here. He's been knifed and he's been beaten up for his pains. But he's also developed a kind of relationship with some of the street kids, and he knows more about what happens in the Tinderbox than anyone who doesn't live there.'

'What's the Tinderbox?' Briony Fellowes had used the term too, also without explaining.

The sergeant indicated with a nod the door Schofield had come through. 'Out there. Where the street lamps end. Where people like you don't go, and people like me only go if it's a matter of life and death, and Sergeant Parker goes a couple of times a week because he considers it his duty.' He shook his head in a kind of wonder. 'Something about the Queen's Shilling.'

Schofield wanted to meet this man. But he wasn't back on duty until the following day, and a six-year-old mystery wasn't the sort of emergency he would give up his free time for. In the end Schofield had to leave unsatisfied. He left some posters at the desk, then went back to his hotel to while away the evening watching television and waiting in vain for his phone to ring.

He returned to the police station, as instructed, at eleven the next morning. Then Schofield understood what made Sergeant Parker different, why he would, not exactly rush in where angels feared to tread, but walk in with a measured pace and unflappable expression. He was taller than Schofield and twice as far round, and his broad face was a showcase of strength, intelligence and massive calm. Schofield felt his hopes tentatively rising.

Parker invited him for a walk around his patch. But he didn't take him into the Tinderbox. He went himself when there was a need, or if it was time he showed his face, but he considered it no place for a civilian. Most of his colleagues considered it no place for a policeman, but Parker was unwilling to accept there was anywhere that a six-foot-five Jamaican couldn't go. He'd been to BNP rallies to make the point, and he went into the Tinderbox. He didn't go looking for trouble. But he didn't go out of his way to avoid it either.

He said, 'You're trying to make contact with the families?'

Schofield didn't understand. 'Families?'

'Tribes, families - gangs. And you want to have a little chat with them.' Incredulity made his bass voice lift.

Schofield nodded. 'Someone knows where my daughter's living. She was seen over by the motorway. I just want to talk to her. I just want someone to tell her I'm here.'

Sergeant Parker sighed. 'Mr Schofield, you must have been told there's people round here who'd love to reunite you with members of your family. The dead ones. You stroll into the Field Marshal's camp, he'll put you in touch with Schofields all the way back to the ones with tails.'

Schofield gave a tight-lipped grin. 'I'm guessing Field Marshal isn't an official position around here.'

The policeman was gaining a little grudging respect for his companion. The man wasn't stupid, and at least he had a good reason for being here. 'There's *nothing* official in the Tinderbox, unless you count me. Rommel, a.k.a. the Field Marshal, is one of the tribal leaders. He's a mad bastard in charge of a lot of other mad bastards, and all he's got in common with his namesake is that he owns a Nazi helmet. Do not go looking for him. Do not admit to ever having heard his name.'

'Where did he come from?'

Parker gave a vast shrug. 'Where did any of them come from? He arrived as a kid, grew up on the street, got bigger and tougher and meaner. Now he's as mean as they come, and the rest of his tribe are as mean and crazy as he is. They're skinheads, yes? And there's nothing a street kid can do that's crazier than shaving off the one bit of warmth he gets for free.'

'Where do they live?'

Parker stopped walking and turned to look at him. 'Didn't you hear what I just said? Get yourself killed if you must, but don't do it on my beat. Mr Schofield, I don't think you have any idea what you're dealing with here. I'm not making this up; I *know* Rommel has killed men. Proving it is something else, but I know it for a fact. One day I'll get him. One day he'll kill someone who can be shown to have existed, who paid his taxes and whose friends are prepared to talk to us, and then we'll go in there with tanks if needs be, and we'll get him.' A cheering thought occurred to him. 'Hey, Mr Schofield, maybe we'll get him for killing you!'

He said it with a grin, but Schofield knew it wasn't a joke. He felt the fear he'd almost forgotten squirm into fresh life in his belly. 'If Cassie's with him...' If Parker told him his daughter was with the Field Marshal, he'd have to choose between leaving her there and going in after her.

The big Jamaican shook his head. 'Rommel's crew wear leather and chains. And they're pretty well all men.' He took another look at the still from *Streetwise*. 'Ethnic is more like the Pagan's family.'

'All right.' Schofield heard the unsteadiness in his own voice. 'So where do they hang out?'

But the policeman wasn't going to tell him that either. 'The Pagan's not a rabid dog like Rommel, but he's still bad news. He's smart, and he's strong, and he doesn't tolerate any interference with his family. You go near Rommel, he's going to gut you. You go near the Pagan, he's still going to gut you but at least he won't make you watch.'

'A nicer class of homicidal maniac,' managed Schofield.

Parker liked that. 'Oh yes, if you had to choose you'd take the Pagan every time. Rommel, I'd have him in Broadmoor tomorrow if it was up to me. The Pagan, I'm not sure. He keeps his family together and he keeps them fed, and I think maybe they'd be more trouble fending for themselves. And he does stop ambitious young thugs from moving in and carving up the Tinderbox. He's not your idea of a pillar of the community, but maybe he's what that particular community needs.'

But he was talking to a man who thought his daughter had fallen into the Pagan's clutches. 'You're not telling me you admire him?'

Parker shook his head. 'I suppose ... he puzzles me. Mostly it's pretty obvious why people come here. They're misfits who can't make it in the real world.' Momentarily he seemed to have forgotten who he was talking

79

to. 'It takes a misfit to come here, a misfit to stay, and a world-class misfit to stay long enough to put together his own family. Mostly they haven't any choice; they wouldn't be accepted anywhere else. But the Pagan could leave if he wanted. I don't know why he lives like that, round camp fires in derelict buildings. I don't know what he gets out of it that makes it all worthwhile.'

'Money?' suggested Schofield ironically. 'Drugs?'

'Sure,' agreed Parker. 'But if that's what he wants, there are easier ways for a smart man to get them. I think having all those people dependent on him, looking up to him, tickles his vanity. You want to be a big fish, you swim in a small pool. It's a control thing. You might want to think about that, Mr Schofield. If it turns out your daughter is with the Pagan, you'll have to be careful how you proceed. I don't know how he'll react if one of his family tries to leave.'

Schofield was getting a tingling sensation up his spine, as if his nerves knew more than they were telling him. 'You think that's where she is, don't you? With the Pagan. Where do I find them?'

Parker turned again and walked on. 'I wouldn't tell you if I knew. And in fact, I don't know. Two months ago they were in a derelict hotel. Then there was a fire and they left. I don't know where they went. They could be anywhere. They could have left London.'

'They could have gone to Clacton for their holidays,' snapped Schofield, 'but the likelihood is they're still here, in the place they know. In the Tinderbox. *Where* in the Tinderbox? She's my daughter, Sergeant Parker, and I haven't seen her for six years! Help me find her.'

The policeman carried on walking with a measured step. 'You're going to have difficulty understanding this. But my prime duty is not to reunite you with your daughter, it's to keep the peace, and I don't think sending you to the Pagan would achieve that. You're a good man, Mr Schofield, and I don't want to be labelling sharp implements with your blood on them. Even more than that, I don't want the Tinderbox blowing up because you've got the families fighting over a reward.

'Years ago,' he said, apparently changing the subject, 'there was a factory here making artillery for the Royal Navy. That's why the place is called the Tinderbox – the locals reckoned it would only take one spark for the whole place to go up in flames. We still call it that, for the same reason. Right now there's a kind of balance between the families – in particular, between Rommel and the Pagan – that keeps the peace. They're just wary enough of one another to avoid starting trouble. If something happens to change that they'll burn the Tinderbox to the ground, and everyone in it.' He turned his head to fix his companion with a stern eye. 'If at all possible I'd like to avoid that.'

'Then give me something,' insisted Schofield. 'If you don't want me talking to the Pagan, tell me who I *should* talk to.'

Parker gave it some thought. 'There's a man called Winston—'

'I've already met him,' Schofield interrupted. 'He says he'll ask around. He couldn't tell me when, or if, he'd get an answer.'

The policeman regarded him thoughtfully. He was surprised, even a little impressed, that Schofield in his good suit had found his way to Winston. 'You could talk to Annie.'

'Who's Annie?'

'The barmaid at The Wooden Wall – you know, the pub on the corner? She knows just about everyone round here. Buy her a lager and lime, show her your family album and ask her if she's seen your daughter. If she has she'll say so. If she knows how to get a message to her she will.'

And it was at The Wooden Wall that they parted, when Sergeant Parker's beat turned down a corrugated-iron fence which had out-lasted the factory it was built to protect. Schofield was beginning to get his bearings: this was the unmarked but still very real western boundary of the Tinderbox. He watched the policeman for a minute, wondering if this was one of the days he'd go inside. Then he realized that, if he went on watching, Parker would certainly go inside, and this just might be the day his luck ran out. Schofield averted his gaze quickly, and turned and went into the pub.

The architect was amazed to find himself in a high-ceilinged Victorian gin palace with all the choir stalls and etched glass still in place. If The Wooden Wall had been in Chelsea, or Limehouse, or almost anywhere else, it would have been impossible to move for City traders and media types. But this wasn't just an image of how London used to be; it *was* London as it used to be, a much more dangerous environment than it is now, where cutpurses and cut-throats waited round dark corners. A BMW parked outside The Wooden Wall would last ten minutes before it was up on bricks and its wheels were gone. Another ten minutes and someone would steal the bricks.

So the place wasn't overrun with expansive young men in sharp suits talking about unimaginable sums of money. It wasn't overrun with anyone. A couple of men, possibly market traders on their way home, were hunched morosely in a corner. A couple of women – Schofield was no expert but he thought they might be street walkers – had kicked off their shoes and were laughing together.

And then there was Annie. She was the licensee's sister. She was born in The Wooden Wall, had lived there all her life, had seen it slowly fail as the area around it failed. Now she was a plump woman of about fifty in a frilly white blouse and black satin skirt, with curly fair hair and the remnants of a girlish giggle. Schofield introduced himself and asked if she'd join him for a minute. Instead of lager and lime she opted for a cherry brandy.

She heard Schofield out in sympathetic silence, and looked at his pictures for long enough that he knew she wasn't just being polite. But in the end she shook her bubble perm sadly. 'I'm sorry, dear. I haven't seen her.'

Although it had been a long shot, Schofield was disappointed. All the indications were that his daughter was living within half a mile of this place. He'd almost convinced himself that Annie, whose whole world was the pub and those who frequented it, who could probably remember every face that had come through the door in the last forty years, would recognize the picture of Cassie and be able to tell him, *Oh yes, Saturday nights, about nine fifteen. Drinks sweet cider.* But she returned his picture with an apologetic smile.

However, there might be other things she

could tell him that he needed to know. He asked about the other denizens of the Tinderbox – the tribes Cassie could have joined forces with. In particular he repeated the names he'd already heard: Winston, Rommel and the Pagan.

Annie's recall appeared to be total and undiscriminating. She remembered Rommel when he was a sullen child begging at her back door for leftover sandwiches. She remembered Winston when he was thin, and the Pagan before he had a beard. Like everyone else, she told him Winston was his best bet. That Rommel was to be avoided at all costs, and that the Pagan was dangerously unpredictable. Schofield asked where they lived, but Annie either couldn't or wouldn't tell him.

Apart from that, he thought she'd told him all she could. Schofield thanked her, bought her another cherry brandy and went to leave. But she put a soft hand on his sleeve, detaining him. She wanted to see the photograph again. The one of Cassie as a girl. 'What's she holding?'

'A clarinet.'

'Oh.' She considered. 'Is that like a flute?'

'Something like that,' he agreed, ill equipped to deliver a lecture on the elements of a wind section. But at the door a niggling doubt stopped him and he turned back. 'Why, do you know someone who plays the flute?'

'No,' said Annie, and her voice was sad and weary. 'Nobody I know does anything like that. Anything cultured.' Her plump pink fingers toyed with the glass. 'Only sometimes in the middle of the night, when everything's quiet and I'm nearly asleep, I hear music. Lovely music. I don't know where it comes from. I thought it was a flute. It sounds like angels singing.'

Six

He phoned Jan. Excitement thrilled in his voice. 'I think it's her. I haven't found her yet. But I've got a still from the programme, and I think it's her. And there's a woman who lives on the corner who hears someone playing music late at night—'

'When are you coming home?' The coldness in her voice hit Schofield like a slap in the face. 'Ken can't run a two-man business on his own.'

He thought she mustn't have heard, or had misunderstood. 'A few days – maybe a week. Jan, I'm close, I know I am. She's just out there. I've talked to people who've seen her. All I have to do is find her. Ken understands.

He wouldn't expect me to leave now.'

'It's a partnership,' said Jan stubbornly. 'You can't expect him to carry your clients as well as his own. Not at half a day's notice. It's not reasonable.'

'It's the weekend, Jan,' he reminded her quietly. 'There'll be nothing to do till Monday.'

'Then can I tell him you'll be back on Monday?'

Schofield knew both his wife and his partner; he knew where this was coming from. 'Tell him Tuesday, with luck. Somebody's making enquiries for me right now. I'll go see him again at the start of the week. If he has some news for me I could be on my way home with Cassie on Monday night. Tell Ken if this guy doesn't come through for me ... No, never mind,' he said, editing the thoughts as they left his head. 'He'll know. He knows why I'm doing this.'

'As long as Ken Broadbent understands,' Jan said tightly, ringing off.

For a long time Schofield sat hunched behind the wheel of his car, staring at the phone in his hand as if he blamed it for his wife's intransigence. He knew that what he was doing had come between them, but still didn't understand how. He didn't know what it would take to repair the damage. But at this point it was almost irrelevant. If he succeeded the situation would change utterly. If he failed and came home alone, perhaps that would mollify her.

It wasn't just that she thought he was wasting his time. She thought what he was doing was wrong. Not for the first time, he tried to work out why she felt that way. She couldn't really want never to see her child again. Then what? Try as he might, he honestly couldn't see why she considered his mission so misguided. As he sat alone in the car the uncomprehending anger died slowly out of his face, leaving only sorrow and a deep weariness.

The last six years had marked his face with lines as deep and permanent as scars. There was almost nothing left of the callow charm that had stayed with him to the brink of middle age, until he was the father of two adolescent children, when he finished growing up in the space of a few dreadful weeks. The horror he had to bring his family through demanded a man's strength more than a boy's charm, and he found it because he had to. He took a certain grim pride in how he had risen to the challenge.

What he never realized was that Jan's grief at her daughter's leaving was compounded by the loss of the gentle man she married. She didn't blame him for the new toughness, the hard shell he'd had to grow against the hurt of that time, or for the bleak single-mindedness that was in him now. She'd never stopped loving him. But after Cassie left he was harder to like.

She'd have been surprised to see how weariness had opened cracks in his armour revealing the emotions he normally kept tidied out of sight. He sat huddled in his car – her car – tired in body, brain and soul, trying to summon the energy to call her back and try to put things right between them, and misery, loneliness and defeat seeped down the seams of his face like tears.

He'd never stopped loving her either, but it was a long time since he'd been able to express it without emphasising the gap that had grown between them. For a long time it had been as hard to talk about them as about Cassie; it had seemed easier to pack the marriage neatly away and put it up in the attic with Cassie's things, and just hope that one day it too would be needed again.

The next day was Sunday, so he went to church. To several churches, in fact, driving round the safe outer margins of the Tinderbox and tracking down every spire he could see, every peel of bells he heard. He handed out most of his posters – making a mental note to run off some more at the first copy shop he saw – and buttonholed a succession of clergy as they finished with their sparse congregations. But no one recognized the pictures he showed them.

'Was she a church-goer?' a couple of them

asked.

'Not when she was at home.'

'Then why...?'

'Because I'm desperate,' he admitted frankly. 'Because things change. Because a young girl alone and adrift in an unfamiliar city just might seek help or comfort in a house of God. Because gathering up lost sheep is part of your job description.'

That didn't win him any Brownie points. He saw the respectable, well-fed faces close down in resentment. When he did the rounds again at Evensong, armed with a sheaf of new posters, they busied themselves with other duties. He returned to his hotel with nothing to show for his day.

From dawn on Monday he was counting the minutes until he could visit Winston again. Too soon and they might think he was a police raid and vanish into the concrete jungle. He planned to arrive at the camp under the flyover at eleven o'clock, which was only a little earlier in the day than Briony had taken him there. In fact the last hour dragged unbearably, and he jumped the gun.

It was ten thirty when he found his way to the improbable tennis court. A light rain was falling, and Winston had fashioned a tent out of a huge sheet of clear plastic to keep his sofa dry. Otherwise he didn't appear to have moved since Friday.

He recognized Schofield but made no move to meet him. 'You're too soon, man.'

'I said I'd come back today.'

'I told you to come back in a week.'

Schofield waved his hand at the barren landscape. 'What's going to take a week? If she's here, she's within half a mile of this spot. You look, you're going to find her. *Have you looked?*'

The fat boy was untroubled. 'It's not that easy. There's a lot of people here. And there's no kind of directory – you can't just phone round. We're talking to people. It's going to take time.'

'Somebody told me she could be with the Pagan.'

Winston considered. 'That's possible.'

'Where are they?'

'Not sure. I know where they were a couple of months ago...'

'So do I,' growled Schofield, 'and I don't even live here. You must have seen them since then.'

'Sure I've seen them,' agreed Winston complacently. 'But they haven't got round to sending out their change of address cards. You don't advertise where you're living, all right? If you do, somebody tries to take it off you. Sooner or later we'll see them, and we'll talk to them and ask about your girl. But I can't tell you when. I've got your poster, I've got your number. I'll call you.'

'Would it help,' asked Schofield, 'if I gave you some money up front?'

'No,' said Winston honestly. 'But it wouldn't hurt either.'

In the end Schofield had to believe him. He gave him fifty pounds and drove disconsolately back to his hotel to pack. If there was nothing left for him to do but wait for phone calls that never came, he could do it at home.

An hour later, as he threw his bag into the back of Jan's car, the phone finally rang. He snatched it from his pocket, tearing the lining in his haste. 'Winston?'

But it was a girl's voice. 'Mr Schofield? Is it you that's been leaving those posters around? 'Cause if it is, I might be able to help you.'

She said she'd meet him after work. He bought himself a late lunch, and stared through it until it went cold. Then he drove around for a while until it was time to meet her. So it wasn't that time was short and he rushed off without thinking. He did nothing but think, for three hours. He remembered the warnings he'd been given, recognized the risk he was running. And decided it was worth it.

It wasn't Cassie who called him. At first he tried to persuade himself that it was. Listening to her he leaned intently over the steering wheel, his body growing warm and shaking softly, and thought *It is – it's her. She's pretending to be someone else to keep her options open until she's sure she wants to do this.* But as she went on speaking Schofield had to acknowledge that he was mistaken. There was no resonance between them. He had to believe that he'd know if he was talking to his own daughter.

So it wasn't Cassie. But it was someone who claimed to know where she was, and was willing to take Schofield to her. She told him where to meet her, giving directions from The Wooden Wall. She said, 'You have to come alone.'

More alarm bells rang. But Schofield was disposed not to heed them. 'I'm not bringing a snatch squad, if that's what you mean.'

'Alone,' she insisted. 'I'm sticking my neck out for you. That's all right, I know you'll make it worth my while, but if we're noticed I won't keep the money long. You don't have to live here; I do. You and me on our own, nobody's going to pay much heed. You, me and a couple of big guys watching our backs – that'll be noticed. Plus, it's the best way I know of making sure your girl isn't where we're going when we get there. Her and her whole family will just vanish if they know you're coming. Sorry, but that's how it is. My way or no way.'

Laurence Schofield was not a stupid man. He'd lived in the world long enough to know that the only sensible reply was *No way*. But this was what he'd come for, and this was the closest he'd got, and if he did this he could be driving home with Cassie in a couple of hours' time, and if he walked away he'd never know. And then, the girl didn't sound like someone to be frightened of.

'All right,' he said softly.

He did as he was told: left the car at The Wooden Wall at five thirty and proceeded on foot. She'd said she'd meet him round the first corner.

Monday night in the Tinderbox, with the sun going down over the elevated sections of the motorway, was like being nowhere at all. A rubble-strewn limbo, it stretched improbably far in all directions. Schofield couldn't imagine how such an expanse of capital-city land could fall derelict and be abandoned, except for a handful of streets – half-streets, rather, one end or one side having crumbled faster than the other – and a few scrubby businesses unknown to the VAT man.

He found the corner the girl had described but no one was there. Disappointment set talons in his heart.

He thought he heard movement in the alley behind him and turned to look, peering into the gloom where the shadows were gathering. Seeing nothing, he turned back to find her beside him.

It wasn't Cassie. She was a wan little thing

who barely came up to his shoulder, dressed like everyone else round here in denims and a sweater, a woolly hat pulled down over black curls.

In the circumstances there wasn't much need to introduce themselves. But the girl wanted to be sure. She said, 'Mr Schofield?' in the half-timorous, half-plaintive voice he remembered.

'Yes.'

'You've got my money?'

'Yes.' It was in his inside pocket. He'd thought of leaving it locked in the car. But if he found Cassie he'd want to be able to leave immediately, without his guide clamouring for payment. 'Are you going to earn it?'

'You'll see.' She walked past him into the alley. 'It's this way.' He hesitated barely a moment before following her.

He tried to get more information as they went but her answers were monosyllabic. She walked quickly, keeping her head down.

'Does Cassie know I'm here?'

'Yes.'

'Is she...' He was almost afraid to put it into words. 'Is she happy to see me?' He awaited her answer with bated breath.

'I suppose.'

'Her – what do you call it? – her tribe. They won't try to stop me?'

'No.'

'Are you a friend of Cassie's? What's your

name?'

It was too dark to see her face now, but the sudden movement of her head was sharp with fear. 'I'm nobody. Nobody.' She was walking so swiftly now he had to stretch his long legs to keep up.

She took him into an entry and stopped. 'Wait here. I'll go get her.' Before he could object she was gone. Even the sharp quick rap of her heels was swallowed by the cliff of rotting brickwork above him.

For in walking they'd left behind the rubble plain where time, neglect and bulldozers had worked their various demolitions, and had entered another kind of desert. Here the buildings towered over the narrow lanes, huddled close like conspirators. They were huge structures, warehouses and mills four storeys high, which once employed thousands of people. And one morning the owner had come on to the factory floor and told people whose families had worked for his family for generations that they would be on the dole from Friday. Decades later, the echoes of that morning were visible throughout the Tinderbox. The little streets died slower than the industries they served, but they died just the same.

Strange music and footsteps in the entry behind him roused Schofield from his anxious thoughts. 'Cassie?' His voice cracked on the soaring hope.

But it was neither the girl he'd come to meet nor the one who'd brought him. It was a man. A moment later a second joined the first. They stood framed by the tall buildings, filling the narrow entry. A chill spring moon threw enough light to reflect a row of pinpoints off something that fell softly, sinuously, from each man's right hand. Then Schofield understood the fragments of anarchic music. The men were carrying lengths of chain.

He'd been naive and foolish. It had been a long day in the course of which hope had vied with disappointment and he'd grown tired swinging between them; and growing tired had grown careless. He'd fallen into the trap that he'd been warned about time and again. He'd broadcast his purpose too widely, and someone had – as someone was bound to – seen a way of turning Schofield's tragedy to his own advantage.

At least he didn't waste time wondering if the men with chains would take him to Cassie. He knew why they were here. There was no point trying to bluff or plead or bluster his way out. He had nothing to bargain with that they could not take from him by the simple expedient of knocking him down. It was a crude trap set to part him from his money, and there was no scope in the situation for subtlety of intellect to triumph over strength of arms. He did the only thing possible: turned on his heel and ran. Boots clattered behind him and the chains chimed.

In the darkness he could see almost nothing. He stumbled over the rubbish piled in drifts along the gutters, sheets of newspaper wrapping themselves around his legs. He turned a corner and ran full-tilt into a row of dustbins. The old metal ones, they clattered down the alley spilling contents too old now even to stink. Schofield danced among them for a long second before gravity had its inevitable way with him and he hit the ground.

Behind him, he couldn't judge how far but not far enough, a triumphant if breathless obscenity split the dank air. Bruised, battered, aware from the ventilation of unexpected places that he'd torn his clothes, Schofield staggered to his feet and lurched on. Sweat ran in his eyes, blinding him. His chest heaved with effort, knives sliding between his ribs, and his throat burned. He was nearing the point where his legs would carry him no longer.

And then they would catch him. He literally could not imagine the effect that heavy chains swung by angry men would have on flesh and bone in a dark alley where no interruption was likely, but he thought he was about to find out.

He turned another corner, and the entry

was blocked. The wall was higher than his head, forming a hard-edged silhouette against the sky.

A small portion of his brain not occupied with the mechanics of flight considered the situation. If there was no way through he was trapped. The men with the chains would catch him and take his wallet, his coat, his shoes and anything else they had a use for before they beat him to a bloody pulp. That calm section of his brain considered it might be better to offer no further resistance. They might just take his belongings and break a few ribs if he didn't put them to any more trouble.

By the time he reached the wall he was panting with panic and exertion. He was a middle-aged professional man who hadn't run since his children were small. He hadn't run like this since he was himself a child.

The pounding steps behind him slowed too, the manic jangle of the chains falling to a steady beat like the metronome for a steel band. The men believed they had him, that there was no need to expend more sweat in the pursuit. Schofield thought so too. This was where push came to shove. He could do nothing about his fear except try not to whimper. He turned to face whatever was in store, and backed until the wall stopped him. His arms spread out along it to brace him against the imminent attack.

Out of the darkness, as if from the very substance of the rotting brickwork, a hand reached out and touched Schofield's arm.

There was a door into the building on one side of the wall. Schofield's heart leapt at the shock of the touch, then thundered on. He didn't know who'd found him, or what their purpose was. He knew he wasn't safe yet, but at least it was a chance. What lay through the door couldn't be worse than what waited in the alley. He followed the hand into the utter blackness of the empty building.

This too had been a factory once. Schofield could see nothing, but the iron arms of dead machines gouged his thighs as he went. He couldn't imagine how his rescuer moved so quickly between them. Schofield felt himself falling behind, was afraid he'd be abandoned to his fate. But the hand reached back to him in the dark, steering him, and occasionally a soft gruff voice murmured an instruction. Schofield followed, obedient as a child. When the hand drew him to a frail wooden staircase, he climbed; when the way lay along a spidery catwalk high up in the dusty air, he crawled on his hands and knees, blanking out the danger.

When the hand pulled him down and a finger on his lips pressed him to silence, Schofield crouched and panted softly through his mouth like a well-trained gun dog. He could hear the men moving below him: the scuff of boots, the clank of chains, intermittently a grunted curse as they bumped into the iron furniture.

At first they searched in silence. But as the minutes passed and they found only more machinery, more rubbish, growing impatient with the task and with one another they traded advice, then instructions, then abuse across the industrial bone yard. One of them was called Shag, the other – if Schofield heard correctly – Average. He stayed near the door to stop anyone sneaking out. Shag worked his way along the lines of dead machines, feeling for places where a man might hide. Schofield wondered what would happen when he found the stairs. But he dared not ask, even in a whisper; and actually he didn't want to know.

Before that Shag had had enough. He brought his chain crashing down on one of the machines with as much venom as if it had been Schofield's body. 'This is frigging stupid!' he screamed, and the sheer hatred in his voice clutched at Schofield's vitals. He knew absolutely that if these men found him they'd beat him to death. 'We'll never find him in here. I don't suppose you brought a frigging torch?'

Average shouted back, 'Did you?'

'He must have got past you,' snarled Shag. Chain crashed in a murderous rhythm as he beat his way back to the door. 'I'm going home. Next time we do this, you can be the bait and I'll use the girl for muscle.' The door slammed and silence descended.

Schofield exhaled in a long, shaky sigh. He started to say, 'How can I thank you?' But a strong hand closed over his mouth and the voice in his ear hissed him to be still. So they crouched together in the dark, ten metres up in the dead factory on a catwalk held together mainly by force of habit, Laurence Schofield and the angel of his deliverance, and they waited.

Ten minutes passed. Then, unseen below them, Average – his was the deeper voice – grunted, 'I reckon he has gone, too. Bastard. Come on, let's see if there's any supper left.' This time when they left Schofield heard the faint ring of boots away down the alley outside.

PART TWO

THE BOY

One

'Schofield,' said Schofield. Already he'd pulled out a poster and was tilting it to the
moonlight in the hope that might help. 'Her
name is Cassie Schofield. Cassandra.'

'Never heard of her,' said Jonah.

'Perhaps she looks familiar?'

'Not to me.'

'She may be using another name.'

'Can't imagine why.' From the tone of his
voice Schofield thought the boy was laughing at him. He glanced sharply sideways but
there wasn't enough light to see.

Schofield suspected Jonah had been laughing at him from the moment he saw him –
that it was only his risible helplessness in this
hard place that justified intervening in what
he would otherwise have considered a private matter. He seemed less concerned with
saving an innocent man from a vicious
assault than with teasing the assailants.
Schofield thought he owed his life to Jonah's
peculiar sense of humour.

When he explained how he'd been tricked he got no sympathy, only derision that anyone could be so gullible. 'I'm new here,' Schofield said defensively.

'Never would have guessed,' said Jonah with an audible grin.

At first Schofield thought he'd misheard when the boy tossed his name over his shoulder as they climbed down from the cat-walk. He wondered if he'd said Joe, or Jones. He even wondered – he could still see nothing – if he'd imagined the slight gruffness of the voice and it was Joan. When they left the factory and a stray beam of moonlight glinted on a tangle of fair, shoulder-length curls he was more than half persuaded that he owed his life to a girl.

But where the entry widened to an alley, more light revealed a stockiness of build and a squareness of jaw that were essentially masculine, if still immature. Schofield guessed the boy was about Tom's age. But he was shorter than Tom and the sturdiness of his frame was deceptive: when they brushed together in the dark Schofield was aware how little there was between Jonah's clothes and his bones.

The boy guided him to the edge of the Tinderbox. 'You'll be OK from here. Turn right at the corner, right again at the viaduct. You'll be able to see The Wooden Wall from there.'

Schofield was hunting in his torn pockets for his wallet. But Jonah was already turning away, and only Schofield's hand on the sleeve of the battered parka stopped him. 'Where are you going?'

'Home,' said the boy. His gaze travelled between his dirty clothes and Schofield's ripped ones. 'We're not dressed for the West End.'

'You can't leave me here!' Schofield heard the terror in his own voice, and didn't care as long as it had the desired effect. 'I don't know where the hell we are. God almighty, what kind of a place is this? Who were those men?'

Jonah contrived to look down his nose at the taller man. 'They're Rommel's heavies, from the abattoir. They live here. They belong here. You don't. You come here with your bulging wallet and you're shocked when someone tries to take it from you? This is the Tinderbox, Mr Schofield. It belongs to people like Shag and Average. And me.' That note of pride in his voice said he felt good about being able to live in this hostile place. 'Go away. Stay away.'

'I can't. I have to find my daughter.'

'You won't find her if you're dead.'

Schofield was still holding his sleeve. Partly as a drowning man holds a lifeline, partly because mere luck had brought him what he'd come here looking for: someone who knew this alien place and its stranger inhabitants. He wouldn't have let go unless the boy broke his fingers. 'You could find her. I'll pay you.'

Jonah shrugged. 'I told you, I don't know her.'

'You haven't looked. I have a torch back at the car...' But Jonah was coming no further with him. 'Then take the poster, ask around. Someone must know her, she was seen near here. Someone thought she might be with the Pagan's people.'

'Yeah?' Then he shook his head. 'I can't just walk into their camp and start asking questions. People round here don't like that. It's kind of rude.'

After all that had happened, that made Schofield gasp. That people who lived like this – like Jonah, like the men with the chains – had a concept of good manners. But he wasn't ready to give up. 'If I don't belong here, nor does Cassie. Help me find her. You *have* to. There is no one else.'

But Jonah was unmoved. 'Then there's no one. Mr Schofield, if your daughter is here, and she's been here for six years, she's part of the Tinderbox now. She's part of a family and she's safe. Don't worry about her. If she ever needs you, she knows where to find you.'

Reaction had left Schofield close to tears. He couldn't make the boy do anything he didn't want to. When Jonah turned back into the darkness of the Tinderbox he'd never see him again, and his best chance of finding Cassie would be gone too. And there was nothing he could do about it.

He let go of Jonah's sleeve. His voice was low. 'At least let me thank you for your help. I think if you hadn't turned up when you did, those men would have killed me.'

'They would,' agreed Jonah calmly. 'Rommel's guys don't take prisoners.'

Schofield winced. 'Then let me do something for you in return. You're living rough, aren't you? Let me help.'

'I don't need your help,' said Jonah dismissively. 'I could use some money.'

Somehow Schofield was disappointed. The boy had saved his life, and thought cash an adequate reward. 'All right. I've got a thousand pounds—'

Jonah hooted with sheer astonishment. 'You're walking round with a thousand pounds? You walked into the Tinderbox with a *thousand* pounds? Man, you don't deserve to live! Anyone that stupid *deserves* to be hanging on a hook at the abattoir. Look, I don't want that kind of money from you. Give me a hundred. Any more than that and I'll have Rommel's heavies after *me*.'

Schofield refused to count it out. He gave Jonah half of what he had. 'It's still only money...'

Jonah's head came up sharply and his voice was hard. 'That's right, money. You buy food with it. You buy boots with it when you've walked the soles out of the ones you've got. You buy industrial-sized plastic bags so everything you own isn't soaked every time it rains. For someone whose life revolves around making the stuff, you're pretty casual about money.'

Miserable and embarrassed, Schofield tried to explain. 'I didn't mean ... Of course ... I just wish there was something more I could do.'

'What, take me away from all this?' Jonah laughed out loud, a rich, hoarse laugh that spoke of too many nights in damp bedding. 'I don't need taking away from all this. I don't *want* taking away from all this. I'm OK here. I know my way around. Nobody mugs me.'

It was time to give up. 'Maybe they will,' murmured Schofield, 'now you're a man of property.'

Jonah flicked him a last grin. Then he was gone, vanished back into the dangerous dark as if Schofield had merely imagined him. There was nothing more to be done. Schofield walked across the first real road towards the pub on the corner. Somewhat improbably, his car was as he'd left it. Schofield was astonished to realize it wasn't an hour since he parked it there.

He returned to his hotel and asked for his room back. He was too shaken to embark on a hundred-mile drive, and there was nothing else he could do. He thought about reporting the episode but knew Sergeant Parker would be even less sympathetic than Jonah had been. He'd asked for trouble, he'd been luckier than he deserved, and he wasn't going to demand justice when taking an arrest warrant into the Tinderbox could get the policeman killed. He went to bed, nursing the pain of being alone when for just a moment he had thought he'd have Cassie with him by now.

In the early hours of the morning his phone rang. It was another policeman, not Parker, wanting to know if Schofield was the Laurence Schofield who'd had the posters printed.

Schofield was wide awake and on the edge of his bed before he finished asking. 'Yes,' he said. 'Yes! Have you some news of my daughter?'

But the phone call wasn't about Cassie. 'According to the young man who was carrying this poster, the five hundred and eighty pounds he was also carrying was given to him by you. Freely, without duress, and not in connection with any illegal activities.'

'Jonah? You arrested Jonah?'

'I had reason to stop and search him,' said

the voice at the other end, expressionless. 'I found an unusually large sum of money on him and asked him to explain it. He told me to phone you.'

'Yes,' said Schofield again, 'that's right; he's done nothing wrong. He helped me. I was lost, some men were threatening me and he helped me. I wanted to reward him.'

'With five hundred and eighty pounds?'

'I'd have signed over my pension fund if he'd wanted it.'

He heard the sound of heavy breathing. 'And did you report this incident, sir? Where the men were threatening you?'

'There didn't seem a lot of point. Are you familiar with the Tinderbox?'

Certainly he knew the name. The tone of the policeman's voice changed. 'You got lost in there? And lived to tell the tale?'

'Thanks to Jonah. That's why I gave him the money. Maybe it was too much. He said it'd get him into trouble. But it didn't seem a lot for saving my skin.' Now he'd had a little time to think, Schofield was puzzled. 'Where did you find him? Surely you don't do stop-and-searches in the Tinderbox.'

'He was going into an all-night cinema half a mile away.'

Schofield's heart gave a little twist within him. With more money than he'd probably seen in his life, all Jonah could think to do was go to see a film. And before he got past the ticket kiosk he was pinned against the wall with someone going through his pockets.

'Is that the only problem? The money? He isn't in any other trouble?'

'Not with me,' said the constable. 'But there's something wrong with him. He's bouncing off the walls down here. We can't get any sense out of him. All he'd do when we questioned him was wave this poster at us. I figured that meant you might know him.'

'Well, you were right. You can let him go now.'

'Not in this state I can't,' growled the constable. 'If he hasn't done anything wrong I don't know why he's in such a panic, but I can't just chuck him back on the street like this.' Then his voice took on a slightly shifty note. 'Of course, if I could get someone to pick him up, take responsibility for him...'

Schofield sighed. It was four o'clock in the morning. But it was a morning he wouldn't have seen but for Jonah. 'Tell me where you are.'

The custody sergeant was waiting for him. 'We didn't know what to do about him. The money was the only reason to hold him, once you said you'd given it him we should have let him go. But ... well, you'll see.'

Schofield heard before he saw. It sounded

like an animal in a trap, beating itself bloody in the effort to escape. There was a low animal wail, half-howl, half-moan, that had the custody suite's other occupants on edge and complaining. One of them whined, 'You're not supposed to keep pets down here, Sarge,' as they passed.

The sergeant checked a spy hole and unlocked the door. 'If you want to get out of here,' he said patiently, 'you're going to have to calm down a bit.'

Against the bare walls the boy was a blur of movement. It was no exaggeration: he was literally bouncing off the walls. His face was bruised and blind with panic, locked into the furious activity as though it was keeping something worse at bay. Schofield thought if they left the door open it would be minutes before he realized.

Schofield turned to the sergeant with fury in his eyes. 'What the *hell*...?'

'Not us, sir,' said the officer, shaking his head. 'I told you – he went crazy.'

Schofield sucked in a steadying breath and moved into the little room. 'Jonah. Jonah!'

But where the boy had gone even the sound of his name, or what passed for his name, couldn't reach him. He hurtled past Schofield as if he hadn't seen him, his eyes wide and blank, red-rimmed in the ashy pallor of his face. The keening continued unabated.

114

The custody sergeant grimaced at Schofield's back. 'See?'

The next time Jonah hurtled past Schofield reached out a long arm to field him, trapping the agitated body against the wall with his own. Instantly the monotone wail rose to a frightened yell that no amount of common sense would penetrate. 'Jonah!' Schofield slapped him soundly across the cheek with his open palm.

The noise stopped as if someone had turned off a tap.

'That's better,' said Schofield. 'Now, Jonah, look at me. *Look* at me. You know who I am, yes?' After a moment the boy nodded wordlessly. 'The police don't need to keep you. Do you want to come with me?'

Jonah nodded again, eagerly this time, the fair tangles dancing round his face.

'Thank Christ for that,' muttered the sergeant – and the whole of the custody suite added an amen.

Schofield didn't even try to talk until he got the boy outside. He steered him by the elbows through the maze of corridors until the front door of the police station closed behind them. Beneath the blue lamp Jonah let his head rock back and sucked in great draughts of gritty air. As if he'd been under water and close to drowning.

The last four days had left Schofield physically exhausted and mentally drained. He'd needed the sleep that was so rudely interrupted. Without it he was tetchy. 'What the hell was that about?'

Jonah avoided his gaze. But at least now he could put words together. He mumbled, 'They thought I stole the money. They wouldn't let me go.'

'Not that. The head-banging routine. Why didn't you just wait till I turned up? My number was on the poster; you knew they were going to call me. Did you think I wouldn't come?'

The boy shrugged defensively. 'I don't know. I didn't know what you'd do.'

'Jonah, you saved my life!' Schofield heard himself shouting and said it again, quieter. 'You saved my life. And you thought I'd leave you in a police cell rather than explain how?'

'I thought you might.' The boy looked down at himself, and defiantly back. 'I know what I am. I'm not your kind of people. You admit to knowing someone like me, those bastards are only going to think one thing. The easiest way would have been to deny all knowledge.'

Schofield sighed, the anger past. 'I don't understand this world you live in. Even if I didn't owe you my life, I wouldn't behave like that. I don't know anyone who would.'

'You know them,' insisted Jonah. 'You just don't know you know them. You get a different view of people from the gutter.' He managed a tremulous grin. 'Boot soles, mostly.'

The shadow of what had happened in the police station was already beginning to fade from his eyes. In there, surrounded by authority, he'd seemed a terrified child. Out here on these cold uncaring streets, where people could die unnoticed, he was almost a man. 'It's too late to go back to bed,' he decided. 'I'll buy you breakfast.'

Too surprised to argue, Schofield followed the boy down the street. Where he turned into an unlit alley the man hesitated, pierced by anxiety; but Jonah said, 'Come on,' encouragingly, and soon they turned a corner and there were lights ahead, flickering as people moved between them.

It was a fruit market. Traders were setting out stalls bright with produce off the backs of lorries which had driven all night. They were working men and women already into their working day, and in a corner of the square were the lit windows of a café which did more business between five and eight in the morning than at any other time.

Now he was back on his own turf the panic that had reduced the boy to a wild animal had entirely passed. Jonah pushed his way inside with a hint of a swagger and appropriated one of the Formica tables. 'Everything you've got, Ronnie,' he said loftily, 'and a gallon of coffee.'

A lean figure wrapped in stained whites looked through from the kitchen. A hawkish eye took in Schofield. 'You got any money today, Jonah?'

Jonah scowled and pulled ten pounds from his pocket. He'd separated it from the rest where the wad couldn't be seen. Schofield took note. 'Of course I've got money. Would I rob you?'

'Yes,' said the man, without much rancour.

'The shepherd's pie doesn't count,' insisted the boy. 'Eating it was an act of charity. You should *pay* people to eat your shepherd's pie. Danger money.'

Chuckling darkly, Ronnie retired to his kitchen.

'We call him Eggon Ronnie,' volunteered Jonah. 'You want to know why?'

Schofield knew he'd regret this. 'Why?'

'There's egg on his apron, egg on his shirt, egg on...'

Schofield passed a hand across his eyes.

In minutes Ronnie was back with market-trader portions of fried breakfast. Then he made another trip with doorsteps of toast and a jar of marmalade. Finally he returned with a big enamel pot and two mugs.

Schofield ate more from politeness than need. But Jonah ate as if the stolen pie was the last hot meal he'd had. He ate everything – burnt corners, greasy bits, bacon rind, tomato skins, the lot. He ladled sugar into his coffee. He cleaned his plate so thoroughly Schofield wondered if Ronnie would bother to wash up afterwards. When he'd finished he sat back with a satisfied sigh, cradling his hands behind his head.

Schofield found himself smiling. 'Better?'

'Oh yeah.'

In the simple pleasure of his expression, for the first time Schofield glimpsed something of the appeal of this feckless way of life. If you could travel, as Jonah had, from the depths of despair to the peak of satisfaction in about half an hour and with change from a tenner, the world was your oyster. Anything could be just around the corner. All right, sometimes it was Shag and Average jangling their chains, but sometimes it was a poor lost soul from the right side of the tracks who'd pay you serious money to show him back to his car. If your life could so easily be improved so radically, there was no need to fear the future and no incentive to plan for it.

Schofield blinked, astonished at himself. The way this boy lived – the way Cassie was living – was appalling. It was reckless and irresponsible. It had been easier to understand when he thought they had no choice. What did it say – about them, about the rest of society – if they had options and this was what they chose? All it took was a warm meal and Jonah thought he owned the world. Of course he didn't, but Schofield, who'd never gone hungry but had also never felt that way, could envy him for thinking it.

As host, Jonah refilled the mugs. Then he said, 'Can I see the pictures again?'

Schofield took out the poster and smoothed it on the table. Then he put the still shot from *Streetwise* beside it. Jonah picked up the still and squinted at it from different angles, and Schofield didn't hurry him. He was in no rush to be disappointed once again.

'I was wrong,' Jonah said at last, handing it back. 'I do know her. At least, I know who she is. That's Casey. The Pagan's woman. You think she's going home with you? Dream on.'

Two

This was why Schofield had come – why he'd done everything. And now the moment was here he didn't know what to do. He went on staring at the boy for more than a minute before he could get his lips to form words. 'You know her? Jonah – you know my daughter? You know Cassie?'

The boy shrugged broad bony shoulders. 'If that's her in the photo then yes, sure. She calls herself Casey now.'

'And she's ... living with someone?' He knew she was twenty-one; in his heart she was still fifteen.

'The Pagan.' He said it as if the name should mean something to Schofield. And to an extent it did. It was one of the two names that had come up in every conversation he'd had about the Tinderbox. Briony Fellowes, Sergeant Parker, even Annie had agreed he wasn't as bad as Rommel. Somehow, Schofield found that less than reassuring.

And Cassie was living with him. Sleeping with him. Perhaps they had children. As nothing else had done, that brought home to Schofield how much of his daughter's life he'd missed. Even if he found her today, even if he had her home for supper, there were still six years of her life about which he would know only what she chose to tell him. That hurt almost physically.

Jonah leaned forward over the table, fair brows gathered in a frown of concern. 'You OK?'

'Yes. Of course.' But Schofield was sitting there with his mouth half open and his eyes stretched and glazed, and any competent first-aider would have diagnosed shock. 'It's just ... You said you didn't recognize her!'

'It was dark; it could have been anybody on that poster.' Jonah explained carefully, as if afraid Schofield might punish his mistake.

'And then...' He shouldn't have started the sentence. It was clear to Schofield that he didn't want to finish it.

'And then,' Schofield hazarded slowly, 'people who live in the Tinderbox don't talk about one another to people who live outside?'

The boy had the grace to drop his gaze. 'Pretty much, yeah.'

Schofield sucked in a deep breath and pulled himself up straight. 'All right. You know her. Do you know where she is?'

The boy shrugged.

The other Schofield, the one his wife didn't like so much, shot a hand across the table that fastened in the front of Jonah's parka before he had time to recoil. 'I said, where is she?'

The boy's eyes flared whitely at him, startled and afraid. 'In the Tinderbox. That's all you need to know.'

'Take me to her.'

'No!' However nervous he was of Schofield, he was more afraid of the Pagan. 'I told you, I don't go into their camp. And if I can't, you sure as hell can't.'

'She's my daughter. I can do anything that'll get her back.'

'She isn't *coming* back.' He saw that resonate in Schofield's eyes like a slap, and some half-remembered impulse of decency made him feel sorry. 'Don't you understand? She's

122

the Pagan's woman. She's the head of a tribe – a family. That's who she is now, not your little girl. She's never going to leave the Tinderbox. Anywhere else she'd be somebody's wife, somebody's mother, somebody's secretary, but here she's the alpha female of a leading tribe. Maybe that doesn't seem like much to you, but it does to her. She's never going to leave.'

Schofield regarded him coldly. 'Tell you what, Jonah. You take me to her and I'll ask her.' He must have seen the flicker of unease in the boy's eyes. 'Unless what you're telling me is that this man – this Pagan – isn't going to *let* her leave?'

Jonah squirmed in his seat, uncomfortable and resentful. 'This is none of my business, OK? You needed help, I helped you; you wanted information, I gave you that too. You want to march into the Pagan's camp armed with a photograph, a birth certificate and a home movie of the Schofield family barbecue, you'll have to do it on your own. You have no idea what you're dealing with here. This isn't your world – it isn't anything *like* your world. If dumb animals like Shag and Average can back you against a wall, what do you think the Pagan's going to do to you? He'll rip your arms off!'

'I'll get the police,' swore Schofield. 'They won't be happy but they'll come. If I tell them this man's holding my daughter against her will, they'll have no option. They'll tear the place apart to find her.'

'You send cops into the Tinderbox and the whole bloody place'll blow sky high!' From the tenor of his voice Schofield had to believe it was the truth. 'People are going to *die*. Maybe you; maybe her. Or maybe you'll get her back, but after you're on your way home someone'll remember it was me who was picked up a couple of days before. Shag and Average don't know it was me that pulled you out of the alley, but they'll work it out. I talked to you, the police talked to me and I had money to spend. Oh yes, they'll know who to blame if the riot squad moves in on the Tinderbox.'

Schofield sniffed impatiently. He thought Jonah was being theatrical. 'You'll just have to keep your head down till the dust settles.'

'When the dust settles, it's going to find me nailed to a wall!' yelled the boy.

The image shook Schofield to his roots. He knew it wasn't a metaphor. 'So get out of town for a week.'

'What, to my little place in the country?' hooted Jonah derisively. 'Join the Chumley-Fanshaws for a week on their grouse moor? I bet Princess Anne'd lend me a horse if I asked nicely!'

'You could—'

'I could starve,' spat Jonah. 'And I tried that already, and I didn't like it. This is my home, OK? It's where I live – where I make my living. So maybe a squat in a damp basement isn't your idea of a home, but it's mine, and everything I own is here, and if I leave it someone else'll take it. And the Pagan'll still nail my hands to the wall next time he sees me. Why do you think they call him the Pagan? Because he's hot on the Christian virtues? Believe me, this man never forgives, and he never forgets.'

Rigid with anger, he shoved himself away from the table. He took Schofield's money from the pocket of his jeans and slapped payment for their breakfast on Ronnie's counter. The rest of the wad he tossed with a sneer onto the table. 'Keep it. It's done me more harm than good already.'

Emotional outbursts were a thing of the past in the Schofield household. You can't afford to unstop the bottle when you don't know what will come out. Schofield didn't shout back. He said quietly, 'I was going to say, you could come to us.'

In the boy's eyes he saw the hot anger turn to mystification. As if he'd said it in Hebrew. 'What? *Why?*'

They understood nothing of one another's thought processes. Schofield was as astonished by the response as Jonah was by the offer. 'Why? Because if you hadn't helped me you wouldn't need somewhere to get away *to*!'

With the anger gone and nothing coming to replace it, Schofield finally saw what he was dealing with. Not Superman with his cloak in the wash; not a wild animal; not even a cocky street kid at ease in a place sensible people were afraid to visit. Just a boy, maybe sixteen years old, cold, not getting enough to eat, not sleeping well enough, who should still have been growing but probably wasn't, pinched, tired, without hope. Clearly a survivor. But surviving isn't the same as living.

Jonah pushed the thick hair off his forehead with one hand. 'This is where I live,' he said again, quieter but insistently, as if it meant something specific to him. 'I'm not leaving.'

He went on standing in the middle of the Élite Café, awkward with big-boned teenage clumsiness, unsure of his next move. With Ronnie in the back they had the place to themselves – no one was watching, no mocking eyes pushing him towards a decision. They could talk if they wanted to. If they were able to.

Schofield too was unsure what to do next. His priority was, as it had always been, to bring his daughter home. No one's problems would distract him from that. But he didn't want to leave devastation in his wake. He didn't want to be remembered as the man who put a match to the Tinderbox. He

126

didn't want this boy to get hurt for helping him.

Yet he was aware that, whatever his other concerns, the major problem in Jonah's life right now was Schofield. His gaunt young face twisted with the effort to explain things that would have been self-evident to everyone else he knew. 'Try to understand. People here don't have the kind of families they want to stay in touch with. It's not much fun on the streets, especially not at the start – anyone with somewhere to go back to would go. But after that, for those who stay, their families are the friends they make here – the people that get them through the cold nights, that look after them when they're sick, that they can have a laugh with however rough things get.

'After six years your daughter has a new family – the Pagan and his tribe. And she's his woman, and he's her man, as much as if they'd married in your parish church, and the kids living with them are their kids. Their responsibility. People owe their lives to one another here in ways you can't imagine. It's like a battlefield: somebody drags you out under fire, you know you owe him your life. You never forget that. You never forget him.'

Schofield thought for a moment Jonah was reminding him of the debt between them. But then he realized he was talking about times when he'd been the one in need of rescue.

'People who save lives by paying for hospitals and policemen and fire engines, that's important too but it's not personal. That's the difference between my world and yours. Your friends pay taxes; mine risk their lives for one another. Casey's friends will have risked their lives for her. You can't take that away from her, it's part of who she is. She'll never be your little girl again. She'll never leave either the Pagan or the Tinderbox.'

'People owe their lives to their parents too,' Schofield said softly.

A coal burned in Jonah's eye. 'Yeah, right. But if you're looking for gratitude you've come to the wrong place. There's only one thing everyone in the Tinderbox has in common, and it's this: where they came from was worse than sleeping out in the rain.'

Schofield felt his cheek burning. 'That isn't true,' he gritted. 'I love my daughter. Nothing I did, or didn't do, drove her away. And I want her back, enough to take any risk necessary. Maybe you don't believe it right now, but there'll be people who want you back too.'

He'd touched a nerve so raw the boy literally jolted. The ember in his eye flared up so that momentarily it engulfed them both in a flame of impotent rage. 'You know nothing about it! You know nothing about my people. You know nothing about me.' He was too angry even to storm out.

Schofield reached out an apologetic hand. 'Jonah, I'm sorry. I didn't mean to upset you. You're right, I don't know what you're doing here, what you ran away from. But I do know about Cassie. She wasn't running away from anything. She can come home today. I want to tell her that. Why should that cause a problem? Are you really so afraid of this man she's living with that you daren't tell her that her father wants to say hello?'

Jonah tossed his straw-coloured head in furious exasperation. 'Yes! No. Yeah, sure. The guy runs half the Tinderbox – I've spent the last year staying out of his way. And now, whether the police raid his camp or his woman runs home to her dad, I'm the one he's going to blame.'

'Then show me where she's living and I'll do the rest. The Pagan need never know you were there.'

'He'll know,' muttered Jonah.

'I won't say a word.'

'All the same, he'll know.'

Schofield hung on to what was left of his patience. It was hard, being this close and still not close enough, but he tried. But if Jonah had tried to leave then he'd have grabbed him, and Eggon Ronnie and half the Tinderbox wouldn't have separated them.

But the boy didn't leave. It was as if there was something keeping him here too. Not gratitude – what he'd had from Schofield was nothing compared to what he'd done for him. Perhaps, thought Schofield, it was a sort of fragile hope. If Cassie's father still loved her enough to risk everything to bring her home, maybe there was hope for them all.

Schofield pressed the advantage cautiously, aware he couldn't afford to get it wrong again. 'Jonah, I can't make you help me. I can ask, I can beg, I can pay you, but I can't make you do anything. But this is the first chance I've had to talk to her in six years. If she slips away from me this time I don't expect I'll ever see her again. Well, perhaps you think I don't deserve to. But what about Cassie? Don't you think she'd like to know how her family – her real family – are? It's not just me, you know; she has a mother and a brother. Tom. He's about your age. He still misses her dreadfully, and I'm guessing that means Cassie still misses him. Do you suppose she never thinks about us – what we're doing, if we're all right? After six years it's hard to pick up the phone, even to post a letter. But that doesn't mean she wouldn't like to make contact again.

'Maybe you're right and she won't want to leave – she'll choose the life she's made here, the family she's a part of now, over the ones she left. But that's her choice, not yours. I don't think she'd ever forgive you if there was a chance for her and me to meet, just once, in friendship, and you came between us.'

The boy was so torn by his dilemma that the blood flowed every way but visibly. If Schofield had been less intent on his own desires he'd have felt badly about that. But he persuaded himself he was only encouraging Jonah to do what was best for everyone.

'All right!' The words might have been wrung from him by torture. His head rocked back and he gazed at the stained ceiling in despair. 'All right. I'll take you there. But you've got to promise me something.'

'Anything,' swore Schofield. At that moment he meant it literally.

'You'll do what I tell you. This isn't going to be easy. People get hurt here all the time. If you think you're safe because you're Casey's father, think again. If the Pagan finds us before we find her, he'll cut our throats and she'll never even know. He has nothing to lose. Remember that.'

Finally he headed for the door. Schofield got up from the table and followed him.

The thing about homelessness is that if you don't have an address you disappear off the radar. Government departments that would hound you for tax arrears, road tax, child support and the TV licence fee if they knew where you lived lose interest if you have no permanent residence. This might be a good thing, except that those bodies that may on occasion be persuaded to help with income support and housing benefit and free glasses and free teeth work on the same principle.

Homelessness is like an iceberg: nine tenths of it is out of sight. It isn't an old man on a park bench or a couple of kids in a doorway. It's thousands of people who figure in no statistics, claim no rights, receive no help, have no voice.

The thing about icebergs is, one of them sank the *Titanic*.

If Schofield's house had burned down there would have been help available. It might not have been what they were used to, but the local authority would have had them in some kind of emergency accommodation by nightfall. But the Pagan paid no rates, no income tax, no National Insurance. When the derelict hotel his family had been living in burned down they warmed themselves at the embers, gathered up everything that was worth salvaging, then melted back into the Tinderbox – a hundred people vanishing into the dark like a rumour. If they'd waited for someone to come and help they'd have frozen to death.

But the one thing the Tinderbox could

always offer was an empty building some-where. There were more empty buildings than there were people. The school dated back to a time when the Tinderbox was a thronging slum of big industry and tiny houses. As the Victorian factories closed, to reopen with EEC grants in leafy New Towns, so the population dwindled; and as the houses followed the factories into dereliction, so the school rolls fell. There was no economic way of using the great crumb-ling building to teach increasingly technical subjects to diminishing numbers of pupils, so in due course it too closed. Schofield doubted there had been much of a campaign to save it. To his trained eye the brutal out-line of the original workhouse was unmistak-able.

When Jonah said the Pagan's family were living in an old school he envisaged a three-room infant school, not a great black block on three storeys with a looming pediment containing the blind eye of a missing clock and the smoke-grimed motto *The Time is Short*. There were bars at some of the windows. It was blacker and bleaker than anything Schofield had imagined. He mur-mured faintly, 'Cassie lives *here*?'

Jonah looked up at it too. But he saw different things. He saw an acre of roof still largely intact, and glass in many of the windows, and heavy doors to bolt against the weather and the neighbours. He'd heard there was running water too, and a boiler. 'The Pagan looks after his people.'

A man less emotionally involved than Schofield might have wondered what could have happened in Jonah's life to make dossing in a a derelict workhouse seem so attractive. But his thoughts were bound up in what had brought him here. 'What do we do? Knock on the door?'

The boy looked at him askance. '*We* do nothing. You stay here. If anyone comes, hide. If anyone sees you, pretend not to see them. If someone asks what you're doing, say you're waiting for someone. *Don't* tell them who you are, and don't tell them I'm inside. If I can, I'll bring her to you. It may take time. *Don't* come looking for me.' With that Jonah snaked through a gap in the iron railings and loped off across the asphalt desert that had been the playground.

Schofield waited. Jonah had left him on the corner of an entry so that he could duck out of sight if someone came. But no one came. It was daylight now, the early sun strengthening through the grey overcast, and he was standing on the corner of a street perhaps two miles from the centre of one of the great cities of the world. And for twenty minutes he had it to himself. It was as if the bomb had dropped and no one had told him.

Finally someone came. He heard the noise

first, a rumble like distant thunder. Then – trundling like a dinosaur with its long boom folded neatly in front of it, pivoting on its tracks like a cumbrous ballerina – a vast yellow digger turned into the street. It drove to the school gates and a man climbed down. He unlocked the chain and drove in. Schofield watched with growing alarm as a dumper truck, a couple of lorries and a low-loader carrying a crane followed in a stately procession up the street and into the play-ground.

Then he understood. Someone had decided there were enough materials in the old school to be worth knocking it down.

For a second he thought he'd have to break his promise to Jonah, to break his cover and rush over to warn them there were people inside. Then he realized there was no need. No one was in any danger. Not Jonah, and not Cassie. If she and her tribe were ever here they were long gone, and the boy knew it. He'd brought Schofield to the school precisely because there was no one here. Not Cassie, and certainly not the man he called the Pagan.

'Oh, you lying little bastard!' Schofield's murmur was vicious with disappointment. But a fairer part of him recognized that he'd put Jonah in an impossible position, where whatever he did – or if he did nothing – he'd be guilty of an awful breach of Tinderbox law. If he'd thought quicker he'd never have said he recognized Cassie. Because once *that* cat was out of the bag, he had somehow to stop Schofield involving the police to get her back. He must have settled on this as his least worst option. If he could persuade him that Cassie had moved on yet again, that the trail had gone cold, perhaps her father would finally leave. It was deceitful, it was unkind, but perhaps it seemed the only way for the boy to protect himself.

'Oh, Jonah,' sighed Schofield, more in sorrow now than in anger. He supposed that in due course the boy would return with a careful pastiche of surprise and apology in place, and say there was no one at home, that the Pagan's family were adrift once more, homeless even in this place of homelessness. And in answer to Schofield's first question he'd shake his straw-coloured head and say no, he'd no idea where they might have gone.

Even if he had some sympathy for the boy's dilemma, Schofield was in no mood to listen to his lies. A better man might have waited for his return and made peace with him. But Schofield was driven. If Jonah would help him no further, he needed to find someone who would. He turned his back on the school and walked away, and tried not to hope the boy would still be wandering the crumbling building when a hundred tons of Victorian brick fell on him.

Three

Schofield drove once more to the camp under the flyover. Now he could go straight there, without hunting.

Despite the fact that Winston had told him to go home only yesterday, he didn't look particularly surprised to see him again. 'Still no news for you, man.'

He was warming himself at the embers of the night's fire. 'Cold's the big problem,' he told Schofield as if sharing a great truth with him. 'Not hunger. You can get enough to eat. There are places and ways, and even if they let you down you can get by on less than you'd think as long as you get something sometimes.'

Looking at the butter softness of his bulky body, Schofield wondered how he had the nerve to talk about hunger. The thought must have showed in his eyes because Winston grinned and patted his expansive midriff. 'I've been hungry,' he assured his visitor complacently. 'When I was new here. Now I know my way round I don't expect to go hungry again.'

Schofield shook his head wearily. 'I'm sorry, I didn't mean ... I have no right to judge. I've never been hungry in my life.'

Winston nodded, unperturbed. He waved Schofield to the sofa beside the fire. 'It's not nice,' he acknowledged. 'But the cold's worse. Nobody starves to death, even on the street. They die of cold. Maybe hunger leaves them too weak to keep warm, but it's the cold that gets them in the end. There aren't many fat men on the streets – not fat like me,' he added with a hint of pride. 'But mostly we're not skeletons either. But oh, man, we're all of us cold. All the time. You wrap up. You wear everything you own. You collect stuff to lie on – to put between you and the ground. And you know you've done enough, that tonight at least you're not going to die of it. But you're still cold. Every minute of the day and all through the night. Even when you're asleep, if you know nothing else you still know you're cold. For eight months of the year. Even in the middle of summer, in the hours before dawn you're going to be cold again. Just to remind you the good times won't last.'

Schofield was ready to leave London. This was his last shot, and he was going through the motions more than expecting anything to come of it. His adventures notwithstanding, he was back where Briony Fellowes had left him, talking to the fat boy.

But he knew more than he had the first time they talked. He asked quietly, 'Is there no alternative?'

Winston smiled tolerantly, as if Schofield had asked the same question of a man in a wheelchair. 'Not now. At the start, maybe. At the start some of us could have gone back – clawed our way back into the world before the gates shut. But if there'd been anything there for us, we wouldn't have left in the first place. And later the gates won't open, however hard you knock. We've got alternatives. Beg or starve; scavenge or freeze. We fell through the holes in the safety net; now there's nothing between us and the pit but our own ingenuity. We live by our wits.' He gave a wry little chuckle. 'You don't call this living? You get used to it. And it's not all bad. Most of us have more friends, and better friends, here than where we came from. We're good to one another, you know? And there's this to be said for shifting for yourself: what nobody gave you, nobody can take away. So maybe most of the people here would move on if they got the chance, but not many would go back.'

The thought of his fragile daughter living like that for six years chilled Schofield to the marrow of his bones. 'You've talked to her? She said that ... that she wouldn't come back? Winston, she didn't mean it – she *couldn't* mean it. Listen to me. She has a chance that nobody gave you or any of the people here: to come back to a clean slate and people who love her. Talk to her again. Please. Don't let her throw away the rest of her life because she's too proud to admit that nothing – not the freedom, not even the friends – is worth all those hours of being cold.'

The fat man was watching him with compassion. 'Sorry, man. I couldn't find her. I found out where she was living, but they've gone. I couldn't have missed them by more than a day. It was an old school. They'd been there for weeks, but now the bulldozers have moved in. Somebody warned them and they moved on.'

Like a fresh loss, the disappointment brought tears to Schofield's eyes. Winston had been his last hope. All along, Winston had been his only real hope. And Winston had nothing to tell him.

Except that Jonah hadn't been lying. He'd gone to the school expecting to find the Pagan's tribe encamped there, and was surprised to find them gone.

Winston said kindly, 'Don't give up. They have got to be somewhere. They won't have left London. Sooner or later I'll hear where they're staying and I'll have another shot at talking to her. I've got your poster – is that still your number? I'll call when I've got some news.'

Schofield had nowhere else to go, nothing else to do. The search was over. He phoned his wife. 'I'm coming home.'

There was a fractional pause before she responded. 'Alone?'

Schofield sighed. The loss of all hope had left him drained. He sat leaden-limbed in the car. 'Yes, alone. She's here. I've spoken to people who know her. I know where she was living two days ago, but nobody seems to know where she is now. I don't know where else to look, who else to ask.'

There was another, longer pause. Then Jan said, 'Come home now. We miss you. *I* miss you.'

He was ready to drive off when it occurred to him that he had one more duty call to make: he should call Briony Fellowes and let her know that his quest had failed. He didn't suppose she'd given him more than a passing thought since they parted, but she'd tried to help and it was a matter of common courtesy to let her know how it had worked out.

He quite hoped she'd be out of the office so he could leave a message. But when he gave his name there was a brief hiatus and then she answered.

'Laurence? What's the news? Did Winston find her?'

He explained as unemotionally as he could, thanked her for her efforts but said he was going home now. There was a pause then that he didn't understand, longer than would be normal and charged in some way, before the reporter said, 'You've made your mind up? You're calling it a day?'

Schofield had expected sympathy, commiseration, perhaps a promise to call him if she learned any more. He was taken aback by her tone. But unless she was being deliberately unkind, what sounded like censure was actually something else. 'What is it, Briony? What's happened?'

Still she hesitated. 'It may mean nothing. I don't know, Laurence – if you're ready to go home maybe that would be best. You can't keep chasing shadows forever.'

But he thought he could. He'd packed up only when the last shadow vanished. 'What have you heard?'

Whatever she thought of his quest, she wasn't going to lie to him. 'One of our camera crews had a strange encounter last night, not far from the Tinderbox. They were covering a Green Revolution rally, which should have been surreal enough all by itself. But as they were coming home, taking one of the sound man's short cuts, they came across ... I don't know how to describe it. Des the cameraman said he'd seen nothing like it since he was in Afghanistan.

'He reckons there were a hundred of them – men, women and kids. They were wearing weird clothes – hippy stuff, ethnic stuff, brass jewellery and little silver bells. They had a lorry piled high with gear but most of the people were on foot, carrying what they could. Pots, pans, bedrolls. Two of the women were carrying a rocking chair, several of them were carrying babies. They weren't in any hurry but they did seem to know where they were going.'

Schofield's throat was tight. 'The Pagan's tribe? Is that where they went when they left the school?'

'Laurence, I just don't know. The crew piled out of the van and set up the equipment, and took shots of them just quietly passing. But when Jackie – the reporter – tried to talk to them, they weren't interested. Everyone she spoke to referred her to someone down the line, and by the time she'd got to the end and still hadn't found the leader they'd gone into an empty depot and shut the gate behind them.

'Stan the sound man drove the van to the far side of the depot, to have another go at them as they came out. But they didn't come out, and when he found a way in they weren't inside either. Obviously there's another exit even Stan didn't know about. He drove round for half an hour trying to find them, but they'd vanished.'

'And you didn't *call* me?' Schofield's voice soared.

'I didn't know what to do,' said Briony stubbornly. 'I thought I'd wait till Winston got back to you. Even if Cassie's with these people, I don't know where they are now, only where they were sixteen hours ago. If the Pagan's tribe were on the move about then, probably it was them. But I don't know how much use that's going to be to you.'

Schofield heard her out in silence, unsure how to react. He felt like a punch-drunk boxer, no longer knowing where the blows were coming from, and every time he was ready to throw in the towel the bell went and somebody sponged his face and pushed him back into the ring.

He didn't want to go on fighting. He was dead on his feet. But every time he went down, a glimpse of the prize coaxed him up again. To be this close, to know where Cassie was just sixteen hours ago, and abandon the search now; did he really mean to do that? Perhaps he should have done. Perhaps a stronger man than Schofield would have done. But the search had taken him over. He was no longer able to judge whether the prize was worth what he was paying for it.

He said, 'Can you take me to where they disappeared?'

He got caught up in rush hour as he crossed the city. She'd been waiting for twenty minutes in the rain, her coat tightly buckled against the chill of the evening. She wasn't alone. Waiting with her were Des and Stan, the cameraman and sound engineer. 'They'll show us the way.'

'Good. Get in.'

But they had wheels of their own, a van parked just round the corner. 'Follow us.'

Schofield would have thought nothing of it, except for the edgy way Briony was shifting her weight from foot to foot. He considered for a moment. 'Are you bringing a camera?'

Briony said quickly, 'It wasn't my idea. But if you find your daughter it'll be thanks to our help. We'd like to be able to film it. It's not a condition; if you say no we'll still take you to the depot and then we'll leave. But it's a good story. Not just good for us. We could show that not all the street kids are unwanted, that every so often there's a happy ending. I think that's worth saying.'

Plus, you'll have the networks fighting for the film, Schofield thought sourly. But he didn't say it aloud. From the TV crew's viewpoint it wasn't an unreasonable request. They'd helped Schofield; if there was going to be a happy reunion they must feel they had a claim on the footage. It was only payment in another form. Schofield was too tired to be genuinely angry, but he was a little saddened. Jonah, to whom he owed his life, had only taken his money when pressed, and then given – well, thrown – most of it back.

And he'd been hungry at the time.

He kept his face expressionless. 'All right. As long as you remember that the priority is not the pictures, it's the outcome. Briony, are you riding with me?' She got into his car without a word.

Stan led them through a number of short cuts: back streets and abandoned yards and rutted tracks beside a canal. More than once Schofield feared for Jan's exhaust. He kept up because, as well as the sense of purpose hanging round his neck like an albatross, there was the fear of getting lost again in this limbo world that most of the millions thronging the streets of working London did not suspect.

The architect in him still wondered why so much dereliction was tolerated. He could understand why nobody wanted to live in the Tinderbox right now. But a fleet of yellow diggers and wrecking balls would quickly remove the most undesirable elements, and after that you could build anything you could imagine. There was – there had to be – a killing to be made.

Which, he realized, was probably why the situation was allowed to continue. However desirable the Tinderbox could be in two years' time, right now it was bandit country. Before improvements could be made, people had to go in there. Survey it, work out what bits belonged to who, come up with a plan.

And do it with Shag and Average peering over their shoulders. Schofield could see how every planner given the task might come to the view that the *really* smart thing to do would be leave it just how it was for a little while longer. With property prices climbing, how could that ever be a bad call? So the Tinderbox survived as a kind of portrait in London's attic, the two impinging so little on one another's daily being that they might have been in parallel universes.

Stan's tail lights took a different route to the one Schofield knew. But he was conscious that the Tinderbox couldn't be far away. He felt it drawing nearer, like a storm. Eventually the van stopped and, looking past it, Schofield saw iron gates shut against them. Des the cameraman got out and walked back to Schofield's car.

'This is where we lost them. They came through this gate and they were walking in that direction.' He pointed. 'So we got back in the van and drove round to meet them on the far side. But they never came out. We looked all round the site, in all the buildings, anywhere you could hide half a dozen people let alone a hundred. There was no one there. OK, it was dark; we might have missed something. But we couldn't have missed a hundred people.'

'There must be another way out,' said Schofield. He wished Jonah was here. Jonah would know if there was another exit – and if so, where it led. But he'd left Jonah at the school, and had no idea how to find him now he was once again in need of his services.

'Well, yes,' agreed Des, lofting one sardonic eyebrow, 'we got that far.' He was a tall, dark, lean man of about forty who tended to stoop even when he didn't have his eye to a viewfinder. 'But we couldn't find it. And we couldn't pick up their trail again.'

By now it was dark. They should have been here in daylight, when there was a chance to see further than torches would reach. They should have agreed to come back tomorrow. But tomorrow was another day, and Schofield could no longer see that far ahead. He rooted in Jan's glove compartment, came up with a pocket torch just strong enough to change a tyre by. 'I'll have a look round. A hundred people can't just disappear.'

Briony shook her head. 'These people can. You have to remember their safety can depend on how quiet they can be, whether they can vanish if they have to. They move like Indians. You'll be lucky to find a footprint in the dust.'

'They went somewhere,' insisted Schofield. 'If I can find where they left the depot, maybe I can find where they went.' He set off round the perimeter fence at a weary stump of a walk.

He found nothing. No one came to help so

148

he searched the buildings alone – inside, behind and between them. It was over an hour before he admitted defeat.

Long before that he heard the toot of the van's horn and saw the headlights arc across the broken tarmac. His heart skipped a beat. If they left him here alone, he had no idea how to find his way back to civilisation. But even that seemed better than quitting. This was his last chance. He wouldn't give up on it until it gave up on him.

When it did – when he got back to his car, and he'd found no one, and no sign that anyone had been there, and no clue to where they'd gone when they left – he found Briony Fellowes sitting in his car with her coat collar round her ears, hugging her knees. She'd locked the doors, and had to open them to let him in. Though she said nothing, her expression said everything. She didn't even ask if he'd had any luck.

Schofield sniffed. 'You should have gone with them.'

'They wanted to wait. But we got a call. An armed robbery in Goodge Street. They had to go. I said I'd wait for you.'

'Why?' he asked roughly, too tired and dispirited to acknowledge his gratitude.

'Because it's my fault you're here,' she said in a low voice. 'If I'd kept my mouth shut you'd be halfway home by now. I should have let you go.'

'That wasn't your decision to make!'

'That's what I thought at the time. But I think I was wrong.'

Only then did he see how miserable she looked. He sighed. 'Let's go. There's nothing here. I'll take you home.'

She lived in the north of the city. They passed over the river. Briony asked him up to her flat for a hot drink. He was chilled to the bone from quartering the depot but he still didn't think it was a good idea. 'I should phone Jan. She's expecting me home about now.'

'Call while I make the coffee. Laurence, you're frozen; if you try to drive like this you'll fall asleep at the wheel and kill yourself. How's that going to help anyone?'

He *was* cold, and tired, and lonely. It would have taken only a fraction more weakness on his part to accept the offer. He knew it was meant honestly; he knew he could accept in the same spirit. But then what? Might a hot drink lead to a hot bath, and then to the kind of indiscretion which comes naturally to some men, but which the suit-wearing Laurence Schofield had not contemplated in a quarter of a century of marriage?

He knew he was in no fit state for a three-hour drive. It wasn't just the cold. The repeated raising and dashing of hopes had built up the frustration until it ran in his veins like poison, needling, plucking at his brain. An hour on a comfortable sofa now, with a hot coffee in one hand and a toasted sandwich in the other, would render him human again.

If he could have trusted himself he'd have taken up her offer. But he didn't. Once a man has sought warmth and comfort in the home of an attractive young woman, it's only a matter of time before it begins to seem silly to stop at tea and toast. A fine sweat broke on his cold skin at the thought of losing himself, of shedding the disappointment and the grief in an urgent foray between Briony Fellowes' thighs. Nothing she'd said or done told him that was an option. But he believed it was.

The thought may not have been classic Schofield, but the response to it was. He put it behind him. However much better it might make him feel tonight, tomorrow the same problems would still be there and there'd be a new one as well. He'd risked so much already – the respect of his wife, the trust of his partner – but nothing he couldn't repair when he went back. Warming himself at the hearth of this woman's loins would cut him off from all that forever.

'I don't think so,' he said, smiling a slow apology. 'If I leave now I'll still be home sometime tonight. If I don't, I may never make it home.'

He wasn't sure if she understood – either

what had been going through his mind or the decision he'd reached. She watched him go without expression. He watched her in the rear-view mirror until he turned the corner.

Then he stopped the car and took out his phone. He wasn't sure quite what to say to Jan. *Sorry, turns out I was lying when I said I was on my way home ... It's probably the truth this time, unless...*

Unless, for instance, it suddenly occurred to him that he knew where, or at least how, to find Jonah. He knew where he dined out when he had money in his pockets – and also, it seemed, when he hadn't. If he could find Jonah he could explain why he'd left him at the school. He was sure the boy would go with him then, back to the depot where a hundred urban gypsies had disappeared like smoke into the night air, and show him where they had gone.

With no idea what to tell Jan this time, he put the phone away.

Four

By the time Schofield had found the little market square again it was after eight. He was afraid that the Élite Café, catering as it did for the early-morning trade, would be shut. But there was a light on and Eggon Ronnie in his stained whites was present, in body if not in spirit. In the absence of customers he'd nodded off with his head on his hand and his elbow on the counter.

The bell above the door jangled as Schofield came in and Ronnie jerked awake. 'It's all gone except coffee and...' Then he recognized his visitor and stopped. 'Oh.'

It was a long time since Schofield had eaten. 'Whatever it is, I'll have it.'

It was the remnants of earlier meals that had been drying out in the oven since trade slowed down hours ago. But right now Schofield was in no position to be picky. He covered the worst of it with vermilion sauce from a gummy plastic tomato and applied himself doggedly.

Ronnie didn't go back to sleep but sat behind the counter watching him. Without looking up Schofield said, 'Has he been in?'

Ronnie said guardedly, 'Who?'

Since they only had one acquaintance in common Schofield didn't bother elaborating. 'I need to talk to him.'

Ronnie shrugged, non-committal. 'He might be by later.'

Schofield was learning not to rush conversations like this. 'Good.' He probed a primordial soup of bubble and squeak for signs of evolution.

Ronnie emerged from behind his counter then and hovered, as if he might have more to say but wasn't sure whether to say it. 'You're not going to make trouble for the kid, are you?'

Schofield met his gaze. 'No. That's the last thing I want.'

'He doesn't need any more trouble with the police.'

Schofield thought he was talking about the money. 'I thought I was helping him. I didn't realize it was a criminal offence for a street kid to have money in his pocket.'

Ronnie looked perplexed. 'What?'

'What?'

So Jonah had been in a police cell before. That wasn't entirely unexpected, and it might go some way to explaining his reaction. Schofield tried again. 'Ronnie, I don't mean him any harm. I need his help, that's all.'

Eggon Ronnie gave a rude snort. 'You got any idea how much trouble you can get into helping someone round here?'

Schofield put down his knife and fork and leaned back, regarding his host levelly. 'If you've something to tell me, it might be best to get it said.'

Reaching a decision, Ronnie slid into the seat opposite, leaning across the table as if he didn't want to be overheard. There was no one else in the café. 'How much do you know about Jonah?'

'Not much,' admitted Schofield. 'I know he doesn't like police stations. I know he hasn't much time for his family. That's about it.'

'Yeah,' grunted Ronnie, 'well, that's pretty much the headlines.' He hesitated again. 'It's not my job to tell you things about him that Jonah'd sooner keep to himself. And I don't know what kind of help you want from him. But you need to know there are things he can't do for you. Things you can't ask him to do.'

Schofield wasn't sure what he was suggesting. He said stiffly, 'I'm a married man and the father of two children. I'm *not* looking for a little friend in the city. I *am* looking for my daughter, who's been a vagrant here for the last six years. Jonah can help me find her.'

Angry-eyed, Ronnie teetered on the edge

155

of a confidence. 'I don't know about your girl. I do know a lot of the kids choose to be here, and maybe she's one of them. But Jonah isn't. He's here because there's no-where else for him. If you make it so he can't stay here, there'll be nowhere for him at all.'

Perhaps it was the hot meal; Schofield found the energy to fuel a little anger of his own. 'If you've something to say, spit it out. Otherwise tell me where to find him.'

The cook – his own mother wouldn't have called him a chef – chewed savagely on his lip. Clearly he wanted to speak; equally clearly, he wasn't sure it was the right thing to do. If Jonah had wanted this strange, tall, suspiciously clean man to know his story he'd have told it himself. But if Ronnie said nothing the man would go on pushing until something gave. Ronnie was afraid that, brimming with street smarts as he was, cocky enough on a good day to make you want to throw bricks at him, the boy was nowhere near as hard as this driven man. If something was going to break, it would be him.

'All right,' he said slowly. 'I don't know everything. I'll tell you what I know. Then you'll see why you have to leave the kid alone. Why he can't afford any trouble. And you'll find someone else to help you, yeah?' Behind the gruffness was a note of pleading.

'Tell me,' said Schofield. It was no kind of

a commitment, but Ronnie told him anyway.

'This is about a year ago, before he came here. The kid was fifteen. He was accused of something. I don't think he did it – I really don't. Neither did the old bill, and they let him go after about a week. But before that he was in some kind of kids' remand ... something.'

The story might have been clearer, thought Schofield, if Eggon Ronnie had had a better command of the English language. But he was following well enough. 'What was he accused of?'

But Ronnie wasn't taking questions from the floor. Now he'd decided to tell the story he was going to get through it without distractions. 'He had a bad time there. He's no criminal. He was from a decent family, he talked proper, his mum drove a people-carrier – of course he was going to get seven kinds of shit knocked out of him. And it was only a few days before the charges were dropped. But when you're scared out of your mind, a few days feels like a lifetime.'

Thinking about it, Ronnie absent-mindedly helped himself to Schofield's coffee – and finding it not to his liking, added sugar. 'Now here's the funny part. When they gave him his belt back and told him to scarper, he didn't go home. They wouldn't have him home. What's that about? The kid convinces the bill he hasn't done anything wrong, but he can't convince his mum and dad? So I don't know. Maybe they knew more than the bill could prove. Maybe they didn't know squat but the damage was done – the kid had got himself into trouble and brought shame on the family. That's what they call it, isn't it, in nice families?' He looked at Schofield as if Schofield might know. 'Then they give you some money and tell you never to darken their door again.'

'His people threw him out? He was fifteen, and they turned him out of the house?'

Ronnie nodded sombrely. 'And he came here. Ended up in the Tinderbox. That great melting-pot,' he added with unexpected poetry, 'of the lost, the unwanted, the hopeless and the downright bloody psycho.'

Schofield stared at him, appalled. He'd lost Cassie when she was fifteen. Maybe she'd gone because she'd done something she was ashamed to tell him. He hadn't cared then and he didn't care now. If she'd killed someone, he'd still have walked over hot coals to get her back. She was his child and he was ready to die for her. He literally could not imagine the circumstances in which he would have turned her away. Bringing the police to his door wouldn't be anywhere near enough to do it, no matter how many lace curtains twitched or how much neighbourhood gossip followed.

He went back to his earlier question. It had

seemed relevant then; now he knew it was fundamental. 'What did he do, Ronnie?

The cook demurred. 'I told you, he was never convicted of anything...'

'What was he accused of doing?' Schofield insisted softly.

Ronnie gave it up. A point comes when you can't prevaricate any longer, when only the truth will do. 'Raping a sixteen-year-old girl.'

People changed their names when they came to the Tinderbox. The boy had changed his to Jonah. The outcast, cursed by God and his kind. Perhaps his family would be pleased to know his education had not been wasted.

Schofield found himself breathing lightly through his mouth. 'Dear God. I had no idea...'

'I told you,' Ronnie said again, doggedly, 'he didn't do it. They let him go.'

'You mean,' Schofield said unsteadily, 'they couldn't prove it. But his family knew, didn't they? *They* knew she wasn't making it up. They knew she wasn't a willing participant who only claimed it was rape when her father found out.'

'It wasn't like that,' growled Ronnie. 'It happened, all right. She ended up in hospital. Somebody raped her – actually, several somebodies. But Jonah wasn't one of them.'

There was a sense in which it hardly

mattered. Nothing would ever be proven now. Whether or not the boy did what he'd been accused of, Schofield would never know for sure. What he did finally understand was the extraordinary terror Jonah had displayed in the police custody suite this morning. His arrest had reopened a chapter of his life which he'd changed every aspect of his existence to close.

'You see?' wheedled Ronnie. 'He can't afford to get into any more trouble. He's OK here. He gets by pretty well on his own. He makes his way doing odd jobs for people – for me, sometimes. And nobody has a hold on him. He doesn't hurt anyone and he doesn't steal ...Well,' he amended with a tiny grin, 'except from me sometimes. He doesn't give the law any excuse to touch him. Most people in the Tinderbox live by petty theft. Jonah keeps his hands clean because he'd rather go hungry than risk being banged up again.

'That's why he's on his own. It's easier with a tribe. You eat better and sleep safer, and there's help if things go wrong. But Rommel's tribe are a bunch of psychos; if you're caught with them they don't just lock you up, they throw away the key. Even the Pagan's family have a pretty flexible attitude to the law, so prison's an occupational hazard. The Pagan would take him tomorrow. He's tried to get him, but Jonah stays out of his way. He can do the cold nights but he couldn't do the time. I honest to God think he'd cut his throat to stay out of jail, and sooner or later working for the Pagan would mean one or the other.'

Schofield shook his head in wonder. 'How do you *know* all this?' He'd spent some hours in Jonah's company. He'd heard him laugh and seen him cry. The boy had saved his life, and he'd tried to repay the debt with money. It amounted not to a friendship but to a certain kind of intimacy. But Jonah had said almost nothing about his past.

He hadn't confided in Ronnie either – at least, not intentionally. 'He was sick. Soon after he came here. He passed out in my Brown Windsor soup. I put him to bed in the back. The doctor gave him antibiotics and he came round soon enough. But he was out of his skull for a time, talking like there was a big reservoir of stuff dammed up in his head. Some of it I couldn't make sense of, but some of it I could.'

'Did you ask him about it when he was better?'

Ronnie looked at him as if he'd suggested something indecent. ''Course not.' His voice hardened. 'And if you tell him about any of this, I'll feed you to our cat.'

It was all added complications Schofield could have done without. He tried to re-assure the cook. 'I don't want to make any trouble – not for you and not for Jonah. I just need a bit of advice. He could probably give me all the help I need without leaving his...' What? Flat, room, squat? 'Do you know where he is, Ronnie? Can you tell me where to find him? I swear to you, I'm not going to get him arrested. It wasn't my fault he was arrested last night – it *is* down to me that they let him go.'

Ronnie got up abruptly, the off-white length of him unfolding like a seagull. 'I'll have to think.' He disappeared into the kitchen.

Schofield knew better than to follow. He thought the cook would come back. It might cost him money, but he thought finally Ronnie would tell him where Jonah was living.

He was wrong. When the kitchen door opened again and he looked up, ready to negotiate, it wasn't Ronnie. It was Jonah.

Framed in the open door, the straw-coloured hair in tangles to his shoulder, his broad young face watchful, his stocky young body poised as if for flight or fight, and he hadn't yet decided which, for a moment he seemed to Schofield to be something other than a plain human boy. He looked at Jonah and didn't see a youth hammered out by hard times to a new rough-edged manhood. He saw some kind of changeling, fashioned of other atoms for use in another place. He'd thought Jonah the master of his environment, alien as Schofield found it. Now he saw that it *was* alien, to Jonah too, that he had no charm to guide him, that he survived here by sheer effort of will. Because he had to. Because he could never return through the looking glass.

A sense of distance hit Schofield so that for a moment he couldn't speak. He'd thought he knew what it was to be lonely; now he realized he didn't know the meaning of the word. Jonah knew. A boy whose only hope of friendship came from people who would betray him into his worst nightmare had no choice but to be alone. To make his own way in these ruins of the world, apart even from the ragged children and the men carving exotic kingdoms out of petty crime.

Jonah saw the shock of understanding in his eyes and his body stiffened with resentment. He didn't want Schofield's pity any more than he wanted his money. 'What do you want now?'

Schofield strove to ignore the aching sense of emptiness. 'You live here?'

'Yeah. So?' His voice was a challenge.

Ronnie came out of the kitchen with a mackintosh flapping over his whites. 'I'm off home. Lock up behind me. And lock up if you go out.' He caught Schofield's eye. He said nothing. But the thought went all the way.

'I'm going nowhere,' said Jonah.

Schofield said, 'We'll lock up.'

Jonah locked the door and turned off the lights. Then he led the way through the kitchen and down the steps that led to the area where the bins were. Under the stairs, under the kitchen, was the basement storeroom where he lived.

It was still a storeroom. The walls were lined with cardboard cartons of tinned soup, tinned beans, instant coffee and tomato ketchup, and crates of soft drinks. Jonah lived in the smaller room between these artificial walls, and much of his furniture was made of crates.

His bed was a thin mattress raised on a platform of crates lashed together with string. A sheet of plywood nailed to a couple made a table, and more crates upholstered with cushions that didn't match served as chairs. Cardboard boxes in a vertical stack open to the room gave him somewhere to keep his things. There were three boxes but only two were in use and they weren't full. The middle one held his clothes, the top one some biscuit tins and a half-used bottle of milk. The boy's larder, kept off the ground to foil the rats.

That wasn't the remarkable thing about Jonah's home. The remarkable thing was how he'd decorated it. The space glowed with a startling blood-red richness. Every piece of red fabric ever discarded by a Londoner seemed to have found its way here. Curtains in velvet, plush and brocade, in burgundy, crimson, scarlet and vermilion, draped the catering supplies like mediaeval tapestries. All were old, many moth-eaten, but they glowed like stained glass in the light of a couple of candle pots.

The boy was watching for Schofield's reaction. He said, a shade defensively, 'There is an electric light. I like the candles better.'

There were rugs on the floor, all of them worn and all of them red. They lay tossed together, edges overlapping, moulting fringes entangled. A red chenille throw covered the bed and a claret velvet cushion was his pillow. It was still dented, threaded by yellow hairs, as if he'd been asleep when Ronnie came for him.

Schofield stood astonished in the midst of it, turning slowly, like a child on its first visit to Santa's grotto. Jonah kept watching him. If anyone had been watching Jonah they'd have seen anxiety in his eyes and the shuffling of his shoulders inside his battered clothes. When he could bear the stunned silence no longer he grunted, 'Go on then, say what everyone says. It reminds you of a cathouse.'

Schofield continued turning until his eyes came back to Jonah, then he blinked. 'I've never been in a cathouse,' he said honestly.

Jonah let out his breath in a gruff chuckle. 'Me neither. But I'm told they look like this.'

Maybe they did. Maybe men who frequented brothels liked to be reminded of the womb. Schofield couldn't imagine relaxing here for a moment. But he could see how it might appeal to a boy whose worldly possessions could be packed into two cardboard boxes.

'I'm not sure,' he said carefully, 'I'd listen to a man who had nothing better to do in a brothel than study the decor.'

After that it was easier to talk. But there was still mistrust simmering between them. Jonah sat cross-legged on the bed and waved Schofield to the crate with the plumpest cushion. 'I didn't expect to see you again. What the hell happened at the school?'

Schofield explained. 'I thought you'd dumped me. It was only afterwards that I found out Cassie probably *was* there until the night before.' He recounted what the television crew had seen.

'I spent bloody ages looking for you,' growled Jonah. 'I thought you must have followed me inside. I thought the place would fall down on top of you. It damn near came down on top of me.'

'I said I was sorry,' Schofield murmured, although in fact he had not. 'Jonah, you know what finding Cassie means—'

'I am getting sick and tired,' Jonah spat

fiercely, 'of you waving that name in my face like a get-out-of-jail-free card. Like it doesn't matter what damage you do, what trouble you cause, how much shit you hurl at the fan, as long as it's for Cassie.'

Schofield tried to answer, and though he meant to mollify the boy he could feel his own temper coldly rising. But he never got the chance to vent it. Jonah hadn't finished.

'I've had it up to here,' he snarled, waving a hand at fringe level. 'Your quest. Your daughter. You walking on other people's faces to reach her. There are thousands of us, Mr Schofield – that makes us common but it doesn't make us dirt. We're not disposable in the interests of finding a girl who could have come home any time in the last six years if she'd wanted to. I'm not going to help you turn the Tinderbox upside down just so Cassie Schofield can sleep alone at night.'

Before he had time to form the intention Schofield was on his feet, his arm swinging from the shoulder. His open hand struck Jonah's cheek with a clap like gunfire and enough force to spill him the length of his cathouse bed. Stunned silent, he looked up wide-eyed as Schofield loomed over him, the narrow scholarly face suffused with fury, the angular body arched.

'How dare you?' hissed Schofield. 'You ... trash. You *nothing*.' He'd snatched up one of the candle pots and held it like a weapon, as if he would smash the boy's face with it. As if only the grinding thud of earthenware against bone and the bright flowering of blood would satisfy him.

If he'd been less startled Jonah could have rolled out of his way and fled the room before Schofield could hit him again. But he seemed dazed by the violence he'd provoked. He cowered on the bed with his eyes round and a thread of blood on his chin where his lip had split.

Schofield's wits began trickling back to him, like a man regaining consciousness after an accident, so that he saw what he was doing. He stared at the heavy pot in his hand as if he couldn't think what it was doing there. He stared in horror at the fresh blood on Jonah's face.

'Oh dear God.' He lowered his hands carefully, replaced the pot – the candle had gone out – beside its fellow and stepped back. His eyes stretched with the enormity of what he'd done. This had been his last chance and he'd thrown it away. Squandered it for nothing, a momentary anger. He'd never hit his own children. He despised men who made points with their fists. He was tired and frustrated, but that was no excuse for knocking a young boy down. Now, when Cassie's trail was just hours old and this boy sprawled on his bed with the imprint of

Schofield's hand hot on his face was the one person in London who might have been both able and willing to find her.

And still it didn't occur to him that risking his mission was not the worst thing he had done.

His gaze fell to the rugs jumbled on the floor. 'Jonah, I'm sorry.'

When he saw that he wasn't going to be hit again Jonah rolled off the bed and on to his feet. His fists were rammed in the pockets of his jeans. His breath was coming fast and uneven. 'Of course you're sorry. You can't find her on your own.'

'You don't understand.' Schofield's voice cracked and he turned away, hiding his face. 'She's my child. I can't bear to think of her living like this.'

'You should never have come here.'

It wasn't the first time Jonah had been struck. The casual blows he collected in the course of his everyday life he accepted philosophically. Most vagrants would share their fire, but occasionally one flung an empty bottle at your head. Most policemen left you alone unless provoked, but occasionally one threw you against a wall and went through your pockets. Mostly if you helped someone load stuff into a car they'd give you a handful of small change, but once a man in a pinstriped suit, his face contorted with rage, had hit Jonah in the face with a rolled-up newspaper.

The unexpected attack is always shocking, but less so to those who live on the rough underside of society. Jonah recovered more quickly from being struck than Schofield recovered from striking him.

'I had no choice,' the man whispered to the wall. 'Not from the start. From the moment my son saw that film I had to act as I did. Briony's help, Winston's, even yours, only drew me in deeper. I couldn't leave. I couldn't stop looking for her. Until today. I was going home today. I called Briony to tell her, and she told me ... So I had to stay. And I had to find you.'

He gave a thin, desperate chuckle, his head rocking back as if in pain. 'And look what a good job I made of asking you to help! Oh God, Jonah, the whole thing's out of control. *I'm* out of control. I'm not running this search any more, it's running me. I think I'm going crazy.'

When there was no response, finally he turned back to the room, uncertainly, like a child expecting chastisement. But for a second, before he hid it, Jonah's face was compassionate. This boy who had nothing, and no hope of anything better, who would be old before he was Schofield's age – assuming he didn't die in a gutter first – felt sorry for the man. Sorry enough to forgive his trespasses and be willing to help him.

He cleared his throat and kept his tone deliberately casual. 'I'm not promising anything. But where exactly did the film crew see them?'

Five

Jonah seemed to know what he was looking for even before they reached the depot, his mind leapfrogging ahead, working out the route Cassie and her friends had taken from the school and, from that, where they might have gone.

Schofield drove into the empty yard, black under a heavy overcast, brooding grimly on the years of neglect and the thousand nameless crimes it must have witnessed. He had suburban man's fear of dark and empty places. His instinct was to park in the middle of the yard and leave the headlights on so they could see what they were doing. But Jonah made him park, lights off, in the shadow of a shed where the car would attract no attention. The dweller in the urban jungle had rediscovered the countryman's wisdom – that, day or night, safety is being alone. It's other people you have to fear.

The boy set off towards an angle of the high wall. Broken glass set in cement along the top glittered in the faint orange glow that was the lights of London reflected by the underside of the clouds. Schofield followed as fast as he dared, the darkness barely troubled by his little torch.

At the perimeter Jonah stopped, rapping his knuckles tinnily on corrugated iron. Sheets of the stuff, three metres high, filled a wide gap in the wall. Schofield had recognized it as a gate when he was here with Briony but he hadn't tried to open it: there was no point. A chain of elephant-tethering proportions secured it to an iron bracket sunk in the wall and an ancient padlock, seized solid with rust, secured the chain.

'They couldn't have come this way,' he said. 'They'd have had to break the padlock.'

Jonah took the torch and shone it on the ground. The gritty surface had been scoured and tyre tracks showed in the scummy residue.

Schofield's voice was incredulous. 'They moved it? How?'

Jonah kept playing the beam over the gate until he found the hinges. Schofield caught his breath. 'Damn it!' he muttered fiercely. The line of dirt pointed not to the hinges of the gate but to the chained end.

Jonah had the gate open in a moment. The hinges had long ago been lifted clear of their pintles so that only its own weight kept the gate closed and only the chain kept it upright. To open it wide for the tribe's lorry would have taken strong hands and several of them, but Jonah needed only enough space to slip through. 'Come on.'

Schofield followed, but slowly. There was something he didn't understand. The TV crew, finding the main gate shut in their faces, had driven round the depot and waited for the travellers to emerge on the opposite side. But they never did, and by then the yard was empty. Where had the nomads gone after shutting the broken gate that the crew, driving round the perimeter of the depot, failed to find them?

Jonah went straight there – an entry across the road, a dark tunnel between two buildings just wide enough to take the lorry. Even a hundred people could have ghosted across the road and into the shadows in a couple of minutes.

Schofield peered into the blackness. It was uncomfortably like that other alley where he'd been in fear for his life, and he was reluctant to enter. 'This is where they went?' he asked doubtfully.

'Oh yeah.' Jonah was as sure as if he'd seen them. It wasn't just that it explained, as nothing else did, how the travellers had eluded the TV crew. Jonah knew where they'd been heading.

The idea had occurred to him as he searched the depot for a hidden exit. Following the black alley between the towering cliffs of masonry would take them to a place which offered all they needed. Shelter, privacy, space. If Jonah had had a hundred people to accommodate he'd have taken them there too – except for one thing.

Schofield probed the darkness with his torch until he found Jonah's face. 'You know where they are, don't you?'

'Maybe.' But he sounded surer than that.

'Close?'

'Pretty close.'

Blood surged in Schofield's veins, throbbed at his temples. His fear of the dark was forgotten. He'd been within half a day of Cassie. Now he was within half a mile, maybe less. Not hours but minutes. If Jonah was right. If she was still with the tribe.

Of course she was with them. Why would she leave now? Hadn't the danger always been that she might not want or be able to leave? He felt an intense, clutching sense of urgency, as if she was waiting for him and would give up if he didn't hurry. 'Come on, then!' He started into the black throat of the alley.

Jonah's hand restrained him. Schofield felt the strong fingers through his torn sleeve. 'Before we go in there you need to understand what we're getting into.' There was a honed edge to his voice. It might have been only caution but it sounded like fear.

Schofield was impatient. 'Jonah, you already made this speech. At the school, remember? I don't do anything, I don't say anything and I keep out of sight. Fine. Now, let's go.'

Stubbornly, Jonah stood his ground. 'This isn't the school. The worst we had to worry about there was upsetting the Pagan. That's still worth avoiding; he's not the kindest, most forgiving person in this city and if he thinks we're after something of his he'll string us up by our balls. All the same, it's not the Pagan I'm worried about.

'This place where they are – where I think they are – it's on the borderline of Rommel's territory. He'd say it's his, the Pagan'd say it isn't. Sooner or later they'll have to settle it, by treaty or by war. Till then this whole area's no man's land. Both tribes will have scouts out, and the fact that they're watching for one another won't stop them seeing us if we let them.'

So it *was* fear. The boy knew what risks they were running, and he was afraid.

'So we do without the torch, anything you have to say you whisper, and if we hear anything at all we hide. OK? You don't need me to tell you that if Average gets us cornered he won't be satisfied with your wallet. He'll want blood on his boots.'

Schofield remembered the sound of the chains. His belly shrank to a cold knot.

There was still time to turn back. Jan would be waiting for him; he was already overdue. If he left now he could head for the M1 and no one need ever know that he'd had one last opportunity to find his daughter and wasn't brave enough to take it.

Or he might tell Jan. It was time they started talking again – about difficult things, important things. Jan wouldn't blame him for thinking of his own safety. She'd say he owed it to her and to Tom. She'd say Cassie had made her choice, and Schofield had no right to imperil himself to give her fresh options now. Once he'd thought her attitude inhuman. But standing here, in this strange emptiness of a great city, looking from darkness into absolute darkness and knowing that crossing the threshold would expose him to dangers he could neither quantify nor control, for the first time he wondered if she was right.

He realized, of course, that was the fear in him talking. He didn't consider himself a brave man. He had a certain moral courage, and the obstinacy that can be mistaken for strength. He could imagine being angry enough and indignant enough to perform one act of bravery in the heat of a moment. He did not know if, even for Cassie, he could find the courage to face physical danger if he had time to think about it first.

Never in his life had he had to make that call. To decide how much pain he was prepared to take, how much blood he was willing to spill, for how dear a cause. He wanted his daughter home. But he could live without her, and she could live as she had these past six years. No one would suffer if he decided he'd done enough. He might have rushed to snatch her from a fire, risking all the flames could do to him. But would he walk on hot coals only to see her, to talk to her? If he did, would she listen? If he didn't, what had the last few days been for?

Jonah saw him waver. 'Or we could call it a day.'

'Could we come back in daylight?' ventured Schofield.

But the boy shook his head vigorously. 'Night's on our side. *I* wouldn't come here in the day. They'd be on us before we could run.'

Anyway, Schofield knew he wasn't coming back tomorrow. Knowing what he now did – that by being here he risked not only the Pagan's displeasure but the renewed attentions of men who'd already tried to kill him – he knew that if he left he would never return. Cowardice or common sense, it hardly mattered which. Schofield knew himself well enough to know that it was now or never. And *never* is a vast, bleak, life sentence of a word.

But then – and only then – it occurred to him that it wasn't just his own life he was gambling with. Until that moment, even with Eggon Ronnie begging him to, he hadn't considered what he was asking of Jonah besides his time. He'd told Ronnie the truth: he didn't want to make trouble for the boy. He hadn't intended to use him either, but finally he saw that he was doing exactly that. Schofield had seen what the loss of his freedom meant to Jonah. He had no right to expose him to that again – and not even deliberately, sacrificing the needs of a stranger to his own, but casually, carelessly, without thinking.

He felt Jonah's eyes on him, puzzled and questioning. He didn't mind if the boy thought it was fear delaying his answer. But an answer he would have to give, and soon. He could call it a day and go home, and if Jonah despised him for that probably only his eyes would say so. Or he could go on. But he'd have to give Jonah a way out. Alone his chances of success were slashed, but he couldn't use a sixteen-year-old boy as body armour.

He stammered the words awkwardly, ill at ease with selflessness after so long. 'Maybe I should go on my own from here.'

He didn't need to see Jonah's face to picture the amazement, incredulity, outrage and alarm paraded there. It was all in the way his body stiffened, his head tilting sideways as if he might have misheard, and in the one word he spoke. *'Why?'*

Schofield stumbled and fumbled, everything he added detracting from what he was trying to say. 'I mean ... Look, it's dangerous, isn't it? If you know where they are you can tell me. It doesn't need both of us risking our necks. You've found them for me; that's all I asked. Talking to her, getting her to come home – that I have to do myself. You'd be putting yourself in danger for no reason.'

'No reason?' The gruff young voice soared. 'Mr Schofield, I've been keeping you alive since I first clapped eyes on you! You'd be five different sorts of dead but for me.'

'I know that,' Schofield said honestly. 'Don't think I'm not grateful. I wouldn't be here but for you. But whatever happens now, afterwards I'll go home. But you'll still be living here. You can't afford to make enemies of these people. Better if no one knows you helped me.'

'They already know! You think those posters you threw around like confetti didn't get this far? They know who you are, what you want, who you've seen and who's talked to you. Rommel knows. He knew when he sent Shag and Average to meet you. You think half the Tinderbox is watching your progress but somehow the Pagan hasn't heard? He's got more idea what you're up to than you have!

Schofield hadn't allowed for that. He'd hoped – naively, he now realized – to slip into the camp unnoticed, locate his daughter and slip out again. 'So the Pagan knows I'm coming. You think he'll try to stop me?'

'Yuh-huh!' said Jonah, with added emphasis. 'Let's put it this way: if your father-in-law sneaked into your house under cover of darkness and tried to take your wife away, you'd be pretty pissed off, yes?'

'That's different,' said Schofield.

'Why is it?'

'Because Jan and I are married, and Cassie isn't. He has no right...'

He knew as he said it this wasn't going to cut much ice with Jonah. Nor did it. 'They're as married as makes any difference. They've been together longer than lots of marriages last. Do what you must, what you can get away with, but don't talk about rights. If the Pagan spit roasts us over a slow fire, everyone here will reckon he had the absolute right to defend his family.'

Which brought them neatly back to where the argument began. Schofield swallowed. 'Please, Jonah, go back now. I'll be careful. I'll avoid a confrontation if I can. But whether she comes with me or not, Cassie won't stand by and let her ... partner hurt her father. From here on I'm safer than

180

you are.'

There was a long silence. Schofield could feel Jonah's eyes on him. When next he spoke his voice was thick, ribbed with anger. 'Ronnie told you that, didn't he? That the Pagan tried to recruit me and I had to fight him off. What else did he tell you?'

'Nothing,' Schofield lied quickly.

'Bollocks!'

The lie wouldn't serve. 'He said you had to stay out of trouble with the police. I promised I wouldn't involve you in anything risky.'

'Mr Schofield, *being here* is risky!' exploded Jonah. 'Talking to you is risky. Going down that alley is as risky as brushing a shark's back teeth. It's all frigging risky! And you think you'd be safer on your own.'

'That's not it,' said Schofield, trying to explain. 'Yes, these people could hurt me – except that my daughter's one of them and I don't think she'll let them. But I'm not vulnerable in the way you are. If the police pick me up, I explain what I'm doing and they let me go. At worst, I call my solicitor. I don't end up bouncing off the walls of the custody suite.'

He heard the sharp intake of breath and the tremor in Jonah's voice. 'He told you. Ronnie, the bastard. He *told* you?'

Schofield groped for Jonah's arm in the darkness. The boy shook him off, violently, but not before Schofield registered the absolute rigidity of him, the muscles clench-ed hard in horror or shame or deep resent-ment. 'Don't be angry. He was trying to help. He thinks you need protecting from me. Perhaps he's right.'

'The bastard!' Jonah swore again, savagely. 'He had no *right* to tell you. I didn't know *he* knew...' He stopped with a strange soft sob, the sound of grief and loss.

Still Schofield was trying to explain. 'He didn't want me getting you into something that you couldn't handle. I said I wouldn't, and I'm trying to keep my promise. If you go back now...'

Jonah wasn't listening. 'How did he know? I never told him, and there *is* no one else.'

'You were ill, apparently. He looked after you. You were rambling.'

'Christ Almighty.' He sounded so stricken that Schofield, concerned, flicked the torch at him. His face was ashen, twisted as if in pain. In the moment before he twisted away from the light his eyes were appalled.

He flung himself at the wall, in the mouth of the alley where the shadows were deepest, resting his forehead on the dank bricks. A thin plaint whispered from his lips. 'He knows? He's known all along? And he's *telling* people? Oh God. Oh Christ.'

Afraid to touch him again, Schofield stall-ed with a hand halfway to the boy's shoulder.

He didn't know how to comfort him. 'Jonah, it's not that important. Lots of people have been inside. I'd have thought everyone here had been locked up at one time or another. It was a misunderstanding. It's not the end of the world.'

The straw-coloured head turned sideways until Jonah's eye appeared. 'Misunderstanding?'

'That's all it was, isn't it? Yes, you were accused of something pretty terrible. But you didn't do it, did you? And when the police realized that they let you go. It must have been an horrific experience – and God knows how your family live with what *they* did – but it's in the past. It's time to put it behind you, to let go. My son's your age. If I thought he was tearing himself apart because of something he had no control over – if I thought it was going to cast a shadow over the rest of his life...'

He ran out of words then, just stood mutely pitying the damaged youth. Because in fact he couldn't have done much more if it *had* been Tom.

Slowly Jonah turned back towards Schofield. His face was no longer racked with despair; the muscles were slack, the eyes half closed. His arms fell loose at his sides and his voice was numb. 'Yes, it was. Horrific. I'll tell you about it, if you want.'

If Jonah wanted to talk, to extirpate the

rage still pulsing in his veins after twelve bitter months by pouring it out in vitriol on a stranger – a man he hardly knew, a man he would never see again – the least Schofield could do was listen. There might be catharsis in the telling, and after catharsis healing. He could have chosen a better time for it, but Schofield supposed the darkness helped. Anyway, he wouldn't stop him. If Jonah didn't talk soon, the magnitude of the emotions he was holding in would break him. So, inconvenient as it was, he was ready to listen. Only...

'Jonah, I already know.'

The tangled hair moved on his shoulders as he shook his head. His tone was expressionless, the voice of a man succumbing to anaesthesia. 'No. I don't think you do. But I'll tell you. I *want* to tell you. I've got to tell someone.'

Six

He was like fifteen-year-old boys every-where: very good at lying about things that didn't matter and very bad at lying about things that did.

He said that morning at breakfast, without a flicker of conscience, that he and Bobby were going to see a film after school. It wouldn't be over till late so there was no point waiting up.

They'd planned this beforehand. The Royalty was showing Branagh's *Henry V*. It was long, it was recommended viewing for students, and as they'd seen it before they'd be able to field any questions that came their way. The lie had so much to recommend it that half the kids at Martin Donnelly's party were believed by their families to be at the Royalty watching *Henry V*.

Jonah – that wasn't his name then – knew them all. Most of them went to the same school. Jonah was in the fourth year, Bobby in the fifth. Some were in bastardised school uniform, collars wide and sleeves rolled back; others had come via home and wore the sort of clothes that parents might see as suitable for a night at the cinema.

They sprawled on the furniture and on the floor, playing music and DVDs. They started on cider, then moved on to explore – in the spirit of scientific curiosity – the contents of the cocktail cabinet. The Donnellys were amiable people who, when they returned from their Personal Discovery weekend in Wales, would either not notice the shortfall or make good-natured jokes about it. They'd taken a tolerant approach to Martin's upbringing. He'd never had a bed time, had been encouraged – since repression is the death of creativity – to vent his temper in rude words, and had been supplied with condoms from an age when the best fun he could have with them was making water balloons.

Someone brought cannabis to the party, someone else brought cocaine. The company divided according to the depths of people's pockets. Jonah could have paid his way at the glass-topped coffee table, cutting coke with a razor blade and snorting lines of it through rolled-up bank notes. But he was more at ease sharing joints, building up an aromatic fug that would have activated fog warnings on the motorway. So the evening passed, and for the most part he was blithely unaware of its passing.

If it had occurred to the revellers to run a

book on which of the girls was most likely to get raped, Sally Burchill's name would have been bottom of the list. She was nice, she was quiet, she was rather plain. She was fond of hockey and dogs, and wore little make-up even at parties. But thinking about it afterwards, the consensus was that actually poor Sally was a natural. She was too nice to see trouble coming, too quiet to yell for help, maybe too plain to have gained the experience to deal with tipsy, randy youths. In the open she could have shown them a clean pair of heels. But she was cornered in the Scandinavian-style sauna beside the Donnellys' swimming pool, beaten unconscious to stop her screaming, and violated repeatedly.

It was Jonah who found her. His head was woozy from the cannabis, the house was packed with tripped-out teenagers, the air smelled like Omar Khayyam's armpit and he thought he'd pass out if he didn't get some fresh air. He padded round the garden, expanding his lungs with the altogether more wholesome scents of a summer evening.

The door of the sauna cabin was ajar. The likelihood was that two or more people had gone inside seeking privacy and recreation. Minded to a little harmless mischief, Jonah went in too. At first he thought the cabin was empty, that he'd arrived too late. But when he turned to go, one bare foot stepped in

Sally Burchill's hair and the other in her blood.

The police descended on the place. They had a comatose sixteen-year-old girl who might not live; who, even if she lived might not regain consciousness for weeks; who, even if she regained consciousness might remember nothing of what happened. They had thirty teenagers, many of them juveniles, half of them potential suspects, most of them high on one illegal substance or another, all of them – including the culprits – in shock. They had the owners of the crime scene halfway up a Welsh mountain chanting mantras, and twenty other sets of parents to speak to – and most of these parents were middle-class professionals whose knee-jerk reaction was to call their solicitors.

Statements were taken from those capable of making them. Among those who were not, half a dozen were considered to be dangerously drunk or drugged and removed to hospital. The remainder were divided in three. Those who couldn't be responsible for Sally's condition and had seen nothing – mostly girls, and a couple of boys who had passed out before anything happened – were sent home. Those who remained sufficiently aware of their own and other people's movements to make useful witnesses were taken aside to calm down and sober up.

That left a group of mainly older boys who

were drunk or high enough, but not too much, to have contributed to the attack on Sally Burchill. They had no alibis except one another. Some had scratches that could have come from playing tag in the dark garden – the state of the roses showed that someone had been – or might have been inflicted by a terrified girl fighting for her life. Initial interviews at the house left important questions unanswered and they were asked to help with further inquiries at the police station.

To start with Jonah was in the second group. He was one of the younger boys present, had spent the evening passing joints and giggling, and his companions were able to vouch for most of his time. He never knew why he was upgraded. Because he was the one who found her, or because of something he said, or someone said about him? But at the last moment, as the second group were being sent home and the third ushered towards the police cars, he was asked to go too.

At the police station they were split up. There was a lot of waiting, before and during interviews. He supposed the detectives were cross-checking what he was saying with what they'd already been told. He tried to be careful what he said. The fact that he hardly remembered what he'd said earlier, that his head still swam from the scented smoke, made this difficult.

His mother was there. She sat tight-lipped at his side, not looking at him. He could feel her fear, her vibrant anger.

He gave a DNA swab, which he expected would resolve the matter. But Sally had been raped by a number of her friends: the medical evidence was going to take time to interpret.

Sometime in the early morning the tone of the interview changed. He was no longer there to assist with inquiries – he was defending himself against an accusation. There was no evidence; if the police believed he was involved someone had lied to them. Someone other than him. He was exhausted and scared. He wished he could talk to Bobby.

The interview ended at dawn. They wouldn't let him go home. Some of the boys had been released, they said, and some were being detained for further questioning. They left him alone but he couldn't sleep. After breakfast they resumed the interview. When he asked where his mother was they told him she'd waived her right to be present. He was provided with an Appropriate Adult, whose job it was to make sure the boy wasn't put under unreasonable pressure, or slapped for giving smart answers.

He lost track of time. They clearly thought he'd done it. They thought he'd raped Sally Burchill, banged her head on the tile floor until she stopped screaming, left her for dead and gone back to finish a reefer with his friends before pretending to find her. He could deny it but he couldn't disprove it. He could have set them on the right lines, but he was young enough to consider that a kind of betrayal. When he'd said all he was prepared to he said no more.

Even when the Appropriate Adult needed a comfort break, no one tried to beat a confession out of him. They eyed him mostly with dislike. They described Sally's injuries in detail. They said that all the other suspects had now been freed. Then they tried sympathy. They knew how girls behaved at parties, how a lad could take her flirting for something more. Even judges understood that. They'd go easy on him if he told the truth now.

Too scared by this juncture even to repeat his denials, he pledged all his remaining effort to keeping quiet. To remembering why it was better for him to sit out this present nightmare, which would pass, than to end it with words which, once said, could never be retracted.

Then the senior investigating officer bustled into the cell where he was toying with another meal – it might have been tea or supper, he couldn't tell either what the time was or what the food was – and charged him with rape and attempted murder. He was sent to the remand wing of a young offenders' institution.

Like Sally Burchill and Martin Donnelly – like most of his friends – he was from a nice middle-class family. It was a nice middle-class neighbourhood. Nothing he'd seen or heard prepared him for the reality of prison. He was overwhelmed by the manic combination of mindless discipline and near mutiny. After just twenty-four hours he understood that the real value of his cell door was not that it kept him in but that it kept others out.

Young offenders' institutions were designed to protect juvenile prisoners from the corrupting influences that turned gauche young men paying mostly for a lack of sense into penal graduates with a thorough knowledge of the criminal way of life. It was hoped they would also cut down the number of youngsters who saw suicide as an escape. But like many good intentions, this one was thwarted mostly by the intended beneficiaries. Many young offenders had a father or older brother serving time and knew more about prison life than working for a living. Lacking more experienced convicts to corrupt them, they corrupted one another.

Sex offenders get a rough ride in all prisons. Men forcibly parted from their girlfriends, wives and daughters worry about their safety and their faithfulness and reserve a particular hatred for men who abuse women. The junior thieves, drug dealers, muggers and card skimmers knew all the prison traditions, including the one that regards a door as locked only when a pro can't open it.

The strangeness of his surroundings, the horror of his situation, the oppressive proximity of so much tacit violence, even the noise that went on late into the night, were not enough to keep Jonah awake. After lights out he lay for some minutes in the darkness, eyes stretched with despair, wondering what he'd be justified in doing to free himself. He seemed to be all out of options. He told himself that, if he waited, it would all get sorted out. He pulled the bedclothes over his head and let the weariness take him.

Because he was asleep he didn't hear the first mouse-like scratchings at his lock. Dully, through fragmented dreams, he heard the door open and supposed it was part of the routine – a head-count or some such. He was still three-quarters asleep when half a dozen hands fastened on him and dragged him out of bed.

They stuffed a rag in his mouth and beat him till he couldn't stand – avoiding his face, sinking their fists into his belly where the bruises wouldn't show. Then two of them held him and the third raped him. Not with pleasure but fiercely, as if it was an obligation.

'That's what it feels like,' they snarled in his ear when they'd finished. 'That's how *she* felt, till you beat her brains in. Talk about this and we'll come back and beat yours in.'

Terrified, shocked to the core, he said nothing. Not to the centre staff and not to the policemen who questioned him again the next day. But still that night the three youths came back and did it again.

They left him sobbing and bleeding, unsure how much more he could take even in the name of loyalty. He could tell the staff but he couldn't identify his attackers, had never seen their faces. And he already knew how much use a locked door was. One way or another they'd make him pay – or if not them, someone would. If it wasn't one set of hard fists sinking into his belly and strong hands spreading him star-shaped on the floor it would be another; until they were satisfied he'd been punished enough.

That night they came back and did it again.

In the morning when the policemen came, Jonah told them all he knew. That Bobby, Martin Donnelly and two other boys were missing from the party for half an hour. That Jonah had run out of money and gone looking for people he could borrow from, and he couldn't find them. He was still looking when he tried the pool house.

He didn't believe Bobby attacked the girl. He thought there was some other explanation, and if he'd known what Jonah was going through he'd have come forward with it, freeing the younger boy from his obligation of silence. Even after he was charged, even after he was raped, he told himself that Bobby couldn't know the trouble he was in, that when he found out he'd put an end to it. When he finally told what he knew it was in the belief that Bobby would sort the matter out from his end.

But he'd misjudged the situation again. Bobby didn't have an innocent explanation. A police car collected the four boys from school, and before the day was out they'd all confessed to the rape of Sally Burchill and Martin Donnelly had admitted occasioning her grievous bodily harm.

By the time the case came to trial Jonah was in London. He never heard what sentences were imposed. He supposed Bobby was behind bars right now, with mice scratching each night at his lock.

When the story was told Schofield stood a long time in silence, thanking God for the dark that spared them having to look at one another. Somewhere during the telling they had assumed identical positions in the mouth of the alley: hands in pockets, leaning their shoulders against the brick wall, each with a foot drawn up against it, staring at the opposite wall.

Between Schofield's shoulder and Jonah's there was about the width of a man's hand. All Schofield's instincts told him to find a way of bridging that gap, as he would have done if it had been his own child telling him about the worst time of his life. But an internal voice urged caution. Jonah was not his son. He was a youth growing to manhood in the hardest of all schools, and quite possibly the last thing he wanted in the whole world was to be touched – even in kindness; perhaps especially in kindness – by another man.

But if he did nothing, would Jonah suppose it was disgust holding him back? This boy who'd learned to deal with pain, humiliation and rejection by taking a pride in loneliness – was he aching for a human touch? Or would he jerk away like a stray dog afraid to accept a titbit for fear it might hide a snare?

Some god of the old world came to Schofield's aid. Not the severe, sober-suited Judeo-Christian God but something Puckish, some half-animal deity of grain and grape smiling in its beard at the dilemmas human beings construct for themselves. It was the last kind of god Schofield would have acknowledged, but then it was the last sort of remark he would have made. He wasn't good at jokes. He never saw the point of other people's and told them badly himself.

So it must have been the humorous old god that made him say, 'Life's a bugger.'

When he realized what he'd said he wanted to die. He screwed his eyes tight and groaned aloud.

For a dreadful moment he thought he'd finally broken Jonah's spirit. Moist, choked sounds came from his throat. His head tipped back and his shoulders shook. But Jonah wasn't crying. Something had indeed broken; not his spirit but the steely thread of tension that had been cranking tighter in him as his secret became less and less something he kept and more something that kept him.

For twelve months it had haunted him, stalking him by day and riding him by night. Now, finally, he'd told someone. The thing was out in the open, where the air could get at it, and it was still ugly but the poison was no longer eating away at him. And there was a funny side to it. It was a bad joke of a tragedy, so execrably sordid all you could do was laugh. So he laughed. He sank down helpless in the gutter, his yellow head against the dirty bricks, and he laughed until tears streamed down his face.

After an anxious moment, still unsure what the joke was, Schofield joined in, though not with the same abandon. He was a moderate man; when he laughed he did so in moderation – and anyway, he was still puzzled. When Jonah subsided in a whimpering heap against the wall, unsure of the ground he was treading, Schofield ventured cautiously, 'But, after all that, why did you leave home?'

Jonah shrugged. The burden had lifted from his shoulders and little rancour remained. 'Not much choice. They changed the locks and wouldn't give me a key.'

Of all Schofield had heard, that beggared belief. 'But ... *why*? Didn't they believe you? Did they think you'd done it?'

The gleam in the dark was Jonah's eye. 'They knew what happened. They'd known all along. But Bobby was the smart one. He was going to Cambridge. I wanted to be a carpenter. If someone was going down for this, it was always going to be me.'

From the tinny taste of cold Schofield knew his mouth had dropped open – knew, and for a moment could do nothing about it. Then: 'Bobby's your *brother*?'

Jonah nodded. 'Didn't I say? Me and Bobby were like that.' Schofield felt him move, knew he was crossing his fingers. 'We went everywhere together. I'd have died for Bobby. But I couldn't do his time for him. I don't know what got into him. Well, actually I do – coke and some single-malt whisky. It's the only explanation. He's not that kind of guy. *I'd* have believed it was me rather than Bobby raped Sally Burchill. And I never blamed him for being scared to own up,' he added stoutly. 'He couldn't undo what had happened, and he couldn't know what was happening to me, and there couldn't be any evidence against me so he figured they'd have to let me go eventually. And he had our parents on his case. If one of us was going down, they didn't want it to be the one who could have gone to Cambridge. Carpentry's all very well but it doesn't have the same ring about it.'

He blew out a gusty sigh. 'You know, every day I wonder if I should have stuck it out. Every day. It would've been rough, but probably I'd have got out before much longer. Got out and gone home. The return of the hero: champagne and kisses, and a new router to play with. Still, you can't go back, can you?' He gave a little snort of laughter. 'Not after they've changed the locks you can't.'

The world turned while Schofield fought for air. When he had a voice he said, as firmly as he could, 'That settles it. I'm on my own from here.'

Now Jonah didn't understand. 'Why? Nothing's changed.'

Schofield's priorities had changed. He still wanted to find Cassie, but not at any cost. He was prepared to risk himself; he was not now prepared to risk Jonah, even if that meant failure. 'You could have joined the Pagan any time in the last twelve months. You decided you were safer alone. It was a good decision – stick to it.'

'I will,' nodded the boy. 'But I can take you to his camp without joining his merry band.'

Schofield shook his head. 'Ronnie said...'

'Ronnie!' snorted Jonah. 'What does Ronnie know? Ronnie's idea of a walk on the wild side is changing his chip fat!'

Schofield grinned. He wanted to believe Jonah could take care of himself as well as he claimed. He wanted to believe he was worrying for nothing. He looked into the black alley, back at the black depot and up at the ruddy glow of London reflecting from the clouds. He was seeking a sign.

Jonah got tired of waiting. He hauled himself to his feet and headed up the alley. 'Come on.'

That simplified it. Schofield knew it was wrong, but he also knew that his chances of succeeding alone were remote. He was glad to have the decision taken out of his hands. The only choice he had now was to follow or stay behind. So he followed, with only a soft sigh that might have been misgivings but was probably relief.

PART THREE

THE GIRL

One

The woman moved through the chaos of the new camp with half a smile on her face. She'd done as much sorting out and settling in as she intended for one day. What remained to be done could wait till tomorrow.

Having made the decision to abandon her own work, she took especial pleasure in watching other people at theirs. The squabbling over the best sites that inevitably followed a move had been resolved, by the Pagan where the parties were unable to resolve it themselves, so that now each group – from couples up to extended families of five or six adults with as many children scrambling round them like puppies – had its own hearth and the makings of a home rising about it.

Erecting the houses was complicated by the fact that the family had stayed so long in a place with a roof. Homes in the hotel had been two or three rooms each; homes in the school had been little enclaves of private space enclosed by screens. Weatherproofing, usually the first priority, had not been a consideration, with the result that carefully hoarded sheets of plastic and squares of tin had been put to other uses or mislaid.

What could not be found would be replaced, but it would take a few days. If the rain held off there would be no problem. They had the hearth fires and a couple of big communal blazes to keep the worst of the cold at bay and dry anything touched by the morning mist. But if the overcast fulfilled its threat and the heavens opened, half the people here would be unable to get out of the rain. Cold and wet were much more dangerous than cold alone. Those with adequate shelter would somehow have to accommodate those without until all the houses could be finished.

They were not houses in the conventional sense. Ordinary people – and people here used the expression with a pejorative curl of the lip, the way tax-payers say *vagrant* – wouldn't have recognized these rudimentary shacks and tepees as houses. There were no amenities, no more furniture than could be tossed on to the back of a lorry at an hour's notice, not enough space to swing even a small obliging cat. Ordinary people expected, as a minimum, a front door that locked, windows, basic plumbing, and furniture on which to sleep, eat and sit.

But if you defined a house as being a place

of safety, where no one would come without invitation, which could be kept warm enough and dry enough for comfort and where the residents could enjoy privacy when they wanted it and entertain friends when the occasion arose, then houses they were, at least as much as shoe-box flats stacked up to the sky. More than that, they had the makings of homes.

In just a few days some of the hearth fires that now glittered across the dark wasteland would be reduced to a faint cherry glow casting shadows on the slanting walls of high tepees, and others would be entirely invisible behind the solid walls of squat shacks. Everyone would be dry and warming up. But the camp would never look prettier than it did tonight, with scores of fires twinkling in the dark, their rosy light washing up on three sides against stone walls and on the fourth against the square tower of the ruinous church of St Jude. Casey, who had an eye for beauty, wanted to enjoy the sight before the camp grew more comfortable but less picturesque.

A gaggle of excited children, bundled in so many woolly layers as to resemble teddy bears in both shape and texture, were learning the topography of the new settlement by the simple expedient of running until they bumped into something. This time they bumped into Casey. She protected herself with her hands, smiling in the darkness. 'What do you think of it so far?'

Teeth and eyes gleamed in the darkness. One of them said, 'Cool!' Another said, judiciously, 'Best yet,' as if his experience of desirable residences was not confined to scenes of dereliction.

Casey was glad they were pleased. 'Remember to tell the Pagan.' They raced on, shouting and bumping into things.

Talking with the others she called him *the Pagan*, as they did. But when they were alone together she called him only Man, and he called her Woman. Not at first. At first he'd called her Child. For more than a year he'd cared for her as a child, finding her a home with one of the extended families, showing her how to find money and food, teaching her how to avoid trouble and how to deal with such trouble as she couldn't avoid.

She was in awe of him then, this tall man, cadaverously thin, with his high forehead and the black beard where lurked a sudden, ferocious smile, and his diamond-grey eyes that could see both far away and deep into people's hearts. She'd had her education at the hands of the Pagan, as did all the youngsters coming new to his tribe.

In return she did his work of begging, stealing and helping in schemes designed to separate ordinary people from their money. She had a talent for this, or at least the kind of sweet innocent face and soulful eyes that made it easy. And the work, once she shrugged off the last reproaches of middle-class respectability, was to her liking. Most of the sheep she fleeced were betrayed mainly by their own lust. Decent men whom she approached either gave her their change or shooed her away. Those who went with her were self-selected victims.

At first she worried it might misfire, leaving her to provide the services she offered. But the Pagan ensured that there was always someone on hand to rescue her. Dirty Mary made a convincing nun and succeeded in shaming the contents of his wallet out of one man after another. Old Hickory's doting grandfather was nearly as successful, and Little Jo's starving kid brother was a nice Dickensian touch. Little Jo was actually Josephine, and made her first appearance as a starving kid sister. But the man offered twice as much if he could have the child as well, so Jo underwent a sex change before they ran the scam again. Like most of these randomly dressed, undernourished children she would not be recognisably one sex or the other until hormones began to change her outline.

When that happened to Casey, in her seventeenth year, the Pagan began treating her differently. He promoted Jo to chief bait and kept Casey about the camp. In a way she missed the thrill of the game – the excitement and dread, inextricably intermingled, of approaching men she didn't know and going off alone with them, and having to hide who she really was behind the mask of tarnished freshness and youthful availability. Privately she thought she did it better than Little Jo, who was too easy. But it wouldn't have occurred to her to challenge the Pagan's orders.

The second year she served him in the role of housekeeper, making a home for him, preparing his meals, mending his clothes. She still slept with the family that had taken her in, and she reached her seventeenth birthday a virgin – an achievement even in societies less chaotic than the Tinderbox.

When he finally took her it was with a certain formality, a due solemnity. He was exactly twice her age. He'd had consorts before, women who'd stayed with him for a time until they grew tired of one another. He'd never before wanted a permanent arrangement. He'd never been willing to wait for a woman before. He asked Casey to be his partner, to share his home and his travels, to bear his children.

By then, if he'd asked her to be his dog or his doormat she'd have agreed. She worshipped his strength, his vision. She knew if he was near by the tingling behind her knees. She knew if he was in danger by the gripping of her heart. She was in love. If she was also a little afraid of him, she trusted this would pass as the barriers between them came down and there was no unknown left to fear.

A little way off in the darkness one of the fires began to dance. For a moment Casey was puzzled. Then she realized it was the Juggler and smiled. She'd seen him fill the air with shimmering balls, with plates, with oranges and once with snowballs. Now he'd thrust four brands into the fire – she thought there were four though they moved too fast for counting – and was making a Catherine wheel of them. They wove intricate patterns against the night, kept improbably aloft by the deft fingers and sinewy wrists of the languid young man they called the Juggler.

Someone had told her he used to be something in the City. Another story was that he was a rich man's son who'd grown sick of privilege and turned for asylum first to a circus, then to the Tinderbox. Either could be the truth, or neither. Casey didn't care who he used to be. The only truth that mattered was that he could draw gasps of joy from the children round him; that the little flames he kept dancing in the night air made them happy and that made him happy.

Casey wondered why ordinary people made such an issue of happiness. She found it easy to be happy. Being with friends, not being hungry, not being cold – all these things made her happy. She thought ordinary people must be a poor lot not to be happy all the time.

When the church was still a church, this had been its churchyard. Presumably the graves were here still, buried under a century of wind drift. Certainly there were tombstones, canted drunkenly and sunk to the depth of *Dearly Beloved*. Most of the names survived but few of the dates and fewer of the tributes. Perhaps that was how it should be. If this was someone's last resting place, did it matter when they came here or who they left behind?

'I must remember to warn the children about yew,' Casey murmured absently to herself.

At one end of the graveyard the ground heaved up in a hillock higher than the wall enclosing it. Casey had no way of knowing if it was a natural feature or a man-made one. All she knew was that it rewarded the climber with a comprehensive view of the settlement, much of the surrounding area, and – strung along the horizon like a necklace of tiny red and yellow beads – the lights of London, vibrant, confident, impossibly remote. They promised wealth and power, and rewards like gems from the hands of princes. The offer applied only to those with access to the magic acres at the heart of the metropolis, but their beauty was free to anyone within a five-mile radius who could climb high enough to see over the grimy between.

Casey loved night in the city. She loved the lights. She loved the way that great ugly blocks fretting the horizon like the stumps of teeth turned with the fading of the day into stacks of diamanté, like Christmas trees or yachts dressed for a regatta. The modest contribution made to the nightly display by a distant traffic light, cycling endlessly between crimson, gold and peridot-green, could fill her eyes with tears. She wondered sometimes if she was a little mad, to take such piquant delight in something as mundane as a traffic light.

Looking the other way there were no traffic lights. There were some street lamps, but none close by. An occasional vehicle drove along under the churchyard wall, weaving between the potholes, but none stopped. There was no reason to. Nowhere to do business, no one to visit. The drivers were sometimes lost, sometimes taking a short cut, but always hurrying out of the Tinderbox as quickly as they could.

It occurred to Casey that a sentry on top of the hill would see any movement towards the settlement in plenty of time to raise the alarm. She thought she'd mention it to the Pagan. He wasn't expecting trouble but it would pay to be cautious for a while. Rommel's abattoir was a shade close for comfort. At some point he would send scouts to test their defences, not so much with a view to war as wanting to see how far they could be pushed before they would push back.

Rommel and the Pagan avoided overt conflict by always circling carefully outside each other's range. Moving this close to the abattoir would put the arrangement under strain. But with the school demolished they had to go somewhere. The graveyard had never been used by Rommel, nor was it clearly within his tribe's territory. Probably the armed truce could be preserved. But there might be raised voices and a little posturing first.

Casey was not much troubled by the spectre of all-out war. Rommel as well as the Pagan could only lose by starting something big enough to bring the police – or if they didn't feel up to it, the army – down on their heads. She was more worried about Rommel raiding the new camp for women. Unlike the Pagan's family, Rommel's tribe was almost entirely male. Such women as lived with them were the exclusive property of the lieutenants, so the squaddies faced a perennial shortage of sex. Like fighting in public, forcing their attentions on ordinary women would leave the police no option but to deal with them and so was strictly forbidden.

Girls in the other tribes, however, were

considered fair game. Homeless people have no rights, homeless women least of all. It was widely believed among the families that, though the authorities would not condone a practice that was both legally and morally indefensible, they saw it as a lesser evil than gangs of frustrated thugs roaming beyond the Tinderbox. Casey was afraid that Rommel might tolerate the new camp because of the opportunities it offered.

She wasn't afraid for herself. Everyone in the Tinderbox knew about her and the Pagan, that any harm to her would mean total war that wouldn't end till most of the protagonists were dead. Rommel's prime directive to any raiding party would be to ensure her safety.

Besides, at twenty-one she was already – so far as the Field Marshal's young guns were concerned – past her sell-by date. If they came here they'd be looking for girls in their mid-teens, still wearing the ordinary clothes that marked them as new in town. Recent arrivals were less adept at defending themselves, had yet to form the strong attachments that led to reprisals, and were more likely to be clean. Girls who'd been turning tricks in dark alleys at a tenner a time for six months would have collected more than money. Others would have acquired drug habits that made them not worth the raiding, expensive and troublesome in camp and dead in bed. It seemed everybody's mother had been right. Boys – even Rommel's boys – really do prefer nice girls.

Casey was letting her thoughts run ahead, worrying about a situation that might never arise. Partly it was the natural anxiety of moving house: *will we get on with the neighbours?* But partly it was the stirring of new feelings in her blood, making her feel protective towards the whole clan. Anyone who thought to carry off Little Jo, or Marie-Claire, or Princess, would have to come through her first. Well, perhaps not Little Jo. Little Jo would enjoy it.

Down in the fire-studded dark the Juggler had finished his performance and the children were drifting away. Casey glanced at the sky, tasted the breeze. She thought the rain would hold off. But if not they'd all have to huddle under the surviving fragments of the church roof, and she would sleep with a child's head on her lap and her head on the Pagan's shoulder. The prospect caused her no grief. She smiled serenely and laced her hands over her belly.

Four years they'd been together in the fullest sense. She'd been pregnant twice before. The first time she miscarried before she was even sure. The second time she lost the child at five months, which was late enough not only to be sure it was there but to have grown to love it. She grieved for it as if it were a real person.

But by then she'd been long enough in the Tinderbox to know that life was easily conceived here but harder to bring to term, that even children born healthy struggled to thrive. She knew that the odds were against this scrap of humanity developing inside her. She knew it was too early to risk calling it a child, to start thinking of names. But all her instincts told her that this time it would hold. She felt unreasonably optimistic. She wanted this child as she couldn't remember wanting anything before. In another week, if she was still pregnant, she would tell the Pagan. When they were alone he'd cried over the last one they lost. She knew how he'd react to the news that she was carrying another.

She saw him walk between the fires, his sharply bearded profile silhouetted for a moment against the flames, his narrow head turning about him. He was looking for her. She knew why. He'd have her flute in his hand. By now everyone had done enough work for one day: it was time for the whole clan, adults and sleepy children alike, to gather round one of the big communal fires for a peaceful hour of gossip, smoking and music.

Back in a time she could hardly remember, Casey had played the clarinet. She played in London too, busking, until someone stole her instrument. The Pagan had given her the flute. It was the first thing he ever did that singled her out from the other children.

Mostly when she played now it was for her own pleasure and that of her family. She didn't need to busk on street corners: the Pagan gave her all she needed. Only a couple of times a year, when she wanted money to buy him something and wanted it to be a surprise, did she venture as far as the Underground and play for the travellers. She avoided rush hours, finding shoppers and tourists more inclined to pause and listen than the time-strapped commuters. Even when she was playing for money she wanted them to enjoy her music, not just toss her some coins as they hurried past.

'Casey?' He was growing concerned at searching and not finding her. She could hear the sharpening tenor of his voice, see how his beard swung through swift arcs as he quested for her like a scenting fox. If she stayed up here much longer he'd get people to help him look for her.

She climbed to her feet, her waist not yet thick enough to make her clumsy. 'Up here. I'm coming.' She saw his head turn towards her as he stood string thin against the fire. She descended the steepest part of the hill one careful step at a time. As the slope level-led out she began to run.

Two

The alley was not the end of the journey, only an entry to a secret network of back lanes that spread through the Tinderbox like veins. Some of the lanes were wide enough for a lorry, though they were probably built to be wide enough for a cart; others were mere passages in which two men would have to turn sideways to pass. Overhead, silhouetted against livid cloud, gantries like the booms of forgotten cranes linked the buildings, the iron skeletons showing through gaps in the corrugated skin. Without maintenance, many of the ties had rotted away and every year a night of strong winds sent more of the rusty cladding plunging into the alley like great disabled birds. Schofield found himself walking on their broken wings.

There was a little wind now, up there among the gantries. He could hear it working the iron, drawing from it metallic groans. He suspected that a sheet of corrugated iron falling twenty metres would cut a man in half. He winced and walked faster, crowding

Jonah's heels.

It was like following a Sherpa into the Himalayas, or an Indian Scout into the Black Hills of Dakota. He had no reason to mistrust his guide, but the place was so threatening that faith was not enough to keep fear at bay. For all his hard-won skills, Jonah was still only a homeless teenager with a bit of street smarts, who couldn't always keep himself out of trouble, let alone someone else. Being better at this than Schofield wasn't enough. He had to be better than the Pagan and his people; better than Rommel and *his* people. If he missed one puff of smoke in the sky, one whistle that was almost but not quite like that of a prairie chicken, the Sioux would be down on them faster than you could say Little Big Horn.

But while they moved quietly there was no attempt at silence. Jonah passed back warnings about the state of the ground and once, when the warning came too late, a sly joke while he waited for Schofield to find his feet again.

It was noticeable how the further they progressed into this nightmare world, the further they strayed from the street lamps and shop fronts and traffic, as Schofield grew increasingly anxious so Jonah's mood lightened. His voice lightened, his steps lightened, and in the darkness his eyes were bright with good humour. Tragically vulnerable in Schofield's world of light, order and policemen, he grew into himself as the trappings of civilisation fell away. Like a forest animal that looks like a hearth rug in a cage and a primordial hunter when returned to the trees.

Perhaps people like Jonah came here because there was nowhere else for them. But they stayed because they were better, stronger, safer here than anyone who might try to follow them. It was *their* forest, the place where they suddenly made sense.

Where the alley widened enough to admit a little moonlight, and Schofield didn't need all his concentration to keep his feet, he murmured, 'I can guess where Shag got his name from. But why's the other one called Average?'

Jonah gave a peal of soft laughter. 'How long have you been worrying about that?'

'Pretty much since I stopped worrying about the size of his fists and whether he wears steel toe caps,' admitted Schofield.

He could hear the grin in Jonah's voice. 'He got it from a weather map. A rainfall chart or something. He saw the words *Mean Average*, knew what *mean* meant and thought *average* meant even nastier. His boot size is higher than his IQ.'

Schofield didn't know whether to laugh or cry. 'And Rommel?'

'Likes swastikas,' Jonah said briefly. His

voice diminished as he moved off. 'Quiet now. We're nearly there.'

A stone wall marched across the end of the alley and the lane turned along it. Because the wall was lower than the buildings it seemed lighter here: they could see each other better than at any time since leaving the depot. Schofield could see Jonah's broad shoulders and the moon-gleam on his yellow hair as he moved ahead.

The boy bent over, peering at the thick scum of road dirt. He said quietly, 'Oh yeah.'

Schofield pulled his torch from his pocket. 'What have you found?'

Jonah's strong fingers gripped his wrist. 'Don't *do* that. Jesus! If you want people to know we're here, why don't you just dance along the top of the wall singing "The Birdy Song"?'

Even on holiday, even on a package holiday in Spain, even on a package holiday in Spain with two under-tens, Schofield had never sung 'The Birdy Song'. No one who knew him would have expected him to. Laurence Schofield, architect, husband and father, never joined in sing-songs on holiday flights or dancing conga lines in foreign hotels. People who knew almost nothing about him knew that. A respectable man, a decent man, a nice man in many ways, but about as much fun as a wet weekend in Whitby.

Fleetingly he wondered what those people

who thought of him as a reliable bore would say if they saw him tonight, crawling round the nether side of the city in the company of a teenage outlaw. Might make them blink, he thought with a momentary satisfaction.

'Sorry,' he murmured, contrite. 'What is it?'

'Tyre tracks. A truck's been through here. It has to be them.'

'So we follow the tracks?'

Jonah winced. 'No. We're not going through the front door; we're going over the back wall.'

Schofield looked up where it loomed above him. The stones were rough boulders rather than ashlar blocks but there were no obvious footholds. Maybe the boy could climb it, but not a middle-aged, middle-class, non-conga-dancing architect. 'I can't do that.'

Jonah looked at it again, surprised. Clearly in his mind a two-metre wall posed no obstacle. Schofield wondered what all his middle-class neighbours who carefully locked their back gates would think of that. ''Course you can.'

'Jonah, I can't climb that wall! I couldn't if my life depended on it. I couldn't,' he remembered, '*when* my life depended on it.'

The boy breathed heavily at him. 'You've got to. We've got to get inside so you can see if Casey's your daughter. We've got to go over the wall because we can't knock on the front door, and we've got to do it here because there's a scrubby little hill inside which means the campsite will be at the other end.'

'None of which alters the fact,' said Schofield tersely, 'that I can't climb a six-foot wall.'

Jonah considered. 'How about a three-foot wall?'

'Probably...'

'Then climb on me.'

'*What?*'

Soft enough that it wouldn't have carried a couple of paces, Jonah's voice was still perceptibly tetchy. 'Don't you know *anything*? Look. Put your hand *here*, and your foot *here*, and...'

Ten seconds later Laurence Schofield was sitting astride the stone wall, trying to erase the memory of treading on another human being to get there.

Five seconds later Jonah was sitting beside him. But he didn't stay there long. Hunters learn not to sky-line, but the hunted are born knowing. He dropped into the darkness, and grabbed Schofield's foot to pull him down too.

The mound was carpeted with brambles and tussock grass. They lay on their bellies while Jonah got his bearings.

The fires of the camp spread out below them were all that Schofield could see.

Perhaps Jonah could see better in the dark that was his natural element, or perhaps he was making an educated guess. 'The Pagan will be in the church tower. That's where he'll make his house.'

Schofield nodded wisely. 'So we give it a wide berth.'

'Not if you want to talk to the woman he's living with.'

As they edged down the hill, still hugging the ground, the dark tower separated itself from the dark churchyard and began to rear up into the sky. By following the wall Schofield thought they could reach it without approaching any of the fires. What he didn't know, what even Jonah couldn't know, was how many people were wandering around in the darkness. Because this quest could come to an abrupt end if they bumped into one of them.

Schofield was afraid they were making too much noise. Every rustle of the grass, every time he disturbed a stone or a wind-blown paper with his hand or knee, he thought everyone in the camp would turn his way. But either they made less noise than he thought, or it didn't carry, or it sounded like the camp dogs rabbiting in the thicket. Or perhaps, believing themselves secure, the people below paid no heed to the sounds of the night in an overgrown churchyard. It was late; they were tired. They'd gathered round the fire for supper and a song or two, and probably wouldn't have noticed if the interlopers had stood up and walked down the hill, laughing and talking.

The sound of the flute pulled Schofield up short. Annie in The Wooden Wall had heard the plangent disembodied notes hanging in the still night air like the souls of men hovering over a battlefield, and Schofield had thought then that she'd been listening to Cassie. Now he was sure. He couldn't have said why. He was no musician; details of technique meant nothing to him. Nor was the music familiar. If he'd heard his daughter play the tune, he didn't remember. But there was a magic to it that stroked his spine. The sweet sorrow of a flute playing in a disused graveyard on the wrong side of any tracks that were ever laid went clean through his skin to shimmer along his nerve endings.

'Jonah ... that's her.'

The boy had stopped crawling when he missed Schofield. Now he lifted his head clear of the undergrowth, looking round in puzzlement. He could see no one. 'Where?'

'The flute. That's Cassie. I know it's her. That's my daughter.'

Then it was as if all the emotions of the last six years, all the emotions he hadn't dared feel, welled up out of the ground he was lying on, out of the heaped-up earth with its ancient burden of bones, up through the dead grass and the knotted brambles, thick as honey, thick as blood, and poured into him through every pore of his body. The fear, the love, the anger, the grief surged over him like a slow tide. He struggled for breath. A knife slid in under his ribs so that gasping sent steely pain stabbing at his heart, and he moaned.

Jonah saw his long narrow body clench. Concern sent him wriggling back to the man's side. 'Are you all right?'

'Yes. Sure,' nodded Schofield. But he was keeping his breathing shallow, and this close Jonah could see the pain twisting his face. 'A bit dizzy.' He forced a grin. 'That bloody wall.'

Jonah grinned too. 'Exercise is good for you. Another week here and you'd be hurdling walls like that.' But what he was thinking was *Oh no. Not here – not now. You want to have a heart attack, do it on your own time. The management regrets that it is not equipped to deal with medical emergencies. The management regrets that if you start screaming and thrashing around it will have no choice but to leave you lying here while it runs for dear life.*

Schofield didn't think it was a heart attack. The pain and tightness in his chest were already easing so it no longer felt like breathing treacle. It had been a kind of emotional firestorm, born of too much exertion and too much excitement. 'I'll be all right in a minute.'

Jonah watched him, troubled. He didn't know how he'd become embroiled in this man's quest. He didn't understand why, after six years, Schofield was prepared to risk injury, illness and worse to find the daughter who'd turned her back on him. And he didn't understand why it mattered to him *what* Schofield did. He was a decent man but not a very likeable one. There was a coolness to him, a remoteness that was the very antithesis of obsession. He was not a hot-blooded, hot-headed passionate man devoting himself to every cause that touched him. He was an intellectual, rational, aloof. Jonah couldn't see why, after so long, he was still an emotional hostage to his errant daughter. Why he couldn't make the sensible decision to consign her to history and let go.

If he'd been a little older, a little more experienced in matters beyond his specialist subject of inner-city survival, he might have realized that the thing he least understood about Schofield was the thing that made him care what happened to him, and whether he achieved what he'd come here for or died trying. The lengths he was prepared to go to in pursuit of his lost child fascinated and confounded Jonah. It was the disproportion between the effort he was investing and any return he could reasonably expect. It was the sheer volume of love this cool, dispassionate man still harboured for the daughter who betrayed him.

And the reason this mattered enough to Jonah to prevent him doing what was in his own best interests – putting distance between him and Schofield, and more distance between him and the Pagan – was how that contrasted with his own experience. He was confused. He wanted to know if it was normal to feel how Schofield felt. Had Cassie been lucky in her parents, or were his significantly sub-standard?

For a long time after coming to London he'd thought that, even if he didn't quite understand how, what happened had been his fault. Normal kids don't get thrown out by their parents, ergo he wasn't a normal kid. Later he realized that was crap. But he thought that was how the world worked: the powerful dumped on the less powerful until the consequences landed on someone too weak to get out from under. Parents – like all adults; like all *people* – were selfish, vindictive, unyielding bastards and he'd been just too young to see it in time.

What was he to believe now? That it was normal to love your children whatever they did? Could Laurence Schofield *really* love Cassie after what she'd done to his family? Could he lose a sweet fifteen-year-old and still risk everything to find the urban guerrilla she'd become? Would he still love her when he knew what she'd had to do to survive? Jonah made no moral judgements, but he thought Schofield would. What if he learned she had a drug habit? What if he learned that sometimes the only way to feed it was with her legs apart? If he found her slender body riddled with AIDS, could he love her then? Because if he could, Jonah had more cause for bitterness than he'd known.

Schofield was recovering. His breathing was steadier, his voice soft and rueful. 'Sorry about that. I'm all right now. Go on, I'm right behind you.'

Too many things were queuing in Jonah's mind to be thought about. What he was thinking now was that maybe Schofield was already as certain as he was going to be that the Pagan's woman was his daughter. He could drag this exhausted man round the campsite, with all the risks that entailed, and never get him close enough to be any surer than he was right now.

'You stay here,' he said. 'I'll bring her to you.'

Hope animated the flick of Schofield's eyes. 'Can you do that?'

'Of course I can,' said Jonah – shortly, because it would be harder and more dangerous than he wanted Schofield to know.

'That's why I came, isn't it? Because you'd have as much chance of wandering through that camp unnoticed as Lawrence of Arabia.'

'I know. But...'

'Keep your head down. Even if there's trouble. *Especially* if there's trouble. I can talk my way out if they think I'm alone, but not if the Seventh Cavalry comes charging down the hill.' Privately, though, he doubted Schofield had a charge left in him.

So did Schofield. He knew they'd reached the point where he could do nothing more without imperilling what they'd already achieved. He had to leave it to the boy now. To trust him. To risk him. 'All right. But Jonah ... be careful. This matters to me. It really, really matters. But not enough for you to get hurt.'

'I can look after myself,' the boy said gruffly. And there wasn't light enough for Schofield to see the tear on the lip of his eye as he backed away into the darkness.

Three

There was a way they walked: half cocky, half defensive, hands in pockets and chins on chests, scuffling their feet in the dust like schoolboys kicking pebbles. Jonah fell into it as he came down the hill. Strolling loose-jointed, he looked round him with the unhurried negligence of someone who had every right to be there. Anyone seeing him would think they knew him because his face was indistinct and his body language wholly familiar. As long as he didn't pass too close to the fires he thought he could wander the camp all night without being challenged.

And he might have to. He needed her alone, but Casey was the centre of a large group by the main fire. Even as he watched more people wandered over to listen to her play. Some were carrying drowsy children. Until the camp was established, the tepees watertight and the bedding dry, the only place warm enough for a baby to sleep safely would be inside its mother's clothes.

'Are you coming over?' The girl passing behind him, whose casual enquiry made the heart hammer at Jonah's ribs like a caged man, had a baby tied in a shawl against her breast, her cardigan and coat fastened round both of them. It made her look, and walk, as if she was pregnant again. Her voice, low to avoid disturbing the child, held the burr of a Scots accent. Jonah didn't know why so many of his kind were Scots. Perhaps the distance lent enchantment. Or perhaps it was that, once they discovered the reality of life on the streets of London, the distance made it hard to get home.

'In a minute,' he nodded, and she nodded back, untroubled, and walked by him, her long skirts flapping softly.

Jonah wandered round until he began to feel conspicuous. Then he found a shadowy spot on the edge of the group and sat down, hugging his knees, listening to the flute, watching the Pagan's family wind down after their busy day, waiting for the party to break up.

He'd get, if he was lucky, one chance to speak to Casey alone. If he missed it he'd have to try again tomorrow or the night after, or until he was caught. If she finished playing and headed towards the church while the Pagan was still deep in conversation, Jonah would follow her. A couple of minutes would be enough. If she wouldn't listen to him – or if she was not in fact Schofield's daughter – all hell would break loose and he'd have to run for it. Surely to God Schofield would have the wit to stay out of sight until Jonah got the chance to come back for him?

He wasn't sure what he should say to Casey. A lot depended on how she reacted. If she raised the alarm as soon as she saw him he'd have to make it quick; if she was willing to hear him out he could make a better case. The one thing he mustn't do until she was ready to meet her father was tell her Schofield was right there, in camp. If things got rough Jonah could hightail it. Schofield couldn't.

In a way he could not explain, he'd come to feel responsible for Laurence Schofield. He was as helpless as a child in the Tinderbox: whatever had made him think he could finish his task here alone? But if it was absurd, there was also a touch of nobility to it. As if the odds against him were so great he could only fail; he couldn't be humiliated. To Jonah, who'd been ground so thoroughly in the dirt that now everything tasted of it, there was something special about that.

The song of the flute stopped, and for a moment he thought Casey was leaving. But she was only making room for the Pagan. Outlined by the flames, the distinctive narrow head and pointed beard made a mediaeval demon of him. He sat with the woman and put a long arm round her shoulders, and their faces tilted towards each other as if they could make a home in one another's eyes.

It wasn't so much a party as an amiable ritual for ending the day among people with no belief in prayer. They stoked the fire and came together, not at a certain hour but when they were tired and ready to rest, and basked in the warmth of companionship, and talked or sang or just let the harshness of their existence run out of their bones. Their days were marred by ugliness, their nights by cold, but this hour round the camp fire, toasting some comfort into their weary bodies, sharing a little food and drink and maybe something even better at taking the iron out of the ground, fitted them to face another night and then another day.

Friendship was what saw them through. They owned nothing that ordinary people would have thought worth taking when they moved. They lived from day to day, from hand to mouth, from wheeling and dealing and stealing. None of them amounted to anything in the eyes of the world. There were a hundred of them, all struggling to survive, all doing things that could get them quietly gutted in a dark alley, and not one of them was an official human being. No safety net was waiting when they fell. They lived as best they could for as long as they could, and then they quietly died. Most of the old dossers found stiff in shop doorways on frosty mornings were younger than Schofield.

But whatever the rigours of their life, here among their own kind they were at home. The hardships were shared hardships, the accumulated knowledge of how to make light of them a communal asset. Pleasures were shared too, and because the hardships were great it was possible to take pleasure in small things. And when the hardship was irredeemable and unrelieved by even trivial pleasures, there remained scope for the humour that is the ultimate human triumph.

Watching from the shadows as the people round the fire joked and passed cigarettes and shared music and sleepy children, Jonah saw just how much he'd given up by doing this alone. He'd learned to live in the most hostile environment in the city without risking things that he feared more than privation, but it wasn't a cost-free option. He'd stayed safe and he'd stayed free. But now, seeing the easy camaraderie that sustained these people, tasting the warmth of the family like the smell of good cooking on the smoky air, he knew he'd paid too high a price.

He was sixteen years old. Apart from staying alive he'd done nothing; apart from the seamy underside of London he'd seen nothing. There wasn't so much as a dog whose face brightened at the sound of his voice. At times he felt like an old man waiting to die, listening for the first stroke of midnight so he could leave the party. He saw no point in what he was doing: getting through today in order to have a shot at getting through tomorrow.

He knew he was lonely. The indifference which was his defence against wanting things he couldn't afford was just a veneer. It might look like the genuine article but from his side he knew how thin it was. When he came this close to people he could identify with it was impossible to escape the brutal truth that his life was an empty shell. In a city of seven million people, thousands of them vagrant like himself, the only friend he had was Eggon Ronnie. If he died tomorrow, the only difference it would make was that Ronnie would be able to store more baked beans.

This was Schofield's fault. It was nine months since Jonah had felt this low, and he wouldn't be feeling it now except that for two days he'd had Schofield on his back. But Schofield was a freak. Real people – real parents, real friends – didn't behave like that. They were happy enough to see you when they had a use for you, when you gave them something they wanted. But sooner or later you let them down and then you were on your own. Friendships, relationships, they all came to the same end, and the sooner you accepted that the less it was going to hurt.

The people round the fire only seemed to be different because of the safe distance between them and him. If he strolled over and joined them he'd soon find out they were a bunch of self-serving bastards like all the other self-serving bastards who'd trodden in his face. Schofield was another. When you got right down to it, he was someone else who wanted something and didn't care who he used to get it.

'So what the hell am I doing here?' he demanded in a savage whisper that would have been just audible to anyone close by. There was no one, but he recognized the danger and went on in an urgent silence, only his lips moving on the words. 'I've crawled into a rats' nest because one rat wants to take another rat from a third rat. It's nothing to *do* with me. But I'm the one who's going to get chewed. However this works out, I'm going to have a rat at my throat.'

A disappointed Schofield could do him no harm, but the Pagan could crucify him. If Casey went with her father, the Pagan would blame Jonah and there'd be nowhere he could hide. The Pagan would hunt him down without caring how long it took, and when he found him he would do things to him that ordinary people never dreamed of. He'd managed to fend the man off thus far because he didn't much care if he had one more kid thieving for him or not. But he'd care about losing Casey. It would take more than fancy footwork for Jonah to avoid him then.

The sensible thing was for Jonah to crawl back into the shadows and leave this place now, this dangerous place with its deadly illusion of comfort, to collect his things from Ronnie's and leave his sanctuary under the Élite Café and go ... anywhere. Somewhere he wasn't known. Use a different name; stay out of the Tinderbox. Let Schofield curse him. He owed Schofield nothing. If he wanted his daughter back, let him take her. Jonah had already done what he was asked: found the girl for him. Even Schofield with his go-to-church haircut and holier-than-thou eyes couldn't ask him to take on the Pagan.

Or maybe he could. He didn't know what the Pagan was capable of. He'd castrated the last man who tried to take Casey from him. Schofield couldn't know that. Or perhaps he knew but put less value on Jonah's balls than his own; which was par for the course in the real world.

He went to get up then, to back away into the shadows, to scale the wall and disappear into the safety of the night, and the Pagan would never know he'd been here. But at that moment the woman with the flute rose too, long and slender in her dark clothes, and bent to kiss the top of the Pagan's head, and his beard tilted as he raised his face to smile at her. But he stayed where he was by the fire, and the conversation resumed as the woman walked towards the ruined church where she'd made her home.

She looked at the sky. There was still a lurid overcast, but if it hadn't rained yet it would probably not rain tonight and they'd have the church to themselves. She particularly wanted to be alone with the man tonight. She was going to tell him about his child. She'd made her mind up while watching the pictures in the fire.

Jonah's mind was made up too. His head was in turmoil but his steps were dogged, his shoulders rounding in that posture that mingled confidence and caution, and said – and lied – that he was one of them. He moved between the shadows and still no one challenged him.

Casey was almost home, past the last of the tepees and the parked lorry and into the deep shade of the squat tower, when someone stepped in front of her. Startled, she caught her breath in a gasp and her hands flew instinctively to her belly. 'Who...?'

It was a man's shape, stocky rather than tall, with a gleam of yellow hair that she didn't recognize. Unease crept up her spine and turned to fear between her shoulder blades.

'Who is it? Say something!'

The voice was so low it barely reached her, wouldn't have travelled a pace further. 'Don't call out. I don't want any trouble. If you call out he'll kill me.' So he was afraid too.

Reassured enough to be curious she said, 'What do you want?' But she kept her voice soft.

'I have a message for you. Let me talk to you for a minute. Then I'll go away. But please don't call him. If you don't want what I'm selling, let me leave.'

Her eyes were adjusting to the deep shadow, and as the alarm faded she realized it was not a man she was talking to but a boy. Something about him was familiar. 'Do I know you?'

'No!' He said it with such obvious horror that Casey almost laughed. She knew her man inspired terror in people, though she'd had only love from him. 'You don't know me. You don't *need* to know me. But there's someone we both know, and he sent you a message.'

'Who? What message? What are you talking about?' The plainer his anxiety, the more confident Casey felt with him. 'What makes you think I'd *accept* a message from someone who needs an errand-boy to deliver it?'

'It's … Look, I know we mostly don't use our proper names. The names we were born with. I mean, no one here does. But I need to know yours.'

It was a rank impertinence and she reacted with indignation. It was the question people in the Tinderbox never asked. She didn't know the Pagan's name nor he hers. This strange, scared boy appearing from nowhere and wanting to know who she used to be was more than she would tolerate.

'That's none of your business,' she said tartly. 'But I know who you are. Jonah the Loner – the kid who's always hanging round the edge of things and never comes in. Oh yes, I know you. You have a roof. You think you're too good for us, don't you? That you'll soil your hands dealing with gypsies and thieves. So you watch us and prowl round the edge of our camp like a dog looking for scraps, and slink away when anyone puts out a hand.'

Her tone had hardened from indignation to anger, and now she was speaking loudly enough to be heard. Jonah glanced round unhappily, hoping to God no one had drifted within earshot. If only she'd shut up long enough for him to say what he'd come to. He wanted to reach out and shake her, but dared not.

'Let me tell you something, Jonah,' she went on, saying his name like a curse. 'We don't want you here. We don't need someone eating our food and turning his nose up at how we come by it. What makes you so superior, anyway? Good family, nice home? Fat lot of good they did you. And just for the record ' – she drew herself up to her full height, a dark and slender Fury – '*my* father is—'

'An architect,' said Jonah in his quiet growl.

And while Casey was still staring at him with startled eyes a hand fell lightly on his shoulder, and a musical tenor voice said in his ear, 'Honouring us with a visit, Jonah?'

After Jonah left, Schofield lay for a while belly-down on the damp earth in an agony of remorse. Was his word worth nothing? Would he perjure himself to get what he wanted? Two hours ago he'd promised Ronnie he wouldn't expose Jonah to any danger. He'd meant it at the time. Now he'd brought the boy into the stronghold of a man whose ways would destroy him. He'd played on Jonah's weaknesses until he had no choice but to walk into his worst nightmare.

Now Schofield lay on the cold flank of the hill, sheltered by the tangle and the dark, and shame boiled over him. His hands fisted so tightly the nails dug into his palms. He squeezed his eyes shut but couldn't avoid seeing what he'd done.

He'd promised – for what his promises were worth – that he'd stay where he was and not follow Jonah into the camp. Clearly, any attempt to extract the boy would precipitate disaster. There was nothing he could do to salvage his honour now. But he could watch. It wouldn't do any good, but he could at least bear witness to what Jonah was doing for him instead of curling up with his own fear until the worst was over. So he inched through the undergrowth until he had a view of the flickering fires below. He didn't think he could be seen. Anyone wandering round up here would fall over him before they saw him.

There wasn't much happening. Most of the tribe were settled around the fire where the girl was playing her flute. The girl. Cassie? He couldn't see well enough to identify Jonah, much less a girl he hadn't seen for six years. But his heart told him it was his daughter. He believed his lost child was less than a hundred metres away, that he could stumble down this hill and fold her in his arms in half a minute. Fear of the consequences was not enough to restrain him. It took all the strength he could muster to keep from breaking cover and going to her.

The flute's plaintive windsong ended. The girl stood up. Schofield hadn't thought she would have grown so tall. She bent over the man beside her and kissed the top of his head; he put a casual arm around her knees and kissed her thigh through the long dark skirt.

So that was the Pagan. Schofield waited for the shudder of recognition. The fury and disgust, because this middle-aged man was his daughter's seducer. The fear, because Schofield knew he was dangerous. And the sense of awe, because the Pagan had tamed the Tinderbox, imposed his rule on it and created a kind of stability, if only by comparison with the havoc wrought by his rival who was not so much a leader of their netherworld community as a predator upon it.

But the expected frisson didn't happen. Anticlimax seeped in through the cracks in the moment. Schofield had expected a giant, an ogre, a towering personality. But all the firelight showed him was a narrow man with a sharply trimmed beard and thinning hair, chatting to friends of an evening, kissing his woman goodnight. Apart from the setting, the scene was entirely ordinary.

He wasn't sure what he'd expected. An orgy perhaps, though the weather was inclement for naked prancing; or knife fights, or drunken oafs arm-wrestling over broken glasses. And a leader who presided over his gypsy tribe with a bit of panache, like the Demon King in a pantomime. The amiable scene below was too domestic for words.

Schofield was ... Yes, he was disappointed.

The girl walked away from the fire towards the ruins of the church and disappeared into the shadows.

Four

One of the Pagan's hands rested on Jonah's shoulder, the other slipped casually around his woman's waist. Jonah's were back in his pockets, knuckle deep and clenched hard. So it wasn't a real hand plunged to the wrist in the pit of his stomach, kneading away at his guts, turning them to water. But it felt like it.

He looked at the broken ground, scuffing with the side of his boot, and mumbled something unintelligible in reply.

The hand patted his shoulder encouragingly and the thin man bent over, offering his ear. 'Sorry,' he said, his voice musical with good humour, 'what was that? Speak up, boy, there's nothing to be afraid of here.' He grinned a sudden death's-head grin. 'Nobody here but us chickens.'

He looked to Casey for confirmation; she nodded soundlessly. The last thing the boy had said before the weight of the Pagan's hand silenced him was ricocheting round her mind. She didn't know what it meant. She didn't remember telling anyone, even her man. It would have sounded like boasting; and besides, they never talked about their pasts. Her troubled eyes scanned Jonah's face, a pale stain in the darkness, and she saw fear but no answers there.

Jonah was trying to get a grip on himself, to get his mind off the hand on his shoulder, the kneading in his belly, and kick it into gear because he needed it to work for him.

He had three options: say nothing, lie or tell the truth. He didn't think he'd be able to say nothing for long. The Pagan would want an explanation – what he was doing here, why he'd come, how he'd got in. He needed to know if the security of his camp was compromised. If Jonah wouldn't volunteer the information it would be extracted from him. The Pagan wouldn't flinch from that, and he was right – he had to be sure his family was safe. But Jonah was afraid what he might say if he was being hurt. He'd have more control if he didn't let it come to that.

If he lied he'd need a story that would stand up to scrutiny. Any inconsistency would be seized upon instantly. The Pagan hadn't become – and more difficult, stayed – a tribal chief by believing everything a nervous teenager told him. The moment he thought Jonah was lying his eyes would go cold, his hand would move from Jonah's shoulder to the scruff of his neck and he'd have a knife at his throat.

Or he could tell the truth. He could tell the woman, with her man standing beside her, that her father had sent him to bring her home. The first thing that would happen was that the Pagan would knock him down. Jonah thought it best to let him. It might cost him a tooth, but hopefully Casey would intervene before it went much further than that. If he tried to run they'd run him down, the Pagan and all his tribe, and once the adrenaline was flowing they wouldn't stop until they heard his bones break and saw him cough blood.

But could he count on the woman to protect him? It might be better for Jonah if she wasn't interested in Schofield's message. Then the Pagan might settle for sending him back with a bloody nose for an answer. But suppose the Pagan asked where Schofield was? With a knife parting his skin, could Jonah keep from betraying the man to his natural enemy?

Casey was clearly puzzled by what he'd said, was trying to work out how he knew. If she told the Pagan he'd know instantly – or he'd guess, and take steps to confirm it. Jonah was trapped. He'd been careless and now he was going to pay for it. Whatever he said, whatever he did, he was going to get hurt. He thought he might as well volunteer the truth as have it beaten out of him. He would lie about Schofield's whereabouts, but otherwise tell the truth and take the consequences. He drew a deep breath, caught Casey's gaze in the desperate entreaty of his own and opened his mouth to tell her why he'd come.

The woman said calmly, 'He's here to join us. He wanted me to put in a good word.'

Jonah stared at her, his expression frozen, his message dead in his mouth.

The Pagan looked at her too, more amused than suspicious. 'What did you tell him?'

Casey gave a negligent shrug. Her eyes never left Jonah's face. 'That it's nothing to me whether he joins us or not. That it's your call, and anything he has to say he can say to your face. He could start with why he wants our company now when he's treated us like lepers for twelve months.'

The Pagan chuckled good-naturedly. 'Don't be uncharitable, Casey. It's been a long, cold winter – I expect he found it tough on his own. Is that right, boy? You're feeling the cold? Family life's attractive when you're hungry, isn't it?'

As his brain thawed and started working again, Jonah realized that Casey had not merely covered for him, she'd put herself at his mercy. If he contradicted her the Pagan would want to know why. In truth there wasn't much danger of Jonah refusing the

247

lifeline she'd thrown him, but it was a conspiracy of a kind. He was grateful for her help, but he wasn't yet sure why she'd take the risk.

The Pagan's hand on his shoulder tightened fractionally; fractionally his voice hardened. 'Isn't that right?'

Jonah nodded, glanced at the Pagan and then quickly down again before the diamond eyes could drill through what he was saying to what he was thinking. 'That's about it. Listen,' he said sharply, because he didn't want the Pagan's attention wandering from him to Casey, 'I'm not here to beg. You wanted me, remember? You wanted me working for you.'

There was a silky quality to the Pagan's voice but no one would have taken it for affection. 'As I recall, you declined my invitation. Harsh words were spoken. You went to some lengths to avoid us after that. I won't pretend we didn't find it hurtful.'

Jonah snorted like a nervous colt. He didn't believe the Pagan could be hurt by anything less than a baseball bat with a nail in the end. But at least he wasn't looking at Casey and wondering about the confusion deep in her eyes. 'OK, you were right. It gets cold here in winter and the pickings get hard. So I'm here. Throw me out if you want – I won't come back. But if you thought you could use me nine months ago, you can sure as hell use me now. I know a lot more.'

He'd decided against lying on the basis that he wouldn't be able to make it convincing. But this was an absolute lie, and it had to convince. He didn't want to join the Pagan's tribe. There wasn't one of them, including quite small children, who hadn't been locked up for something, and for most of them it was a regular occurrence. What being part of the family meant to them was that there were people to keep their bedding dry until they got back.

Sometimes they didn't get back. Sometimes they went down for months, even years, and were never heard of again. Jonah knew this. He knew it was a risk they accepted with a certain philosophy because you could live in the Tinderbox but you couldn't make a living here, not with a whole lot of mouths to feed. Belonging to a tribe inevitably meant leaving the safety of the slum for the perils of a London where people called the police if they felt threatened.

Jonah could do lonely. There was safety in it. Cold and hunger can and do kill, but he was young and strong and he knew he could survive as long as he remained always and only dependent on himself. What he couldn't do – what he couldn't risk; what he would genuinely rather starve than face – was being locked up again. And that, not the uncertain temper of an unpredictable tyrant, was the real price of joining the Pagan's family.

But somehow he had to wipe the knowledge of that out of his eyes so the Pagan would believe it was what he wanted. He had to forget what he could never forget, what he always slept and woke remembering, and swallow the terror of surrendering himself to the horror again. And not because he had no choice but because this *was* his choice, to put Laurence Schofield's needs above his own. And now, with the infinite weight of the Pagan's hand on his shoulder and the endless fear of what he was facing, he couldn't even remember why. But if he didn't do it well enough the Pagan would know, and he'd reduce Jonah to a bloody whimpering heap in order to know everything. And when he did...

He mustn't. This time Jonah had to keep faith with the lie in the way that the boy he had been before had ultimately, disastrously, failed to do.

Rosy in the backwash of the firelight, the hawkish face peering into his own spread in a slow smile. 'Ah, Jonah, but do you know enough?'

'I've made it on my own for twelve months. I can still make it on my own. But maybe there's a better way. This is a big city to have no friends in.'

'That's certainly true.' The smile had an

odd quality. 'Go on.'

But Jonah couldn't think of anything else to say. 'That's it. Do you want to talk about it, or do I leave?'

'Oh, you don't leave,' the man said softly. He linked his arm through Jonah's and walked away, towing the boy with him. Over his shoulder to Casey he said, 'You go inside. I'm going to show Jonah round the camp, have a chat ... You know, man to man.' The smile was growing more wolfish every time he did it.

This wasn't what Casey had wanted. She needed to hear what passed between them, and at some point to get Jonah alone again. But events had overtaken her. If she insisted on joining them the Pagan would wonder why. 'Don't be long. I'll put some coffee on for when you're done.' She went into what was left of the church by the chancel door.

They strolled arm in arm like friends. Only Jonah would have known that he was under restraint. 'You'll like that, won't you?' asked the Pagan. 'A nice cup of coffee?'

'Sure.' Whatever it was he wanted to talk about, Jonah was sure it wasn't coffee.

'My woman makes good coffee.' The sharp eyes slid out sideways. 'You like Casey too, I expect.'

The boy felt the ground quake under his feet. 'I don't know her.'

'No?' The Pagan sounded surprised. 'She

251

seems to know you.'

'We never met before tonight. Anything she knows she must have heard from you.'

The Pagan pondered that for a moment, then nodded. 'Could be. When you gave me the slip I may have said something ... unfriendly. You understand.'

'Sure,' Jonah said again. It seemed the safest response.

The Pagan gave a musical laugh. 'Truth is, I'm not used to people telling me where to go. It might do me good to hear it more often.'

Jonah dared a fractional grin. 'Could be arranged...'

The Pagan looked down at him. The eyes were less friendly than the words. 'Don't push your luck, little man.'

They walked between the fires. Everyone noticed. Jonah saw the heads turn as they passed. But no one voiced a query or came to join them. The Pagan had raised his family well. They knew when to leave him alone.

He said, 'You have to see it from my point of view. I'm the father of a family. People depend on me. I can't take chances that someone on his own – someone like you – might take without a thought. I have to look all around things, see what they could mean besides what I'm being told they mean. Take you, for instance.' His grip tightened on

Jonah's arm almost, but not quite, like a hug. 'Last summer I said you'd find it hard here on your own. I outlined the benefits of belonging to a family, told you I'd get you work, look after you ... And you said you weren't interested.'

Jonah didn't remember it quite like that. It was before he lived under the café. He was squatting in a disused railway carriage. Very early one morning he woke to find three men collecting his belongings. When he protested they hit him. They said, 'You're coming with us.' He didn't know who they were – police, the mob, one of the more militant charities. He asked and they hit him. He asked where they were taking him and they hit him again.

The thin man with the beard said, 'You're going to work for me.' Then Jonah knew who he was. He hadn't been in the Tinderbox for a week before he heard the Pagan's name. Even then he knew what working for him would mean.

He hardly knew how he got free. He went for their eyes with his fingernails, for their shins with his boots – people living rough don't undress to go to bed – for their groins with his knees. He left behind his squat and everything in it, including one man bent double, one with a hand clasped to his clawed cheek and one pouring soft erudite curses on his name. He never returned to the railway carriage. He saw the Pagan again, but only from a distance. He had hoped never to be much closer.

If anyone had asked how it happened he could not have said. It happened by inches. Nothing he'd done, until he came here, had seemed that dangerous, but everything led on to something else. He kept saying *Maybe* when he should have said *No*. Now he was lost in the heart of darkness, getting a guided tour of his camp from a man who sounded like he was ready to bury the hatchet and looked like he wanted to bury it in Jonah's back.

'Now you turn up here,' the Pagan went on. 'The day after we arrive, before anyone else even knows we're here, late at night I find you inside my camp talking to my woman. You say you want to join us.' He did the vulpine smile again. 'But anybody caught spying would say the same thing.'

The hand in Jonah's gut knuckled away. The contents surged to his throat so he had to fight them back. He said, 'S-spying?' and it took him two breaths to get it out.

The Pagan was watching him attentively, interested in his answer. Like a cat so sure of its mouse it's prepared to play a little. The soft chuckle deep in his beard was not itself an evil sound, but there was something a little evil about a man taking such obvious pleasure in another's fear.

'Indeed,' he said solemnly. 'I can't ignore

the possibility. The only law in the Tinderbox is what I create – my family have no security except what I give them. This is a bad place, Jonah. There are people just waiting for me to drop my guard so they can move in and take over. I don't want that. I don't want old Hickory and Aunty Lucy to starve because they no longer earn enough to be worth feeding. I don't want the children forced into prostitution because some new broom thinks it's the quickest way to make money. I don't want them turned from pickpockets into muggers because it takes time to make a dip artist and only a pick-axe handle to make a thug.'

His eyes were mesmerising. Jonah felt them drawing him in. Even in his own brain there seemed to be nowhere they couldn't see.

'This is the deal,' said the man. 'My family work for me and I protect them. We pool what we earn, and I find work for them and keep them safe. If someone gets into trouble I get them out of it. I've run this family for eight years and the longest anyone has spent in jail is three months. Ask around: that's a record.'

Jonah's eyes were glassy. He needed to blink and was afraid to. He was thinking *That's ninety-three days. Ninety-two nights.*

'You understand?' asked the Pagan. 'If I allowed someone to take over this family I'd have let them down. I'd have taken their money and failed to do what they were paying me for.' He did the smile again. 'So I have to be a nasty, suspicious bastard. It's in the job description. I have to wonder why, after you made it so clear you wanted no part of us, suddenly I find you wandering through my camp asking to sign up. My *new* camp,' he added with a little careful emphasis, 'just a stone's throw – and this may not be coincidental – from territory claimed by the Field Marshal.'

Jonah didn't want to join the Pagan's family. The temptation he'd felt watching them gather round the fire had been mere loneliness. The thought of three months locked up – with those special locks that keep you in better than they keep other people out – brought him back to earth with a bump. But now his safety required that the Pagan believe the illusion.

'You have to be wary – I can see that. But I'm not working for Rommel. Why would I work for him rather than you? What you've got here is better than what I've got alone. What he's got is a gang of brain-fried spacers beating the crap out of one another because they can't find real marks any more. What could he possibly offer me that would make spying on you seem like a good idea?'

The Pagan nodded thoughtfully. 'That's a point. You're more our kind of people than

Rommel's. I told you that nine months ago. Maybe you've just come round to believing me.' For a few steady paces he said nothing more. But Jonah knew better than to think himself safe. He kept quiet and waited, and after a few moments the Pagan went on, musing aloud.

'Of course, a man like Rommel has ways of making people do things they don't want to. Things that aren't in their own best interests. Someone like that might be given a certain amount of leeway. Sooner or later most of us meet someone we can't deal with. But the thing is –' he looked keenly at Jonah, making him jump – 'that person would have to think quickly. Decide who he should trust and throw himself on the man's mercy. That would be the smart thing to do. Tell the truth while there was still time to rescue the situation. Because he could only expect one chance. If people got hurt while he was still trying to be all things to all men, he couldn't expect to be forgiven.'

Now he wanted an answer. He stopped, and looked Jonah full in the face, and waited for one.

Jonah tried to keep his voice level. 'I know you've no reason to trust me. But I'm not stupid. I haven't survived on my own for twelve months by being stupid. Rommel didn't send me here. Rommel hates my guts more than he hates yours.'

'Really?' The Pagan's expression was quizzical. 'Why?'

Jonah couldn't tell him that. If he told him that the Pagan would get everything else out of him as well, one way or the other. He shrugged. 'Because I wouldn't work for him either.'

'Jonah the Loner.' The Pagan smiled. The boy could detect no warmth in it. 'But in fact you do have a friend.'

Jonah thought he meant Schofield, and for a moment he panicked. The Pagan looked at him in surprise as he felt the boy's muscles contract. Then he denied it. 'No. I haven't.' It didn't occur to him what a devastating admission that was.

'But you have,' insisted the Pagan gently. 'The man who owns the café. Who lets you live in his store room.'

Jonah hadn't known that the Pagan knew where he lived. A chill ran through his veins. But there was no point lying. 'He's just someone I know.'

'He nursed you through pneumonia, boy,' said the Pagan reproachfully. 'He gives you a home. How much does a man have to do to be your friend?'

Jonah flushed and said nothing.

'My point is, if the Field Marshal threatened to burn down the Élite Café with Eggon Ronnie inside, you might think you had no choice but to do as he told you.'

Jonah said flatly, and truthfully, 'Rommel's been nowhere near me. He has nothing on me and I'm not spying for him. But I can't prove it. If you don't believe me you'll have to do the other thing.'

'Well,' said the Pagan pensively, 'sometimes it's possible to ... shall we say ... demonstrate goodwill. Show that you want something enough to pay for it. So that people know you're serious, and committed, and suitable.'

Jonah felt himself stiffening from his spine outward. His bones locked, his muscles clenched; his very skin seemed to freeze and the blood coursing through him to still and curdle. His voice was rough. 'What the hell are you talking about?'

The Pagan smiled solemnly. Finally he released Jonah's arm. They'd come back to the big fire where many of the family were still gathered. Every eye was on them. The tribe knew what was coming if Jonah didn't.

'Rites of passage,' said the narrow man. 'So that the boy may be admitted to the privileges of manhood. So that the stranger may be admitted to the fold. This is our family – our home. If you want to share it, you have to show you're worthy.'

Jonah's throat was so tight with fear he could barely get the word out. 'How?'

Five

Up on the hill, flat on his belly among the
brambles, Schofield knew something had
gone wrong. All Jonah had had to do was get
Cassie on her own for a minute and ask if
she would see her father. If she'd said yes
they'd have been here by now. If she'd said
no, Jonah would have returned even quicker.
Schofield couldn't imagine what turn of
events had sent him off on a tour of the
camp with its commander-in-chief.

His eyes had followed the girl when she left
the fireside and he saw Jonah approach her.
But then the bearded man rose and went to
join them, and up on the hill Schofield's
heart thundered. His daughter and his
messenger were both in danger, neither of
them knew it, and he couldn't warn them
without betraying them all.

But all hell had not broken out. Instead,
the girl continued into the ruined church
and the man and the boy went for a walk.
Schofield couldn't think what they were
talking about. If Jonah had told the Pagan
where he was hiding, people would have

come for him. So maybe he was still safe. But he didn't think Jonah was.

Minutes passed, slow as old men on sticks. Schofield considered leaving his place of safety and attempting to make his way to the church, to confront his daughter while the Pagan was otherwise engaged. All that stopped him was the thought that, if he was successful – if she gathered her things quickly and left with him – Jonah would be left an unwitting hostage to her man's fury.

So he waited, watching them circle the camp and return at last to the fire. There was no shouting, no violence. He began to wonder if Jonah had managed to broker an amicable agreement on Cassie's future. If the moment Schofield had been told would set the Tinderbox alight had come and gone without fireworks.

'Nothing worth having comes free,' said the Pagan. His long narrow fingers were toying with something he'd found in his pocket. 'Children, for instance. They enter the world in pain and blood, and they cost you pain and blood at intervals thereafter. But if you want children you don't care that it hurts. The hurting is part of the having.'

Jonah said nothing. His throat was too tight for talking and his brain had split, half racing, half frozen. The racing part was wondering just how literally he should be taking this. The Pagan talked about a blood rite bonding the child to the family. Maybe he meant every word of it. But maybe all he required of Jonah was the willingness to submit, would accept that as initiation enough. If he bowed to the idea, might he be excused the reality? He didn't know. The Pagan was an unfathomable man.

But whatever was required of him, he'd have to go through with it. He dared not back away now. So he said nothing, waiting in dumb fear like a beast before its butcher.

Amused by what he saw in Jonah's face, the Pagan gave a soft little chuckle. 'Don't look so scared. I'm not going to harm you. I just need to be sure that you're telling the truth. That you're here because you want to join us, not because you're running from something worse.'

He looked at the thing his hands were toying with and for a moment seemed surprised, as if he couldn't remember how he came by it. Jonah looked too. Oddly enough – since the Pagan had no front door to fix it to – it was a little metal numeral of the kind sold by hardware shops, with a long screw at the back. It might once have been brass; now it was black. It was a number 6, or perhaps a 9.

The Pagan saw Jonah looking at it, smiled and dropped it into the cinders of the fire. His manner was sober. 'Jonah, I need you to be straight with me. If Rommel's behind this, tell me now. We'll sort something out and no one need get hurt. But I can't afford to let him get a foot in here. We have to stay here; we've nowhere else to go. I don't want to fight Rommel, but if I have to I don't want to find he knows my strength and all my plans. Is that what this is all about, Jonah? Tell me. I promise you won't suffer for it.'

Jonah didn't believe his promises. He didn't know if the Pagan was a wicked man or just a ruthless one, but he didn't believe that confession was an easy way out. He shook his head. His face was white, his voice low. 'I don't work for Rommel. I told you why I'm here.'

'To join my family.' The Pagan's voice fell very soft. 'You realize what that means, do you? People in this family, they don't work for me. They belong to me.'

Jonah said nothing.

The Pagan leaned forward and whispered in his ear, 'And just so no one's in any doubt about that, I put my mark on them.'

In the last moments two young men had placed themselves either side of the boy. Now their hands reached for him – not violently, almost with respect. They slipped the parka off his shoulders and put it carefully aside. When they went to pull the sweater over his head, momentarily he resisted. But he felt from their steady unforced

263

movements that they were too strong for him – and it was his good warm sweater, he didn't want it getting damaged. Reluctantly he let it go.

When their hands moved to unbutton his shirt, in a sudden flush of anger he slapped them aside. But one of them held his wrists behind him while the other carefully opened the shirt and eased it away from his body, leaving him exposed to the night and the cold and the gaze of the narrow man. Jonah's lips parted and the breath came swift and shallow between them.

The hands that held him were not fierce but they were firm. He might struggle but he wouldn't escape. The night caressed him with cool fingers of wind and warm breaths from the fire. The Pagan's eyes ran him up and down, up and down, and they too were hot and cold, hungry and bleak. Jonah's body shook as if with fever, spasms of terror running through him.

There was a girl of about his own age kneeling beside the fire, looking up at him with undisguised excitement. Jonah might not know what was coming but she did. Her face was luminous with anticipation. Perhaps unconsciously, she licked her lips.

On the hilltop Schofield watched without understanding. He saw the tribe gathering – everyone, so it seemed, except the children

264

and Cassie. He saw Jonah being held and he saw him stripped. Confusion gave way to horror. He couldn't believe what he was witnessing. Couldn't believe that he was letting it continue. *What are you doing? You can't ... he can't ... not again! He's just a boy. A child. And he's only here because of me.*

He rose to his knees, feeling them tremble. And there he stayed, poised on the brink of a counterattack he couldn't quite find the courage to launch.

The Pagan was winding a rag around his fingers. Holding it by the long screw at the back he retrieved his toy from the fire. The metal number was beginning to glow. He held it one way, looking at it, then turned it upside down and looked at it some more. Then he smiled gently.

'The thing about a number nine,' he said, 'is that it's a letter P back to front.'

Then Jonah understood. His jaw dropped – not with shock, though it was a shocking thing, but because relief had suddenly loosened muscles keyed taut as banjo strings. His shoulders slumped, and for the first time in minutes he took a proper breath. His eyes half closed and the corner of his mouth twitched something like a tiny smile.

The man frowned. His eyes travelled quickly from the boy's face to the hot metal in his hand and back, and still he didn't follow. Jonah knew what he intended. He'd been expecting something worse. The Pagan's thin lips framed a question mark.

Jonah's voice was a gruff murmur that barely reached the Pagan, that no one else would have heard. 'Is that all?'

And as the bewilderment deepened in the Pagan's face, so that he glanced again at what he was holding to check that it was indeed what he believed it to be, the boy drew a deep breath and his bare chest swelled towards the brand.

After that things happened so quickly that, looking back, it was impossible to put them in sequence, or to say which were causes and which effects.

The Pagan, aware of having lost the initiative to a sixteen-year-old boy, clenched his teeth and thrust his hand forward as if striking a blow. The metal number, hot as coals in his bound fingers, met the bare skin of Jonah's chest with a sigh like a ghost exhaling.

Up on the mound Schofield shot to his feet with a sharp, inarticulate cry and didn't care if the whole camp saw him.

Behind him, four young men in the kind of clothes the Pagan's family threw out appeared on top of the stone wall, heads and shoulders outlined briefly against the overcast before they dropped into the brambles and their places were taken by four more.

Pain transfixed Jonah like a lance. His body arched with it, tugging at the restraining hands, and a choked gasp of a cry escaped him; then the eyes rolled in his head and he dropped, limp as sacking.

The Pagan followed him down. He snatched a handful of Jonah's tangled hair with his left hand to keep his head off his chest, and while the men on each side kept him on his knees the Pagan crouched over him, mantling him as a hawk mantles its prey, pressing the metal to his breast so it burned its message abidingly into his flesh.

The girl on her knees beside the fire leaned so close she almost overbalanced. Her eyes shone. Then a soft moan slipped between her moist lips, her eyes quivered and her body slumped, drained nerveless by excitement. Little Jo was no stranger to the initiation ceremony, and it gave her an orgasm each time.

Someone else, less captivated by stigmata on the body of a helpless boy, was looking away, towards the mound, and saw movement and the shape of a man up there. He touched the Pagan's arm. 'Who...?'

The man who got his name from a rainfall chart led his band round one side of the hill at a powerful, thick-legged run. Another man led a second group the other way. They expected to overrun the camp almost before their presence was detected.

In the same moment that he was seen, Schofield saw the intruders. He didn't know who they were, but everything about them – the way they moved, the urgent silence they moved in – told him they belonged here no more than he did. For half a second, fear for himself and fear for his daughter warred in him. But if there was going to be trouble he had to try to protect Cassie. He didn't care about the rest of them, was happy for them to resolve their differences with boots and chains and let the worst man win. But Cassie was his child, and at the last the trite old cliché was true: he would die to save her. And God help him, it might come to that.

He began shouting, leaping up and down and shouting and pointing. 'Over here! You're under attack, damn you! Leave that poor bloody boy alone and go fight with men.'

Losing the advantage of surprise, the invaders broke cover. Flailing weapons beat a path through the startled family towards the Pagan.

The Pagan was not a coward – men don't achieve dominion in a lawless world by cowardice – but he had too much imagination to be a brave man. When he looked up and saw Schofield his worst fears appeared to be confirmed. Rommel had come calling.

Whether he was after girls or all-out war he'd have come mob-handed. And whatever his ultimate objective, his first move would be to put the Pagan out of action. He was mistaken. Neither Schofield nor Jonah had anything to do with Rommel. But thinking it gave him some seconds' head start he wouldn't otherwise have had.

The flicker of the fire caught a mathematician's look on his narrow, intelligent face. He was calculating percentages. The answer came quickly but brought him little joy. With his tribe scattered through the churchyard, the children asleep and the adults so preoccupied at the fire that some of them still didn't realize they were under attack, the camp was indefensible. If they withdrew to the church they might be able to protect themselves, at least for a while, but the outcome was certain.

This was his fault. He should have posted guards. He shouldn't have assumed that Rommel would continue to avoid confrontation. He'd failed in his duty. Anger surged through him, drowning even the fear. He was still crouched over the slumped boy with the livid P emblazoned on his chest. The beginnings of awareness were creeping back into Jonah's face.

The Pagan shook him by the hair. The hooded gaze was implacable, the musical voice harsh with hatred. 'You did this. That's why you came here – to keep me occupied while he got in. Oh, you ... *enemy*! I'll have your eyes for this.'

Too much heat had gone out of the brand into Jonah's flesh. The Pagan threw it aside and snatched a stick from the fire. His left hand was still knotted in Jonah's hair and he wrenched the boy's head back, brandishing the flame in his face.

The men holding Jonah exchanged an uneasy glance. One of them muttered, 'This isn't...'

Schofield was halfway down the hill and running hard – harder than he'd run with Shag and Average behind him, running not like a middle-aged architect but like an athlete, hurdling the tangle where he could not pound through it. Twice he fell, rolled and was back on his feet, still running. He was covering ground faster than he had for twenty-five years. But he wasn't going to get there in time.

Too weak to struggle, Jonah whimpered.

Consumed by passion, rapt in the blasphemy of his revenge, the Pagan was shaken to the core by a shriek – not the boy's cry but the shrill scream of a woman coming from the church. The man knew the voice at once although he'd never heard her scream. He dropped his victim, dropped his weapon, staggered to his feet and lurched round, wild-eyed. 'Casey?'

Then he began to run, and his young men ran with him.

She'd gone into the church but she hadn't made the coffee. She sat on the piled-up bedding, chewing her fingernails, trying to make sense of Jonah's presence in the camp and what he'd said. He must have wanted to see her desperately. The way things lay between him and the Pagan, he could hardly have expected a welcome. He'd come anyway, and he'd got caught, and now he was in for a bad time. Casey hoped her man would know when to stop. She wanted to hear what Jonah had to say.

When, watching from the church door, she saw Jonah's chest bared, like Little Jo she knew what was coming. He didn't do it every time someone joined them. But occasionally, when he doubted their motives or it was time to demonstrate his authority, the Pagan would perform this subjugation ritual. No crueller than branding a calf, psychologically it was devastating. She accepted the Pagan's explanation that a degree of fear was essential to family discipline. But it gave her no pleasure to watch, so she stayed in the church, waiting for the wail that would say it was done.

Then the Pagan would bring him here – his hands gentle now, his voice reassuring. He'd have to help him because the boy would be

271

too weak to walk. Expressionless, she took out the little medicine chest of which she was custodian. She could treat the burn on his chest. She could do nothing about the humiliation branded into his soul.

She was still waiting for the howl, and the general mutter of approval that would greet it, when without warning the other door – the vestry door behind her, nailed shut as it was – crashed inwards and men poured over it. They were big men with shaven heads, dressed in rags and black leather, and they surged through the ruined church with blank, maniacal eyes, hands full of weapons, and a monumental sense of purpose.

Casey let out one piercing yell and fled before them.

Six

There are soldiers and there are street-fighters, and they follow different codes. If the man who called himself Rommel had been a soldier it would have been a battle of Titans. They were very different bands led by very different men, but on level ground they might have been expected to pack a similar sort of punch.

The Pagan's family was much larger but more than half its number were women, children or what passed in the Tinderbox for old people. These were not vulnerable suburban dependants – some of the children qualified as offensive weapons – but they were no match for Rommel's shock troops.

Given the chance to prepare for the attack, the Pagan would have devised stratagems to even the odds. Strategy was his forte. He was as ruthless a man as his opponent and cleverer, but he was best at the kind of battle that could be planned in advance and directed from a high point. Rommel, by contrast, was not the biggest but he was the toughest member of his tribe. He led from the front, and his idea of strategy was to steamroller anyone who got in his way. The smart money would have been on Rommel to win battles and the Pagan to win the war.

But in the face of a surprise attack by heavily armed men there's a limit to how much strategy can achieve. There was no time for the Pagan to deploy his people, no time for them to arm themselves except with whatever scrap materials lay to hand. The battlefield was where they stood, the enemy the men hacking at them with chains and machetes. Their only tactic was to defend themselves as best they could while the initial assault rolled over them, in the hope that there would be time then to organise either a counter-attack or a secure withdrawal.

Rommel's troops stormed through the camp leaving carnage in their wake. By now the children were awake, screaming hysterically or venturing into the tumult in search of the adults who had kissed them goodnight in another world where the loudest noise was the crackling of the dying fire. Women trying to find them and gather them to whatever safety they could devise set up a harpy screeching and went at the intruders with blazing sticks from the fires; but their desperate courage was no match for ironmongery and they fell before the Field Marshal's troops like a bloody harvest. Within minutes the churchyard was like a charnel house, the ground thick with the injured, the air thick with their moans. It wasn't a battle but a slaughter; only the high stone walls stopped it being a rout. Those who could ran; those who couldn't crawled on their bellies to escape the murderous assault.

The Pagan running towards the church tower and Casey running towards the fire met by great good fortune at a point midway and gripped each other, letting the battle rage past them.

'What's happening?' gasped Casey. 'Is it Rommel?'

'It's Rommel.' The Pagan had to shout to be heard. In the frame of his beard his face was white with fury.

'What does he want? Girls?'

'I haven't asked. But he seems to want blood more than sex. I think he means to destroy us.'

The woman clutched his arms. 'You have to get away.'

He stared at her. 'How can I? This is my fault. I promised to protect these people. They trusted me. I should have known he wouldn't tolerate us this close. At the very least I should have been ready. I can't slink away and leave them now!'

She shook her head fiercely. 'There's nothing else you can do. When this is over, that's when they'll need you. To look after them, to make them feel safe again. You can't stop what's happening. Die with them if you must, but it'll be over quicker if you aren't here for him to find.'

'I won't run!' Even an imaginative man may be brave enough to die in the last ditch for something he cares about.

Casey took his face in her hands, made him look at her. 'You must. It's what we require of you. All of us, but me especially. I need you to survive. Our child needs you to survive.'

It wasn't how she'd wanted to tell him, shouting over the roars of men and the screeching women, side-stepping to avoid being trampled. She'd wanted to enjoy the

275

slow comprehension dawning in his face, then the shining joy. It wasn't fair to tell him now, like this, and expect him to change his whole mind-set in consequence. But there might not be another chance. If he didn't come with her now, slipping away under cover of the chaos regardless of what that did to his self-esteem, she might not see him again.

She saw comprehension in the window of his face. The diamond eyes flicked to her belly, luminous, infused with a kind of holy terror. Any other time her news would have filled him with pride, but right now it only added to his potential for loss. His tribe, his woman, his life, and now also his child.

Casey shook him. 'We have to leave here, right now. Before they stop us. There'll be time for vengeance later. If you survive, you can come back later and put things right. Re-establish the family and nail Rommel to a wall. But only if he doesn't kill you in the next five minutes.'

Still he hesitated. He knew how it would look. She was right, if he stayed all he could do for his family was die with them. But there were a hundred people here who look-ed up to him, who would be stunned if he left them in the heat of the battle.

If it had been his skin only, he might have given them what they wanted rather than what they needed: a calm voice in the midst of the tumult, an act of courage for them to fix their eyes on as the madman hewed them down. But there was Casey and now the child to think of, and he wasn't prepared gallantly to throw their lives away too.

'Yes,' he said thickly. 'We'll go – now, while we can. If we still can. I'll take you where you'll be safe. And then I'll start calling in some favours. Everyone who ever owed me anything is in for a busy couple of days.' The beard twitched as his lip curled. 'I mean to end this, Casey. We're not living like this any longer, constantly watching our backs – our homes, our children, our girls always in danger from that animal. I'm going to end him.'

'Yes,' she nodded. 'Yes. Come now.'

'And then,' said the Pagan, 'I'm going to roast that cub of his over a slow fire.'

Of all the people in the bedlam of the churchyard – Rommel and his crew in rags and black leather, weighed down by home-made weaponry and buoyed up by adrenalin, crazy-strong men running down the camp, empty-eyed, flame-eyed, hungry for blood; other men trying to oppose machetes and iron flails with sticks; women torn between helping their men and sheltering their children – only Laurence Schofield saw the Pagan and his woman leave.

He'd stormed off the mound like a minor

act of God, roaring his anger, his heart bursting and his mind stretched with horror because he knew that even if he drove his body to destruction he would still arrive at the fire too late to save Jonah's eyes. With the din surging across the camp he couldn't even hurl curses ahead of him.

As he lost the advantage of height, running men came between him and the shocking scene, fire-lit like a vision of hell from a mediaeval psalter. He didn't expect to hear Jonah's shriek over the cacophony, but he knew what he'd find when he finally elbowed his way through the scrum.

When he reached the fire, all those who had gathered round it were gone. The Pagan, the young men who'd served as his acolytes, even the girl who'd been kneeling at their feet, radiant-eyed, had fled. All that remained was Jonah, left lying beside the fire like garbage, his half-clothed body twisted to one side, his face turned to the ground and veiled by his yellow hair. He made no movement that Schofield could see.

Oblivious to the madness raging round them, ignored by the warring factions as he ignored them, Schofield knelt and touched his fingers to Jonah's throat. He couldn't find a pulse and the skin was cold. Schofield tore off his coat and gathered the boy up in it. He heard himself sobbing and knew it wasn't just exertion. He steeled himself to part the straw-coloured tangles with his fingertips.

The mark of the flame was on his face, a rosy track that ran diagonally across his left brow and right cheek. The eyebrow and the hair above it had shrivelled in the heat, but the translucent skin of the eyelid was intact. Hope fluttered under Schofield's breast bone. 'Jonah, open your eyes.'

The boy was profoundly shocked, wandering in the pathless limbo between consciousness and oblivion. He whined, 'My eyes...'

Schofield held him tight, felt deep tremors shudder the length of him. 'Jonah, listen to me. I think they're all right. I don't think he did it. Open your eyes, Jonah, let me look.'

And when he opened his eyes and Schofield searched them for signs of damage, the worst he could find was that the left one was a little bloodshot. They filled with tears at the realisation that he could see.

There was nowhere safe to leave him but Schofield couldn't carry him. There was no reason now not to pursue his quest to its conclusion. If the Pagan wanted to kill him he'd have to get to him before Rommel or Average, or any of these lunatics could. It wasn't that Schofield was no longer afraid, more that with danger on every side he might as well do what he'd come for. Or keep trying until he was stopped.

If he could find Cassie in the midst of all

this it might work for him. She must be terrified: if he found her alone she'd cling to him as any frightened girl would cling to her father. Then he could take her away before she could wonder whether she wanted to go with him or not. There would be no time to talk, to argue, to trade recriminations or bicker over terms; no time for her to ask how Jan felt about this, for Schofield to have to lie. If he found her alone she would return with him. This he believed.

But he couldn't hunt through the melee for her with a shell-shocked teenager under his arm. So he dragged Jonah away from the fire and left him bundled up in his coat in the shelter of the wall where he might be overlooked. 'Don't move from here. I'll come back for you.' He didn't wait for a reply. He was afraid it wouldn't be the one he needed.

He'd seen Cassie go into the church. She wouldn't be there now, because a few minutes later he'd seen Rommel's men come out of it. But only the invaders were ranging the length and breadth of the site: the Pagan's people were clustered together in terrified little groups anywhere a piece of solid masonry would guard their backs. So maybe she hadn't strayed far. That was where he'd begin his search.

Lurching between the skirmishes at a half-run, Schofield evaded attention for so long that he began to think his life was charmed.

The vanquished lay all around him, while the victors charged past him time and again without sparing him a glance. Then someone hit him very hard between the shoulder blades and he crashed to the ground, face down in the mud, with a peculiar kind of numbing agony exploding through his bones.

For an incalculable time he hadn't strength enough to rise out of the mud, and he expected every moment that a second blow of the iron-shod cudgel would smash his skull or his spine. But his assailant had kept travelling, clean over the top of him, and when at last Schofield got his face off the ground there was no one near. He staggered up and pressed on towards the church.

That was when he saw them. The Pagan had reached Cassie first. That made it harder, but nothing would have stopped Schofield now. He stumbled on, stepping over the fallen, ignoring their groans, his eyes on his daughter's dark head and the gaunt shape of her seducer. Nothing but death would have kept him from them.

He was barely a dozen metres behind, and neither was aware of him, when a sudden uproar made all three of them spin round. Schofield's heart turned over once and sank like a stone. 'Oh, Jonah,' he sighed. 'Didn't I tell you to stay out of trouble?'

★ ★ ★

In all honesty, Jonah was not to blame for what happened. He did his best to stay out of sight, crouching by the wall with Schofield's coat pulled up to his eyes. But luck was against him.

As the heat went out of the battle, the defenders encircled and disabled, the assault force was able to turn its mind to the second phase of the operation: finding women. The third time Little Jo, her skirts round her thighs, ran shrieking in front of a muscular stalwart of Rommel's army he had the grace to run after her, bellowing rampant masculine boasts and unaware that she was running slowly in order to be caught. He got his hand to the hem of her skirt. The garment flew off and the girl tumbled, shrieking and giggling, into the bracken at the foot of the wall. Tugging at his own clothing, the man dived on top of her.

At which point Jonah, concealed just a few paces away, made a fundamental miscalculation. If he'd recognized the girl he might have reconsidered; and if he'd had his wits about him he'd have heard the note of lust in her squeals and concluded it was none of his business. But he thought he was witnessing the violation of a terrified child, and some instinct of chivalry he didn't know he possessed brought him to his feet, shedding Schofield's coat and fisting a stone fallen from the wall.

The man's head snapped over with a sick thud and his thick leathery body collapsed heavily on top on Little Jo's. The girl swore in surprise and disappointment. Then she levered herself out from under the unconscious man and set about her rescuer with screams of fury.

Jonah thought she was hysterical, tried hushing her and pulling her away. But she flew at him like a demented parrot, claws scratching at his face. Startled, once more afraid for his eyes, he staggered back – and bounced off the solid torso of the man who took his name from a weather map.

Average recognized Jonah before Jonah recognized Average. Passing, he looked to see what the yelling was about and saw one of his soldiers lying leaden on the ground and the boy with straw-coloured hair dropping a stone. Average wasn't too concerned that Barkiss was lying as one dead with blood on the back of his shaven skull. He would probably recover; if not he would be replaced. He was more interested in the presence here of the man-cub, the little lone wolf.

Average had worked out who was to blame for the debacle in the alley. He'd meant to exact payment for that, had not expected his chance to come so quickly. But he thought Rommel wouldn't thank him for beating Jonah to a bloody pulp before he could discover what he was doing here, in the camp of his rival, with a fresh new letter P scorched on his chest.

So rather than starting with a hay-maker that would have broken Jonah's jaw and rendered him useless as an informant, he fixed both hands on Jonah's shoulders and lifted him off the ground. Jonah wriggled like a fish, but with his back turned there was no part of the big man he could reach either with his hands or feet. Perhaps it was just as well. When Average's arms grew tired he threw Jonah against the wall and held him there with one hand in the middle of his back.

'Boss? Over here. Got something for you.'

The worst of the din was dying down, all the frenetic chasing and being chased slowing to a breathless standstill. The attack had been an unqualified success. Rommel had taken the enemy camp with only a few minutes' ruthless effort and minimal casualties among his own forces. Now he had time to count his spoils. Peering into the shadows, he walked towards the sound of his lieutenant's voice.

Rommel was not a big man in the way Average was a big man. But he was thickset and solid, and – at around twenty-eight – as powerful as he would ever be. Muscle bulged in his clothes, a higher proportion of black leather to rags than some of his crew, but the same basic uniform. He was so muscular he managed to look squat, almost dwarfish.

Like all of them, under the Nazi helmet his head was shaven. Some were quite bald, some had a five-o'clock shadow and some had a crew-cut that would soon need further attention, but essentially they were skinheads. It did nothing for their personal charm but reinforced the sense of strangeness, of alarming difference. It made their faces look heavy, fleshy and crude, oddly emphasising earlobes and nostrils. To those who didn't know them – perhaps also to those who did – they appeared inhuman; none more so than their leader.

As his eyes adjusted to the shadows he saw what Average had for him. He was surprised to see Jonah here but the yellow hair was unmistakable. 'Turn around.' Sure enough, it was the man-cub. 'Well now,' said Rommel heavily, 'look what the whale's sicked up.'

'Look at his chest,' said Average.

Rommel wore leather gloves with no fingers. He reached out and, quite delicately, with his fingertips, picked the open shirt away from Jonah's body. The shaven head nodded ponderously. 'So you finally decided which team to cheer for. Bad choice, boy. *Baaad* choice.'

'What do you want to do with him?' asked Average.

If there was one thing to be said for the

Tinderbox, it was that firearms had no place in it. They cost too much to acquire and to use, made too much noise, attracted too much attention. It would have been harder to keep the police out if the tribes had settled their differences with guns instead of chains and cudgels. So the proudest symbol of manhood in the Tinderbox was a knife. Good ones changed hands for large sums – as large, occasionally, as a man's life.

Rommel had the most coveted knife in the Tinderbox: an SS dagger. Knowing nothing of its history, he liked to imagine the deeds it had witnessed, the blood it had tasted – though quite possibly its very darkest memories were of him. He wore it in a sheath at his belt. He took it out now, slowly. He tested the blade with his finger. Then, bizarrely, he tasted it.

'The first thing,' he said thoughtfully, 'is to change that brand. Then Shag can have him. The rest of you are going to have a good night – just 'cause Shag doesn't like girls is no reason to leave him out.'

There was no fight left in Jonah. His strength drained, his vision dimming in pulses, he watched the tip of Rommel's knife. Rommel watched him watching and a mad smile played on his thick lips.

Schofield was watching too. He was dizzy with watching. He was watching Rommel and Jonah by the wall, and he was watching

Casey and the Pagan edging behind the ruined church. They made no sudden movements that might have attracted attention but made steadily for the lychgate, and all the people who might have stopped them were too interested in the floor show.

Schofield knew that if he wasn't right behind them when they reached the street he would lose them forever. After this they'd cover their tracks carefully. He too would be more cautious another time. If he had it to do again, he couldn't imagine taking the same risks, or having the same help. He'd go down in history as the man who'd set light to the Tinderbox – no one would aid him now. So this was his last realistic chance to reach his daughter, and if he vacillated undecided for half a minute more it too would have passed.

And what was Jonah to him anyway? A chance acquaintance, a vagrant boy he'd paid to assist him. Something like this would have happened to him sooner or later. He was a juggler, keeping the plates in the air by luck and fancy footwork, but sooner or later he was going to let one fall. This was Jonah's destiny. Perhaps no one could save him from it; certainly Schofield couldn't be expected to. Perhaps, since the only future for him was with one tribe or the other, it would be no kindness to try.

The Pagan and the girl had passed through

the ruined building. Unless someone saw them now they would escape. If Schofield meant to follow he had to go too, do as they were doing and slink away under the gaze of Rommel's distracted soldiers. He had to turn his back on the churchyard, on Jonah and what might become of him, and slip away into the darkness. Only that way could he finish what he'd risked so much for. Only that way could he hope to rescue his daughter and so justify all that he had done. She was his redemption. He'd done things he couldn't forgive if they'd been for nothing.

He sighed. He turned away from the church and made himself walk towards the knot of figures by the wall. As he drew close he had to elbow a way through them. 'Excuse me. Excuse me, please.' Sheer astonishment made them part before him.

Seven

Of all things, it was his suit – or rather, the remains of his suit that had been hauled over walls and through brambles and rolled in earth enriched by centuries of burials – that protected him. Rommel couldn't remember the last time he'd spoken to someone in a suit. A magistrate's court, probably, but they were like Christmases: over time one tended to blend into another.

'Piggin' hell,' he said in genuine surprise. 'It's Beau bleeding Brummell.'

When Schofield turned back from following his daughter to try to help the boy, he'd no idea what he was going to say to Rommel to persuade him to free them both. A more accomplished liar might have posed as a policeman – and got his head smashed in for his pains. He might have appealed to the man's better nature – except that, judging from the scene, he didn't have one. Only as he stepped through the ring of men admiring Rommel's art work did a solution occur to him. It would take some acting on his part, but not much. Really all he had to do

289

was keep calm, sound happy and convince Rommel that he brought good tidings. It might misfire. Rommel might want to finish the steel-point etching that was converting the P on Jonah's chest into an R and then start a companion piece on Schofield's. But he might want what Schofield was offering more.

When the Field Marshal recovered from the shock of meeting a suit, he looked beyond it to the man inside and got another surprise. The man was smiling at him. A diffident smile of course, most people had the sense to be nervous round him, but the man seemed glad to see him. Rommel couldn't remember the last time anyone was glad to see him.

'Congratulations, Mr Pagan,' said Schofield fulsomely. 'That is indeed the boy. You have most certainly earned your reward.'

For ten metres all round everything went quiet. Schofield could almost hear the slow grind of machinery as men unaccustomed to doing much thinking tried to work out what he meant. He saw them look to Rommel for guidance. Did he want them to pulp the interloper for mistaking the Field Marshal for his enemy? Or did he – and this was the approach favoured by what passed in Rommel's camp for an intellectual – want to find out about the reward and *then* pulp him?

Rommel took the initiative. 'Yeah, that's me. I'm the Pagan. You managed to find us, then.'

'It wasn't easy,' said Schofield, inventing wildly. Except for the anxiety. The anxiety was real. 'If I'd known what kind of place this is I'd have had you bring him to me. Still,' he looked around, taking in the surrounding mayhem and making no effort to disguise the horror in his eyes, 'I suppose I'm here now.'

'Damn right you are,' said Rommel cheerfully. 'And here's your boy.' He scruffed Jonah and held him out for inspection as if he was selling a puppy. But he didn't let him go, and Jonah – blood washing down his chest from a dozen little pin-point wounds – would have slid to the ground if he had. 'What about my reward?'

'In my car,' nodded Schofield. 'It seemed unwise carrying a thousand pounds into a place like this. I was afraid I'd be robbed before I could find you. If you'd like to see me back there – I'm parked by a pub called The Wooden Wall – we can conclude our business and I'll be on my way.'

Now he saw Rommel thinking. But the Field Marshal kept the machinery better oiled than most of his crew. 'I'm a bit busy right now. My associate Mr Average will escort you to your vehicle.' He pronounced it *vehicule*. 'He'll sign a receipt for the reward once he's counted it.'

Yeah, right, thought Schofield. *The only way Average is counting higher than ten is by taking his shoes and socks off.* Finding the temerity to mock these people, even in the privacy of his own head, astounded him.

Rommel passed the goods not to Schofield but to his lieutenant. And that seemed to be it. Schofield thought he'd got away with it, that they were on their way home. He wasn't sure he could put together the full thousand pounds in cash, but he thought he could get close enough to wing it. Write down the discrepancy to VAT. It was still going to be the biggest sum of money Average had ever seen in one place.

But as Schofield turned to go Rommel said, 'Just remind me,' and his heart plummeted.

'Just remind me,' said Rommel, 'what this was all about. Why you're paying good money for ... *that.*' He flicked Jonah's ear with a fingernail.

Schofield replied with as good a grace as he could muster. 'As I said in my letter, I'm the Burchill family's solicitor. A year ago their daughter was subjected to a vicious assault by this young thug. Before he could be charged he'd disappeared into the Tinder-box, and we couldn't find anyone willing to pull him out. Not the police, and none of the private operators.' He saw Rommel preening at this tribute to his rule. 'It occurred to us that the simplest thing was to employ one of the senior figures in the area to find him. You've done an excellent job. My clients are most grateful.'

Rommel was unhappy about something. '*One* of the senior figures?'

'Well yes,' agreed Schofield with a nervous little smile. 'The other person I was told would have sufficient status in the area was a gentleman called Mr Rommel. But I was warned against going anywhere near him. Even by the standards of this place, I was told, Mr Rommel is a mad bastard.'

Rommel's face cleared like the sun coming out. 'Quite right, Mr Solicitor,' he agreed happily. 'You do not want to go anywhere near that mad bastard Mr Rommel.'

Average knew the shortest route to The Wooden Wall. He led the way to the lychgate behind the church. Everyone in the camp – victors and vanquished both – watched them go. At every step Schofield anticipated the change of heart that would bring an outcry behind them and the ranks of men lining their passage clapping together like hands. But there was no protest. Neither curses nor missiles flew after them and there was no thunder of running feet. After all the mistakes he'd made, finally Schofield had guessed right. Even a man like Rommel would sooner have money than revenge. As long as it was enough money.

Jonah managed to stay on his feet until they were out of the churchyard. Then, between one step and the next, the last of his strength was gone. Uncomplainingly, he slumped to the cracked pavement, a soft and shapeless huddle in Schofield's coat, and couldn't rise.

'Whoops-a-daisy,' said Average briskly, and lifted him and threw him bodily over his shoulder, and walked on no slower than before.

They were back at the car in minutes. Schofield hunted through his wallet and his pockets and his glove compartment and his overnight bag and came up with a thousand pounds exactly. But only – and this was something of an irony – because Jonah had thrown some of it back in his face.

He emerged with the money, a beam, a pen and what was in fact a bill for servicing his car, but which he hoped would look sufficiently like a receipt given the shortage of street-lighting. 'If you'd just sign for it...?'

He expected the brute to scrawl illegibly across the page, take his money and leave. Or do something quite different with the pen. Instead he spelled his name out carefully – *Average* – like a child practising joined-up writing.

'Thank you,' said Schofield politely.

'Thank *you*,' said Average, and he turned

unhurriedly and disappeared back into the night and the Tinderbox.

Finally Schofield was able to pay Jonah some attention. He was bloody, he was shocked, but he wasn't in any lasting sense damaged. Schofield poured him on to the back seat of the car, then got in and drove away. Anywhere. Anywhere there was light and traffic and people who didn't put their initials on other people the way you might on a favourite trowel.

When he found a place like that he stopped and pulled out his phone. A mile away were a hundred men, women and children who'd had their dream of a tiny civilisation on the edge of the known world trampled by the barbarian. People had been hurt and killed; for some of them the worst wasn't over yet. If she'd stayed, Schofield's daughter would have been one of them. He'd seen her leave, but that didn't excuse him the obligation of getting some help for those who remained.

The fact that he'd left it twenty minutes while he made good his own escape disturbed him. Now everyone he cared about was clear of the churchyard, its high stone walls seemed like the frame of a picture: what went on within them was less real than events outside. Already he felt detached from what had happened there. Only the boy on his back seat was proof he hadn't imagined it.

But if the boy was real then the disaster was real too, and real people were suffering and in need of help. He called the police and reported the battle. He gave his name – when the news reached Sergeant Parker he'd guess anyway – but rang off before the flood of questions swept over him. He'd done all he could; it was up to others now.

Then he phoned Jan. The last she'd heard he was on his way home. He should have been there before this, she must have been worried. But she only asked when she could expect him now, and he said he wasn't sure, sometime today, and that he'd explain when he saw her. She didn't slam the phone down but the line went dead before he could say any more.

In the rear-view mirror he saw Jonah sit up, picking the shirt gingerly away from his monogrammed chest. Schofield turned round in his seat. 'Hello.'

Jonah smiled. 'Hi.'

'How're you doing?'

'I'm fine.'

'No, you're not.'

'No, I'm not,' agreed Jonah, 'but I will be when I get my breath back and eat some breakfast. Fancy some breakfast? Ronnie'll be opening up soon...'

Schofield nodded at his wound. 'We need to get that seen to. Where's the nearest hospital?'

Jonah shook his head. 'I'm not going to hospital. Take me home.'

'It'll get infected. It needs cleaning – you need shots—'

He was interrupted by the clamour of sirens a street away that rose and then dropped abruptly as they passed. *'That's* why I'm not going to hospital,' Jonah said. 'If I show up in A&E with an initial branded on my chest the police'll be all over me.'

'You haven't done anything wrong.'

'You do have some funny notions,' said Jonah in weary exasperation. 'Right and wrong – innocent and guilty – they don't *mean* anything here. What you saw tonight, you think that'll be on the front page of your paper in the morning? That it'll get a mention on the breakfast news, with the Lord Mayor down there expressing concern for the cameras? Dream on. The Lord Mayor doesn't admit to knowing about the Tinder-box. If he did he'd have to do something about it, so he doesn't.

'None of us exists, officially. And if you don't exist you can't be hurt, you can't be killed and you can't make a pig's ear of the Metropolitan Police's clear-up rate. Convenient, really. We'd be a lot more of a problem if we weren't invisible.'

Schofield was watching him with a troubled mix of compassion and impatience, of puzzlement and regret. Finally he said,

'Jonah – what do you want?'

'I told you. Take me home.'

Schofield shook his head. 'I mean, after that. How do you see your life shaping up? Do you want to stay here? Do you want to be invisible for the rest of your days? Do you want – I don't know – a beach-combing concession on a Caribbean island? You're sixteen years old. Where do you want to be when you're thirty? When you're fifty?'

It was clear from the look on his face that Jonah had never contemplated being thirty. He lived from day to day because that was as far ahead as he dared look. He knew – they all knew – he could be dead in a ditch this time next week. Not just as a theoretical possibility, the way Schofield knew that every time you start across a road there's a chance you won't reach the other side. Violent death was an everyday possibility in the Tinderbox. Jonah didn't know what he wanted to be doing when he was thirty because he'd no expectation of living that long.

He shrugged. 'Beats me.'

Schofield felt a serious urge to slap him. 'You have to give it some thought. I want to know if there's anything you want that I can give you. That I can help you to get.'

Jonah considered dutifully. He looked down at his chest. The blood was drying, crusting on the edges of the ugly wound. He said, 'Paracetamol?'

Schofield found an all-night chemist and bought burn dressing, antiseptic and painkillers with the small change from his pockets. All his notes had gone. The chemist watched with undisguised suspicion as he counted the coins out.

Back in the womb room under the Élite Café he turned on the one-bar fire and set water to heat on the one-ring burner. Jonah suffered his ministrations without comment, only the occasional sharp intake of breath. By the time Schofield was finished there was a little colour back in his face. He was sitting on the bed with the chenille throw wrapped round him, like an old man in a shawl. His voice was a throaty drawl, slowing as the painkillers took effect. 'Explain something.'

'If I can.'

'You paid them. To let me go.'

'Yes.'

'Why?'

Schofield stared at him. 'They were hurting you!'

'Yes.' He was waiting for the real answer.

Schofield spread his hands. 'That's it. Because they were hurting you.'

'You gave them a thousand pounds!'

'I gave them what I had. If I'd had more, I'd have given them more.'

'*Why?*'

'Because they were...' This was getting

them nowhere. They lived in worlds with different currencies. In Jonah's, pain was everywhere and money was hard to come by. In Schofield's, money could be earned and one of the best reasons for earning it was to avoid pain. 'Look, Jonah. You wouldn't even have been there except for me. What was happening to you was my responsibility. Fortunately, the one thing I could offer Rommel was the one thing he wanted more than hearing you yell. For which I'm eternally grateful. If I'd had to arm-wrestle for you, you'd still be there.'

Jonah sighed. It was clear to Schofield that he didn't understand any better now; he was just too tired to pursue it further. 'In the morning we'll start looking again. She'll have got out, you know. The Pagan will have got her out. For one thing, Rommel wouldn't have been bothering with me if he'd got hold of them. Tomorrow I'll start talking to people, see if I can find out where they've gone.'

'No,' said Schofield.

The boy stared. 'You mean ... after all that, it wasn't *her*?'

'Yes, it was her. But ... it's over. It wasn't an impossible dream. I got pretty close, thanks to you. If our timing had been just a little better I could have talked to her. But in all honesty, what would that have changed? She knows where we are. If she wanted to come home she wouldn't have waited for a chance encounter with a TV crew making a film that mightn't have been seen by anyone she knew. She could have picked up the phone at any time in the last six years. Jan was right all along. Cassie made her choice. I can't alter that.'

From the way Jonah went on watching him, Schofield was afraid he was putting it together. That he knew his freedom had cost more than money. That Schofield too had had a choice to make.

'What will you do now?' asked Jonah.

'Go home. Mend some fences with my wife and my partner. Get on with my life. You?'

'Get on with mine.'

Schofield had reclaimed what was left of his coat, wrapped it round him and, hunched on Jonah's makeshift chair, turned his feet to the tiny fire. He was waiting for enough hot water to make coffee. But before that Jonah was asleep.

Schofield went on regarding him in a way he could not have done if he'd been awake. In the quiet of the early morning, too soon even for the market traders, an idea began to take shape in his mind. Maybe it was absurd. But maybe it wasn't. He couldn't actually see anything wrong with it. It was a way of snatching something from the jaws of failure. It was worth doing, and not only because he had debts to pay.

The sun wouldn't be up for hours yet. But when the sounds of activity in the market square started filtering down to the store room Schofield saw Jonah beginning to stir. He lit the ring again, and tried to think of a way of saying what was on his mind that the boy might go for.

Jonah stretched himself cautiously as his straw-coloured head emerged from the red tangle of bedclothes. He peered down at his chest, picking at the edge of the dressing.

'How do you feel?' asked Schofield.

The young recover quickly. Now the shock had passed Jonah was buoyed by the knowledge of how closely he had shaved disaster. 'Fine. I'm fine.' He grinned.

'Good.' Schofield chewed nervously on the inside of his cheek. 'Jonah, I want to talk to you...'

'No,' said Jonah.

The man was puzzled. 'No what?'

'No thank you,' said Jonah politely.

Schofield shook his head, confused. 'You don't know what I'm going to say.'

'Yes, I do. And the answer's no.' There was no doubt at all, in his face or in his voice.

But Schofield tried to believe he'd misunderstood. 'Hear me out. I guarantee this is not what you're expecting...'

Like a man in the first flush of alcohol, Jonah's good mood gave way quickly to annoyance. 'Mr Schofield, I know exactly what you're going to say. You've been building up to it since we met. You want me to do something with my life – to be somebody. You think I've had a rough deal and you want to make it up to me. So like I said, thanks but no thanks. I'm too old to need adopting.'

A flush – of anger, embarrassment or pique – warmed Schofield's cheeks. He said stiffly, 'Can we talk about it? I don't want to run your life. I don't want to curb your independence. But I *can* help. You could go back to school if you wanted. Or maybe I could get you an apprenticeship. You talked about being a carpenter. We could find you somewhere to live. Your own place, but close enough that I could help if you needed anything.' He looked around him. 'You can do better than this. You *deserve* better than this. I want you to have—'

'A chance in life?' Jonah interjected sarcastically. 'Mr Schofield, my life's nothing *but* chances. What do I need with another one?'

'You're talking about the chance of not eating today. Of running into someone who wants your boots more than you do. I'm talking about the chance to make—'

'Money? You want to see me put on a suit and make money?'

'Why not? You'd have been buggered within an inch of your life last night if I hadn't put on a suit and made some!'

Already they were shouting at one another. Schofield realized first and backed off, biting his tongue. Jonah's eyes were hot with anger and humiliation. It was true, and he knew it was true. It didn't need to be said aloud.

Schofield did nothing but breathe until his breathing steadied. Then he said softly, 'I'm sorry. I shouldn't have said that. It's just ... I want to help, Jonah. Tell me how I can help you. Tell me what you want.'

'I don't want anything you can give me,' cried Jonah; and seeing Schofield recoil, now *he* felt the pangs of conscience. He knuckled his eyes and tried again. 'I didn't mean that. I meant, I don't need the kind of things one person can give another. I don't need things that you own because I've nowhere to put them. I don't need a family: I had one of those and it was crap. And if I said, *Yeah, OK, find me a job*, we both know how long I'd stick it. Clocking in at eight every morning and minding my manners with the boss? I'd blow it in a week, and be back here as soon as I could get a ride. The truth is, I live the only way I can. So I'll stick to what I know. I make out all right.'

Quietly, grimly, Schofield said, 'The life you know is going to get you killed. Never mind Rommel and the Pagan – they're the least of your problems. I've seen a lot of people living your kind of life these last few days. They grow old fast. Stay here and you won't make forty.'

The boy shrugged defensively. 'Maybe I will. Maybe I'll get lucky.'

'*I'm* the best luck you're going to get!' yelled Schofield. 'Come with me. Let me help you!'

'I can't!'

'Why not?'

'Because I'm scared!'

That hit Schofield like a fist in the belly, pulling him up short. At least it interrupted the way their voices were climbing again. 'Of what?'

'I don't know!' the boy said desperately. 'Getting swallowed up, I guess. I can cope with life here. I understand the rules. I don't know how to cope with anything more complicated.' He struggled to explain. 'You know how you felt when you found the laws you live by don't apply in the Tinderbox? That's how I'd feel anywhere else.' He gave a sudden despairing snort of laughter. 'Your world didn't treat me well even when I belonged there. I don't want to go back.'

'I can't...' Schofield heard his voice cracking and tried again. 'Jonah, I can't believe you want to stay here. I'm not saying it's going to be easy. I'm saying it'll be easier than this.'

But Jonah shook his head obstinately. 'You don't see what I see. Sure there's dirt here, but at least it's obvious. There's dirt where you live too, but you don't see it till it sucks you under. I feel safer with the dirt I know.'

And that was the bottom line. However much Schofield wanted to help him, he couldn't force Jonah to accept anything, including his view of what was best for him. He'd watched Cassie walk away from him, twice, and now he was going to have to let Jonah go too. Disappointment gnawed at his heart.

While they'd been talking – shouting – sounds had started coming down from above that suggested the Élite Café was getting ready for business. Partly to hide his distress, Schofield went up to order breakfast.

He found Ronnie stooped over the sink with a lugubrious expression that stretched all the way round the back of his neck. He was washing up as if he held a personal grudge against every plate, every cup, every piece of cutlery *and* the water in the bowl, which was the colour of tea.

Schofield would have tackled the drying, but the only cloth he could find looked as if Ronnie used it to strain the chip fat. So he leaned against the counter, watching and thinking.

At length he said, 'Ronnie, what would you do with a bit of money?'

Ronnie glanced round at the cash drawer

where he kept enough change to break the first couple of notes that came in each morning. 'Put it in there.'

'More money than that,' said Schofield.

'I've got a bank account,' said Ronnie. Then, overcome by honesty: 'Well, sometimes I have. Sometimes I've got an overdraft.'

Schofield nodded. 'OK. Good. Now, suppose you didn't have an overdraft. Suppose you had some capital. How would you spend it?'

It might have been an odd, even an impertinent question, but Ronnie didn't even have to think. He said immediately, 'I'd buy a mobile.'

Schofield was puzzled. 'A phone?'

'A mobile catering outlet,' said Ronnie with disdain. 'A fish and chip van. Hot pies and sausages. Chicken legs. Hamburgers with fancy dressings, and baked potatoes.'

'A chip van,' echoed Schofield. 'You could make that pay?'

Eggon Ronnie looked round at him, his eyes haughty. 'Make it pay? Do you know what the big problem with a café is?' Schofield shook his head. 'It doesn't move around. Do you know the difference between a mobile and a licence to print money?'

Schofield saw where the rhetoric was going. 'It moves around too much?'

'Exactly. But the man who's got both – who's got regular custom at his permanent outlet and can also cater for the casual trade by being here today for the darts match, there tomorrow for the karaoke night over the pub, round the corner a week on Wednesday if the Save the Squid demo materialises – that man's going to end up being quoted on the Stock Exchange.'

It was far and away the most he'd heard Ronnie talk. Schofield was impressed. 'So why don't you do it?'

Ronnie's muddy gaze returned to his washing-up. 'Do I look like a man with ten thousand quid to spare? The only way I can buy a van is if I sell the café. Then I'd be worse off than I am now. So maybe my fairy godmother's going to happen along with the money in a pumpkin? Great – so long as she can run the café while I'm out in the van.'

'You've no family to help?'

'Help with what? I haven't *got* a van. Besides' – his tone darkened – 'the wife don't do catering.'

'What if you knew someone with ten thousand pounds to invest? What if he all he wanted was, say, a half share in the mobile side of things, and he could even provide you with someone to run this place while you were out on the road?'

Ronnie was staring at him, washing-up forgotten. He wasn't sure what he was hearing except that he knew Schofield wasn't joking. He squinted suspiciously. 'You mean, he can't drive?'

Schofield smiled. 'Not yet. He'll learn. What do you think? Would there be enough income for two wages? Would you want to share your business with even a junior partner?'

Ronnie was giving it serious thought. It wasn't his experience that life presented him with unexpected good fortune. Still...

'I'd need to know a bit about him. You've got to be careful in catering' – he blew his nose absentmindedly on the tea-towel – 'dealing with people's health and all. You don't want no axe-murderers.'

'It's Jonah.'

Then Ronnie understood. His gaze studied Schofield, wondering about him. Wondering what Jonah had done to earn his generosity. 'Ten thousand quid? What's in it for you?'

Schofield shrugged. 'Satisfaction. A debt paid.'

'What does Jonah say?'

'He doesn't know yet. I'm going now; I'll write him a note and leave you the cheque. If I give it to him he'll tear it up in front of me just to show he can. You won't rip him off, will you?'

'No,' said Ronnie simply.

Schofield believed him. 'Listen, Ronnie. You're the best friend he's got. Look out for him. If he'll let you.'

Ronnie smiled. It wasn't much of a smile – a little sour and a little sad, and rusty from lack of use – but a smile was what it was. 'He'll let me. He won't know I'm doing it. That's the secret, Mr Schofield – never let people know you're helping them. That way they don't hate you for it.'

Eight

He left London with nothing. No one in the car beside him, nothing left of the money he'd brought to fund his quest – and, in the end, no regrets. Perhaps there was a small leaden disappointment somewhere under his heart, and he kept wondering if he'd done right by Jonah – if he'd done enough to ensure the boy's future, if he should have done more. But mostly he was just glad to get away. To know that he'd done his best and it was finished. To have the great city with its secret other life dropping away behind him like shedding a load, a little more with every mile.

Halfway home he began wondering what he would say to Jan. The truth, of course, that was her right, and anyway he lacked the imagination to fabricate another lie. But what words would he use to tell it, and how many, how soon? Should he sit her down and spend three hours telling her all that had happened, or let a brief synopsis serve until she asked for more details?

He reminded himself, when his nerve wavered, that a man who could talk his way out of Rommel's clutches could certainly talk to his own wife. But it wasn't that simple. He'd bought Rommel's co-operation. If he tried to buy his way into his wife's good books she'd leave him.

It was midday when he got home. Jan was alone in the house. She heard the car and came to meet him. Her face was expressionless. She was waiting to see what he had to say. She noted, of course, that he was alone.

He didn't put his arm around her. He carried his bag and they went inside.

He'd decided to start with the bare bones and see how far they got him. 'I found her. I saw her. I wasn't able to talk to her. Then we got separated and I don't know where she went. I don't think I can find her again. Anyway, I shan't try.' He waited to see what questions she would ask.

For some minutes, as she moved round the kitchen, making a light lunch – he was too tired to face a proper meal – it seemed she had no questions, that she wasn't interested.

Then, without looking at him, she said, 'How did she look?'

It was like a chink of daylight through a stone wall. He felt the heart swelling within him. 'She looked all right. Thin, but well. I think she's happy. She's got a man. Not the perfect son-in-law – for one thing he's my age, for another he's the local godfather – but they seem to think the world of one another.'

Over the next few hours he gave her more information, as it occurred to him, as she asked for it. And he told her about Jonah. It was hard to know where to start so he started with the bit that he thought would send her ballistic – his investment in the boy's future. But Jan gave only a rueful little smile and shook her head.

'What?' asked Schofield, puzzled.

'Other men blow ten thousand pounds on a night's gambling, an exotic holiday or a yacht. My husband's grand romantic gesture consists of buying a second-hand chip van.'

He shrugged awkwardly. 'I wouldn't be here now if it wasn't for Jonah.'

'I suppose I should be grateful,' said Jan. 'You might have brought him home on a length of string and asked if you could keep him.' It was a joke, and Schofield had sense enough not to tell her how close he'd come to doing just that.

And then he found he wanted to tell her

the other thing. The thing that troubled him more than the money, that might be expected to trouble her. 'I was so close,' he murmured. 'I could have reached out and touched her. But I turned back.'

Jan slipped into the chair across the table from him. 'Why?' she asked quietly.

'Because...' He heard the crack in his own voice, struggled to control it. 'Because Jonah needed me more. Cassie was safe, or near enough, and someone was taking care of her. Jonah was already in trouble, and it was going to get worse fast.'

Jan nodded. 'All right.'

'Is it?' There was a fractious whine in his voice, like a child in need of reassurance. 'I don't know. I went there to bring our daughter home. I left you upset, and Ken snowed under, and my justification was that finding Cassie mattered more than any of us. But I let her go for the sake of a boy I hardly knew. *Is* that all right?'

'You said it yourself,' Jan said softly. 'Except for the boy, you wouldn't have got home. He put himself in danger for you. I don't think you had any choice.'

'But I let her go!' Suddenly he was crying. All the strain of the last few days dumped on him like a cloudburst and there was no shelter. He sat at the kitchen table and tears ran down the lines of his narrow face.

Jan reached across the table top and took

his hand. 'But you held on to Jonah. It was the right thing to do. Cassie doesn't need you now. But right then and there, Jonah did.'

'Another ten metres and I'd have been in the church. I'd never have seen or heard what was happening behind me. I'd never have known.'

'That still doesn't make it a choice.'

It hadn't seemed much of one at the time. But the further these events receded, the harder his decision weighed on him. 'It's just so unfair! It was the only reason I was there. Finding her meant everything. It was worth upsetting you, it was worth imposing on Ken. It was worth risking my life for. And in the end, just seconds away from success, I let her go. I lost her because some damn boy couldn't keep out of trouble for five minutes!'

'That damned boy saved your neck.'

'Oh yes.' Schofield hadn't forgotten.

'And found Cassie for you.'

'Yes.'

'And got caught to save you the risk of approaching her?'

It was nothing but the truth. But it made him sound a coward. 'Yes,' he whispered.

'And you still don't understand why you gave up what you'd set your heart on in order to save him?' Jan's head was tilted quizzically to one side. 'Because you're a

man who pays his debts, Laurence Schofield. You're an honourable man. You're a
pain in the arse sometimes, but you are an
honourable man. And, in honour, there was
no choice to be made. You couldn't let the
boy be savaged when you were in a position
to help him. No one who knows you would
have expected anything different. No one
who loves you would have wanted anything
different.'

A week passed.

The day after Schofield got home there
was an angry phone call from Sergeant
Parker. But Schofield believed he'd broken
no law and invited the policeman to prove
otherwise. Emboldened by the silence, he
pointed out that events in the Tinderbox
hadn't occurred because he'd gone in there
but because the Metropolitan Police had
made a point of staying out. The rise of
warlords like Rommel and the Pagan was
not Schofield's responsibility, and the attack
at the church would have happened whether
he'd been there or not.

Sergeant Parker knew perfectly well that he
was right, wasn't going to argue the indefensible. He bade Schofield a frosty good day
and rang off.

Schofield rang Briony Fellowes, to let her
know how things had turned out. She apolo-
gised for not being more help. But the

315

passage of a little time allowed Schofield to acknowledge that he'd have achieved nothing without her. He asked her to thank Winston for him, too.

He asked her what, in a friendlier phone call, he should have asked Sergeant Parker: how bad the casualties at the churchyard had been.

'Bad enough,' she said sombrely. 'A couple of people died. Both from the Pagan's family. Another twelve or fifteen were treated in hospital – broken bones, machete injuries. God knows how many were raped, and how many needed treatment but were too scared to go to hospital. It was bad enough. But it could have been worse. The police arrived just in time to drive off the Field Marshal's gang before they could get stuck into some serious vengeance. I take it that was you?'

'Who called the police? Yes, of course.'

Briony Fellowes smiled down the phone. 'I knew it. No one else in the Tinderbox would have thought to.'

He asked – and he didn't want to but he couldn't let the chance pass – if she knew where the Pagan had gone. But all she'd heard was that he was gathering the remnants of his family and keeping them safe while they licked their wounds. She had no doubt he'd be back, and sooner rather than later. Then there'd be a rematch that would shape the future of the Tinderbox for years to come.

A week passed.

He got home from the office one evening to find Jan waiting on the doorstep, the oddest expression on her face. Before she would explain she had a question for him. 'When you saw Cassie, did she see you?'

He frowned. 'I don't think so. No, I don't think she could have. Why, what's happened?'

She shook her head. 'Probably nothing, then. A wrong number. One of those call-centre things. It's just ... well, after everything. I'm overreacting.'

'To what?'

'I had one of those silent phone calls. You know, you pick up and whoever's at the other end won't say anything? I kept saying, *Who is that? Who are you looking for?* No one spoke. But I had this really powerful feeling that it was her. That it was Cassie, and she wanted to speak but couldn't find the courage. Then after a couple of minutes the connection was lost.'

Schofield tucked her in the crook of his arm as they went inside. 'Coincidence, I expect. Only...' He hesitated. 'If it goes again this evening, should I answer it?'

He thought over and over about what he'd said – that she couldn't have seen him – and

over and over he came to the same conclusion. All the time he was drawing closer to
her he was keeping out of sight and she was
keeping out of trouble. But she had spoken
to Jonah. With all the ensuing drama, Schofield had never asked the boy what or how
much he'd said.

But what if he'd said, *Your father's looking
for you. I have a message from your family?*
Even if he never got the chance to deliver it,
Cassie would know they were still thinking
of her, still looking for her. They lived where
they'd always lived and the phone number
was the same. She could have called them.
To say she was all right; to ask how they
were. To ask what message the boy Jonah
was supposed to deliver except that they
were interrupted and she didn't know what
became of him afterwards.

Or, of course, it could have been a wrong
number.

They went into the house and waited; and
at about eight o'clock that evening the phone
rang again.